TO THE DEATH

MELISSA WELLIVER

HODDER

AF128764

HODDER CHILDREN'S BOOKS

First published in Great Britain in 2026 by Hodder & Stoughton Limited

1 3 5 7 9 10 8 6 4 2

Text copyright © Melissa Welliver, 2026
Cover illustrations copyright © Paul Blow, 2026

The moral right of the author has been asserted.

*All characters and events in this publication, other than those clearly
in the public domain, are fictitious and any resemblance to
real persons, living or dead, is purely coincidental.*

All rights reserved.
No part of this publication may be reproduced, stored in
a retrieval system, or transmitted, in any form or by any means, without
the prior permission in writing of the publisher, nor be otherwise circulated
in any form of binding or cover other than that in which it is published
and without a similar condition including this condition being
imposed on the subsequent purchaser.

A CIP catalogue record for this book
is available from the British Library.

ISBN 978 1 444 98076 9

Typeset in 11.75/14.5pt Dante MT Std by Six Red Marbles UK, Thetford, Norfolk
Printed and bound in Great Britain by Clays Ltd, Elcograf S.p.A.

The paper and board used in this book
are made from wood from responsible sources.

Hodder Children's Books
An imprint of
Hachette Children's Group
Part of Hodder & Stoughton Limited
Carmelite House
50 Victoria Embankment
London EC4Y 0DZ

The authorised representative in the EEA is Hachette Ireland,
8 Castlecourt Centre, Dublin 15, D15 XTP3, Ireland (email: info@hbgi.ie)

An Hachette UK Company
www.hachette.co.uk

www.hachettechildrens.co.uk

TO ALL OUR INNER MONSTERS – BECAUSE SOMETIMES THEY NEED A STAKE THROUGH THE HEART ... AND SOMETIMES THEY JUST NEED A HUG.

CONTENT WARNING: STRONG LANGUAGE, GORE, VIOLENCE AND DEATH.

PROLOGUE

The stage lights flicked on and they burned my skin like I was a Pyre and they were the sun.

'OK, sixty seconds until showtime,' Cresta said, holding a manicured finger to her earpiece.

I looked around the floodlit courtyard of the ruined castle. It was an old tourist trap from before the fall, crumbling from neglect.

Well, that was about to change.

'Forty-five seconds,' Cresta called out.

The make-up artists buzzed around us like flies on a corpse. The one assigned to me tried to push some sweet-smelling brush against my cheek, but I batted her away.

Nine other contestants sat in the semicircle of chairs that the production team had laid out in the courtyard. Cinta was checking the work of her make-up artist in a mirror, and when she saw the results she threw the compact at the girl and told her to start over. Mills and Decke were deep in conversation, whispering to each other. Mills drew a line across his throat, pointed to me and laughed. I caught Cass's eye and she gave me an attempt at a reassuring smile.

The glint of the gold-rimmed chairs seemed senselessly

gaudy against the dull stone of the ruined castle grounds. Maybe it used to be like this, when there was a king or queen that lived here. But crowds of people would have been here too, instead of on the other side of a camera lens across the sea. Away from here. Safe.

Before the mainland abandoned us and let Bloodwatch farm us out for entertainment.

'They're estimating five million viewers for the premiere.' I couldn't tell if my make-up artist was talking to me or herself. 'Five million people. Can you imagine?' She snapped her make-up bag shut and walked away.

Five million people. And Bloodwatch wouldn't exist without them.

'Thirty seconds,' Cresta called over her script, eyes down, checking her notes. 'We'll have around a minute to do the show introduction, and then we'll leave you to it.'

'It' was an interesting term for 'leaving you to fight for your lives'. In the distance I thought I heard the shriek of a Pyre waking up for their evening hunt.

I looked at the long shadow cast by the floodlights. The sun was setting, painting the sky pink and orange. Being out after dark with no weapon was the stuff of nightmares. This was it. Bloodwatch were really doing this.

I glanced at the group sitting with me. These nine other islanders might be the last people I would ever see. I didn't count the make-up artists, or the armed guards just beyond the cameras, or the drivers ready to wing the production crew out of here as soon as the sun disappeared below the horizon. Mainlanders didn't count.

'Ten seconds.' Cresta put down her notes and smiled at

us. 'You know, I can't wait to see who survives. Our winner's interview is going to make cracking television.'

Glaed shifted in his chair, but he didn't say anything. He had a thousand-yard stare that told me he was scared shitless. Smart. How some of the others were acting vaguely like their normal selves, I couldn't fathom. But, hey, we'd all 'volunteered' to be here.

It was scant consolation, but Cresta had a small smudge of lipstick on her teeth that would show up beautifully on-screen. The cameras were all remotely operated to keep the crew safe – must be nice. They wouldn't last two minutes after the sun went down.

I would.

Winning was my only chance out of here. I had to stay focused on that or everything else would overwhelm me. And as Dad always taught me: a panicked Pyre hunter was a dead Pyre hunter.

'And that's five . . . four . . .' Cresta mouthed the last few numbers, and little red lights appeared below every camera. 'And we are live.'

Cresta winked at me before turning to face the sea of lights.

'Hello, world. My name is Cresta Golding and welcome to the first-ever episode of *Escape from Blood Island*.'

In the distance, a chorus of Pyre screams echoed in the night.

CHAPTER ONE

Three days earlier

'You ever wonder what the difference is between us and the Pyres?' I asked.

Hild and I were sat in the armoury, detailing the crossbows. The name in itself was a bit grand for what the armoury actually was: a small wooden shack, slightly larger than a garden shed.

'Well, seems pretty obvious to me. We're alive and they're not,' Hild said, rubbing wax into the crevice of a crossbow. 'They were unlucky enough to get bitten and we weren't.'

'Yeah. But I mean, they were like us once, right? As you say, they were bitten, got sick, turned, we know how it goes. But they're basically infected humans. They're unwell. Do you ever think about that before putting one down?' I pressed.

Last night had been heavy, at least a dozen Pyre attacks on the walls, and the lack of sleep combined with the busy work of the armoury was making me go cross-eyed.

'Where is this coming from, Astrid?' Hild asked.

I shrugged. My heart hammered against my ribs every time I thought about last night.

Hild narrowed her eyes at me. We had known each other long enough that sometimes it felt as if she could read my mind, and she knew that if she didn't push, I would come to her.

'You know, there was this one Pyre that was driving me barmy last month,' she said. 'Kept coming back, night after night. One of the smart ones, you know? I swear, this bitch had it all figured out. She would watch the stupid Pyres run at us, get caught on the fence and shot through the heart, but she wouldn't do nothing. Just sat there, waiting.'

'One of the smart ones? Please. Sure, some manage to avoid the traps . . . but watching and waiting? You saw some Influencer girl.' I pulled on the repaired string of the crossbow in front of me. The old shoelace held strong as I tested the tension, so I put it to one side with the others.

Hild spread out her hands. 'I'm serious. This bitch was a Pyre. Look, I thought I was imagining it too, some scrawny girl on the edge of the woods watching us. But after a full week, she came out from the trees and I saw her through my scope. Pale skin, black eyes, sharp teeth. Covered in blood. She was a Pyre, Astrid, I swear on my life.'

'All right, fine. Not that smart, though. You can hit a Pyre at a hundred paces. No way you didn't nail her then and there,' I said.

Hild tapped the side of her head. I rolled my eyes. In another life, in another place, she'd be a storyteller.

'No, my friend. Because I saw something that turned my blood Pyre cold. This Pyre didn't run at the wall, shrieking like normal. She went into the field where the corpses were, and she picked one of them up. She struggled, like, but she got that son-of-a-bitch off the floor and started dragging its arse back to the treeline.'

'One of ours? Maybe she thought there would be blood left in them?' I asked.

'Nah. The attacks had been non-stop; we hadn't had chance to go out and move the Pyre corpses. This mad cow was going to collect *one of her own*. Like she was a war hero or some shit. You ever seen anything like that?'

I blinked. 'No, I haven't. You sure? That sounds kind of wild, Hild. Maybe the lack of sleep finally got to you.'

'Well, I guess we'll never know. She may have piqued old Hild's curiosity for a while, but I wasn't about to let some Pyre get what she wanted. So I nailed her when she had her back turned. Right through the heart too; I checked during clean-up the next day. Best shot I've ever made, that was.' Hild shrugged.

'Yeah, yeah,' I said, half laughing.

'I swear. And I know this is really thick of me, but it's taken me eight years to realise we call them Pyres because they're corpses that burn in the sun.'

I snorted. 'Are you serious? Why did you think we called them that?'

'I don't know. It was when I saw my score lying there in the morning sun, cooking, and I was like, damn, she's like her own funeral pyre.' Hild laughed. 'I thought Pyre was a scientific acronym or some shit.'

'Standing for what?' I said, laughing louder.

'Like . . . Pretty Yucky and . . . Really . . . Evil?' Hild replied, and we both chuckled.

'Yeah, super scientific, Hild,' I said. 'To be fair, wouldn't zombies be more appropriate?'

Hild snorted. 'Shows what you know. First of all, they're not *dead* dead like zombies. Remember the one that got stuck on the fence that week we weren't allowed to go out? Would have survived if it hadn't shrivelled up and died of blood thirst, poor sod.'

'I'm not sure we can prove that theory with one test subject. That they need to feed to live, I mean.'

'And the second thing,' Hild continued, 'is that if they were zombies, we wouldn't know the word zombie. That's the rule in all my zombie comics. Everyone knows that with proper zombies, they're never called that. So, no, obviously they went with Pyre. Sounds like vampire, they drink blood and sometimes munch on human flesh, burn in the sun, the whole shebang, innit?'

I held my hands up. 'I'll bow down to the horror queen on that one. I mean, one bite is a pretty fast way to spread a disease or whatever this thing is. If scientists on the mainland had had time to name Pyres, they might have had time to find out where it all came from and . . . Sorry, I'm just being morbid today. Maybe Pyre stuck because it's all us survivors could come up with. Maybe they have some fancy name on the mainland for them that they won't share with us. You know, alongside all the possible information on where this thing came from, or anything else they might have gleaned from watching over us twenty-four-seven.'

We both went quiet, and Hild started fidgeting.

'Come on, let's go for a walk. I've got splinters in places that you do *not* want to know about from doing this all day,' Hild said.

We put away the last of the crossbows, keeping one each for ourselves. Judith, the leader of the Burgh, made sure everyone had a ranged weapon at all times. It wasn't just the Pyres we were armed against. We'd had raiders before, desperate people who came even in the danger of the night to take what was ours so they could feed themselves, their families. Take what little medicine they could find. Life on the island was tough, even with Bloodwatch's precious crates. Many people took food from them in exchange for changing a camera battery or replacing a lens in a Pyre cave, only to get turned into food themselves. Bled to death for the sake of a chocolate bar. Community raiding was just safer and easier in most cases.

We headed out into the small courtyard. The rules were strict in the Burgh, but fair. It was a small community in comparison to the towns the island supported before the fall, but there were around two hundred of us in all – and no under-sixteens allowed, so we all carried crossbows within the walls. The Pyre attacks were getting more frequent, so having our weapons at all times was practical. It used to be maybe once a week there was a Pyre attack, but in the last week alone it had been five nights in a row.

Hild had her own theories about Pyres getting smart to our ways and coordinating, but it was summer. If I could smell the stench coming off some of the Burghers during our water-rationing months, then the Pyres absolutely could. It was probably just attracting more of them.

The Burgh itself was a secondary school before the fall, and someone way before I arrived had reinforced the chain-link fence with a wooden wall. Right in front of the weapons hut was the old school playground. We used the main building for sleeping quarters, but the community had built a medium-sized wooden hut directly opposite the gates, where the council met and took in any potential new recruits. They had even installed the old school bell in the top parapet, like a church steeple, so a lookout could check for Pyre broods and warn us if they needed more guards on the walls.

It was simple, but it had been home for the last two years.

'So, you gonna tell me what has you so spooked? Except for, obviously, the monsters trying to kill us every night?' Hild asked as we walked a rough circuit of the yard. There weren't many people around at this time. The night guards were already in position and the day shift had turned in for bed.

'Hey, the undead I can handle,' I said, but the anger burning in my veins had me balling my fists. 'It's Bloodwatch I can't stand, but I still gave them a good show. I put down a Pyre kid last night.'

Hild reached out and grabbed my closed fist.

'You didn't put down a Pyre kid. Bloodwatch not only let that happen, they made it happen. How can you not put on a show when we're trapped on a televised prison island?' Hild asked.

Tears pricked at the back of my eyes and I bit my lip hard, my anger giving way to guilt.

'I just hate that staying alive means giving them what they want. The whole spectacle of killing a kid, you know? She had red hair, Hild. She had Wynn's hair.' I looked up at her, Hild's big brown eyes seeming even bigger now she had shaved her head.

'No, she didn't. She had red hair, not Wynn's hair. Not like yours either. And she's not a kid; she's not even alive any more. And that's Bloodwatch's fault, all right? Bloodwatch and our whole supposed government over on that bloodthirsty mainland that let this happen. You have to put it out of your mind, mate. Don't let Bloodwatch get in your head,' Hild said.

I swallowed the lump in my throat. We were just trying to stay alive. It wasn't our fault that we were completely abandoned, fighting on camera to the delight of millions of mainlanders, no doubt. Families, people like me and Dad and Wynn used to be, settled in to watch us on their televisions. It made my blood boil.

'When I was little we watched soap operas and silly dating shows. What sort of monsters get kicks out of watching people fight for their lives by killing undead kids?' I said, spitting as I spoke.

Hild opened her mouth to respond, but the clang of the town bell ringing cut through the stillness of the early evening.

There was only one reason for that sound – to signal a problem outside the walls. Hild nodded at me and we set off at a run.

We jogged across the yard as the bell continued to ring, and reached the nearest ladder that led up to the top of the wall, scaling it two rungs at a time. Half the Burgh was already up there, not that I knew anyone much better than I knew Hild. No one asked questions at the Burgh because most of us were running from more than just the Pyres: Bloodwatch. Not everyone on the island was keen to be 'entertainment'.

Hild pulled herself up and smoothed down her leathers. Even when we were on the wall, we made sure our arms were covered. It only took one bite to turn.

'Hey, Griff,' Hild called out to a stocky guy with dark curly hair. Griff had arrived in the Burgh a few months ago but was already a valued sharpshooter. 'Any idea what's going on?'

'Have to assume it's something to do with that,' Griff said, pointing to the field beyond the wall.

Out in the long grass, beyond the spiked outer fence stained with Pyre blood, there was a huge wooden crate. I looked up to the darkening sky and could see the silhouette of a plane, disappearing out of sight over the treeline.

'It's an Influencer package,' Hild said. 'Why would they drop an Influencer package off here? They know our rules.'

This had never happened in the two years I had been in the Burgh. We only had three rules: no Influencers, no cameras and no kids. Bloodwatch employees were too precious to set foot on the island, so all cameras had to be put up by people already here. None of us wanted the cameras in the Burgh, so nobody put them up. Bloodwatch weren't forcing us to have them – but that was probably a matter of time. For now, it was one of the only places on the island without the bloody things, and that's what made it the perfect place for someone like me to hide. I spent two years in the woods surrounded by cameras before I turned sixteen and was allowed through the gates. No escape.

'Maybe it's a mistake. Farmers' Guild are coming tomorrow to top up our food supplies, right? Maybe one of them will be interested. Let's leave it,' I said.

The thought of going that far outside the gates at this time of night, even in plain sight of Hild and the Burgh, made my blood run cold.

Hild squinted through her scope. 'Not sure we can. Take a look.'

She passed it to me and it took a second for the image to focus. Since we had been standing on the wall, three remote cameras had crept out from the woods, all focused on the package. The cameras were like big, black, lifeless eyes mounted on metal rods for legs. Each one had the familiar label on the side: PROPERTY OF THE BLOODWATCH NETWORK.

I didn't know what was creepier, the cameras or the Pyres. At least the lenses in the forest were mounted to the trees. There were thousands of them out there, but clearly this required a close-up. What was in this box? Teeth whitener? Unchippable nail varnish for us to test? Most of the Influencer deals had beauty products inside. I guess being a survivalist just wasn't pretty enough for television.

'You don't see it, do you?' Hild said gently from my right.

It was getting dark fast, and soon the Pyres would be out of their dens, but I could make out the label on the Influencer package. When I was young, and still had my family, we'd even tried a couple of packages. They were always labelled with the rules of usage, how often the user had to show the results on camera, and where to collect their rewards, which were usually food or medicine.

But not this one. This package had a huge sticker over the side, almost as big as the box itself. Maybe I was deluding myself by not reading it until now, or maybe my subconscious was trying to protect me from something I knew would come one day.

The label read: FOR THE EXECUTIONER.

'Astrid,' Hild said when I didn't move. 'It's addressed to you.'

CHAPTER TWO

What do you do when your worst moment, your lowest ebb of humanity, was caught on camera?

I hadn't seen or heard that name for a long time. It wasn't a secret, but no one in the Burgh called me that. At least, not after the first day when the council decided to let me live here. Everyone at the Burgh had a reason for avoiding the cameras. The Executioner was mine.

Right after the incident that earned me that nickname, our house was bombarded with Influencer crates, offering all sorts of shit from medical supplies to gourmet food. One even had fan letters inside. I was halfway through reading the first one before I threw up.

Violence sells, apparently.

The same sour bile crept up my throat and I tried to swallow it down. Why were they bothering me now, after years of peace? With the Bloodwatch Network's coverage, they knew I was here the whole time, but I wasn't the only 'celebrity' on the island. The cameras caught all sorts of heroics, both accidental and intentional. They had entertained the masses for nearly two years while Bloodwatch left me alone.

'You don't have to go out there,' Hild said as I lowered the scope.

All the other guards were staring either at me, the package or their own shuffling feet. It wasn't like they had seen the footage of what happened, obviously. None of us had access to television screens. But news travelled fast on the island, even without the footage. The first time I heard the nickname was during those two years in the woods, when I came across a small survival group. I was looking for food, I hadn't eaten in days, but they knew who I was right away. The red hair gave it away. They were so terrified they threw their dinner at me and ran.

I blinked back tears and watched wordlessly as the package burst into flames.

'Shit,' Hild shouted. A few of the other guards cursed and raised their crossbows. 'Dammit, it's too dark. That fire is going to draw every Pyre for miles around.'

She was right. There was no way we could hold up against a whole brood.

The words barely left Hild's mouth before the first few Pyres appeared from the treeline. It was fully dark now, but the flames lit their pale bodies as they raced towards the package. One of them got too close and set itself alight, screaming as the shreds of what was once their dress burned up first, and then their skin. The other three Pyres held back, unsure. One of them was right in front of the nearest camera. Bloodwatch must be loving this. After a few seconds, the Pyre that was alight keeled over on to the grass and stilled.

Then the other three looked up at the wall.

'They've seen us. That bloody package just rang the dinner bell,' I said.

Instead of lifting my crossbow, I holstered it on my back. Hild raised an eyebrow.

'We have to get that fire out. There's only a few right now, but this could be a bloodbath. If we get any climbers . . .' I trailed off.

Hild nodded. 'All right, but I'm coming with you, and we need cover. Griff, you're with us.'

Griff pinched the bridge of his nose and nodded. Guilt twisted my stomach into knots. It was my fault that this was happening, but the quicker we stopped it, the more lives we would save. The council could argue about kicking me out later.

'OK. Hild, you and I will carry the fire blanket. It's too big and heavy to handle on my own. Griff, we need you to cover us at close range from incoming Pyres. Everyone else, defend as you would. The walls can't be breached.'

Griff, Hild and I ran back to the ladder and jumped down the rungs, making for the gate. The first set of doors was already opening for us, and someone had run over from the town hall with our fire blanket. We had bought it from a travelling trader a few months ago after he demonstrated how well it could starve our bonfire. We hadn't needed to use it yet.

The gate was an airlock – once the inner doors were open, we had to step into the space beyond, and then the guards could open the outer ones. Then we were on our own.

'I've never been outside the walls after dark since being

here,' Griff said nervously as we waited for the gates to close behind us.

'Me neither,' Hild and I said at the same time.

There was that guilt again, gnawing at the pit of my stomach, mixing with the anger that came every time I felt unsafe on the island I once called home. These people were putting their lives on the line because of my past, and none of this would be happening at all if it wasn't for Bloodwatch abandoning us in the name of television ratings.

'Hey, we will see the sun rise.' The island's mantra. Whether you're passing someone on the road, or holding a dying man in your arms, it was the thing to say. Sunrise was the best and safest part of any day on the island. There was no better time to feel at peace.

The sun felt a long way away right now, though.

Hild and Griff nodded at me. Hild grabbed one end of the fire blanket and I adjusted the other over my shoulder so I could have access to my bolt gun, which was in its holster on my hip. You never knew when a Pyre might climb up the wall for a face-to-face meet-and-greet, and I knew as well as anyone that a chest-shot to the heart was a better target from a distance, but a headshot would do just as well close up. Dad had used the bolt gun to slaughter animals on the farm my grandma had outside the city, once they were old enough to butcher. It fires a high-pressured bolt of metal outwards, then retracts again for the next use. No ammo required.

The thought of Dad made me light-headed and I blinked.

Focus. The door behind us had snapped shut and the front gate was opening. Bolts were raining down from crossbows above our heads.

'Looks like the brood is incoming,' I said. 'Keep your heads out there.'

'We will see the sun rise,' Hild and Griff said.

Outside the walls, it was chaos. Usually it would be pitch black by now, but the light from the full moon and the raging bonfire lit up the path in front of us with ease. A Pyre ran straight at us, only collapsing when Griff aimed a perfect shot at its head.

'Let's go. Nothing we haven't seen before,' Hild said, snapping Griff and me out of it. We cleared dead Pyres from the fence all the time. We just didn't often see them moving up close.

'OK, let's go,' I said.

Hild and I had to walk in unison, carrying the blanket between us. It would have been easier for Griff to carry it instead of me as he was the same height as Hild, but I couldn't be the one with a clear weapon and a free runback if things went bad. I'd never forgive myself.

Griff was doing a superb job, firing off rapid rounds of bolts from the satchel that hung at his waist. That said, his bag was looking lighter by the minute; the quicker we got this fire out, the better.

The brood was in full force now. Bolts flew over our heads from the wall as we headed to where the fire was. The ground was littered with Pyre corpses, and Hild and I tripped over a stray arm or leg a couple of times. The smell was the worst part. Some of the Pyres had been as stupid as the first and caught fire, and the smell of their burning flesh made my stomach heave.

'Nearly there,' I said out loud, more to myself than to Hild or Griff.

The heat from the fire was fierce. Sweat made my shoulder slick and holding up the blanket became more and more difficult, but I couldn't let Hild down, so we kept moving. I tried not to register the filthy bodies of the corpses as we walked. If there was another child, I would lose it, and this wasn't the time.

'OK, we're here,' Hild said.

I looked up and shielded my eyes from the inferno in front of us. We dropped the blanket on the floor so we could grab one end each to lift it over the package. The box itself was taller than Hild, so I needed to run round the back to cover it.

I grabbed my corner of the blanket and nodded to Hild, who nodded back. I ran round the far side of the box. This was the most dangerous part of the mission; I was out of the sightline of the guards up on the wall, and right in front of the treeline, where the Pyres were running from. Griff was covering me, but he had Hild to protect too, so I had to have my wits about me. I'd been in worse situations.

'OK, ready?' I shouted.

The roar of the flames and the screeching of the Pyres almost drowned me out. I peered round the flames at Hild and saw her eyes grow wide, her finger pointing at something behind me.

Griff raised his crossbow but he wasn't fast enough. The Pyre had me on the grass in seconds, flat on my stomach and winded from the fall. It dug long nails into the shoulders of my jacket but it couldn't pierce through – thank you, leathers. The Pyre clocked what was going on and leaned down to bite my wrist.

'Astrid!' Hild screamed. I could see her standing with her part of the blanket next to Griff, who was aiming the crossbow at me but was too scared to shoot in case he hit me.

I had to act fast. I twisted my head from where the Pyre was holding me down and watched as it chomped again and again at the leather on my wrist. Its long dark hair had fallen out in clumps, exposing patches of flesh underneath. I could see the whites of her bloodshot eyes as she tried to tear through the cuff. She smelled like death.

In one swift movement, I moved my right hand down to my holster, grabbed the bolt gun and twisted away from her. The Pyre screamed, her grip on my shoulder and wrist tighter than ever, furious I had interrupted her. She stared at me, millimetres from my face, her teeth spilling out of her mouth at jagged angles.

And behind her head, on the side of her skull where her hair was missing, one of the cameras that had arrived with the package leaned in for a close-up. So Bloodwatch wanted a money shot? I'd give them one.

I brought the bolt gun up, placed the barrel between her eyes and pulled the trigger.

Pyre blood wasn't like human blood. It was always black and sticky, which made it unbearable when it was smeared across your face with pieces of skull and brain tissue. I pushed the corpse off me and swallowed down a mouthful of vomit.

'Astrid?' I heard Hild calling out to me. We had to get this blanket over the blaze before another Pyre tried their luck.

'I'm good,' I shouted back, jumping to my feet and reholstering my bolt gun. The camera that had caught the close-up of me blowing the Pyre's brains out was still zoomed in on the corpse, but the other two had moved round and focused on me. Hild was fighting off Pyres with her crossbow in one hand and the blanket in the other. Griff was nailing chest-shot after chest-shot. But all the cameras were looking at me. One was so close I could see my pale face reflected in it, my red hair spilling out of the tight bun I had woven it into that morning.

I pushed past the cameras and grabbed the fire blanket.

'Ready?' I shouted.

Hild nodded. With Griff covering us, we heaved the thing with one joint throw over the crate, and the light from the fire vanished in seconds. And then the darkness came.

'Shit!' Griff yelled, swinging his crossbow around wildly. Bolts still flew overhead so the gate was clearly able to see something – we had the full moon to thank for that. As for me, Hild and Griff, being so close to a bright light and then having it taken away was messing with our vision.

'Just get back to the gates,' Hild said, blinking in the darkness.

I grabbed her hand. 'Good idea.'

'Uh, guys,' Griff said, nerves shaking his voice.

Hild and I followed his gaze as my eyes adjusted to the gloom. Out of the darkness, a dozen or so skeletal bodies loomed ahead, slowly moving towards us.

'I'm out of arrows,' Griff said, pointing at his empty bag.

'Same,' Hild said, her fingers squeezing together around mine.

I gulped. This was it. Another two names to add to the Executioner's death count – but at least the Pyres would get me before I could add any more. I closed my eyes.

'I'm sorry,' I said.

The sound of gunfire cut through the moans of the Pyres and made all of us drop to the ground. I squeezed my eyes shut in anticipation of my death-by-Pyre. I hadn't heard a gunshot in years; the ammo was scarce and too difficult to manufacture. That's why my own reusable bolt gun was so precious.

We were supposed to be dead, torn limb from limb, but after a few seconds the noise stopped and the night was silent.

I opened my eyes.

CHAPTER THREE

I'd only ever seen cameras before, never the people that control them.

On the island, for as long as I can remember after the fall, there have been the cameras. Some of them are fixed on to trees or on the side of ruined buildings. The mainland used to send boxes of aid to us. Several planes a day would drop huge crates with parachutes to the ground, usually filled with freeze-dried rations and medicine.

Then we started fighting over it. As time went on and resources became scarcer, people got desperate. Dad said he would go to the drop sites and there would already be a group there with weapons, killing anyone that came close. And it wasn't long after that the Bloodwatch Network sent their first shipment of cameras.

Obviously, the crate gangs got to them first. Dad found a couple of the enclosed notes after they had gone, describing the contents of the box: dozens of cameras, and promises of more food and medicine if the person who found the crate installed them at various locations. There were even tools and equipment to make it easier.

Next came the shipments of batteries to replace dead ones in the cameras, which eventually turned into specially made batteries that worked indefinitely. Then the planes started targeting crates more carefully and dropping off the traveller cameras that could move around on their own. Pyres were drawn by the noise, but they ignored the cameras. They were interested in blood, not battery acid.

And every single camera had the same sticker across it: PROPERTY OF THE BLOODWATCH NETWORK.

Dad assumed that the world had grown curious about what was happening on the island. Soon there were cameras in every nook and cranny. The Influencer deals were a weird thing to get my head around, but Dad said that before the island fell it was pretty common for companies to offer famous people free stuff in return for something they needed. Then it was money. Now it was food.

Dad knew a lot of stuff. I was ten when the fall happened, and Wynn was only four, so it was hard to remember.

Focus. The present. Thinking about Dad and Wynn was not the way forward.

I opened my eyes and looked up at the group of people who'd just saved our arses. They were all dressed in black T-shirts and cargo trousers, and were holding guns. The T-shirts all had a logo on the right-hand chest pocket with the letters TBN on them. The 'N' had a red smudge of what was supposed to be blood dropping off the end of the letter. Three guesses who these lads worked for.

'Please tell me you got that?'

A woman with long pink braids was talking to a man holding a camera on his shoulder. I raised an eyebrow; the three traveller cams weren't enough?

'We got it, Nova, absolute gold,' the cameraman said.

The woman, Nova apparently, lifted up a smartphone to her face. I hadn't seen one of those since I was too young to own one. It lit her up from below and reminded me of when I used to use a torch to tell Wynn scary stories at night, to drown out the Pyre screams. Nova smiled.

'Excellent. The gaffer will be pleased with this,' she said.

'Erm, hello? Anyone want to tell us what the hell is going on?' Hild asked.

One of the men with the guns tapped Nova on the shoulder.

'Nova, satellite imagery has a new brood incoming. Drawn by the gunfire. We should move this conversation indoors.'

'That's a shame. I was hoping to get some noddy shots to bulk out the promo, but I guess we can get those tomorrow,' Nova said.

Noddy shots?

'Can we come into your little fort?' Nova said, addressing Hild. She spoke very slowly.

Hild worked her jaw. She was trying not to say something she would regret later, and she knew as well as I did that we needed answers from these people. For whatever reason, they'd brought a brood down on our heads.

'Nova? Brood is two minutes out,' the gunman prompted.

Hild gritted her teeth. 'Sure.'

'Lovely,' Nova said, clasping her device to her chest.

We got up off the floor and headed through the group of people. There were ten of them – five gunmen, two carrying cameras, two holding weird sticks with furry bits of fluff on the end, and Nova. We headed back to the Burgh at a jog and they followed us, trying not to trip over any corpses on the way.

'Lovely? Who speaks like that in the middle of a Pyre attack?' Griff mumbled as we ran across the field.

'Not islanders,' I said.

By the time we reached the gates, the first one was already open. The guards must have been watching the whole thing through their scopes. They couldn't hear us, obviously, but they knew guns when they saw them. It wasn't exactly like we could say no and fight firepower with wooden arrows. When the inner gates opened, I wasn't surprised to see the whole council standing there, including Judith.

'Oh, hello,' Nova said, flashing Judith a wide white smile. 'My name is Nova. We're here on behalf of the—'

'We know who you are,' Judith interrupted, raising a scarred eyebrow. Judith was a politician in the before times, so we deferred to her when something was up.

Nova's smile faltered, but she pushed on. 'Right, yes, I know you have been benefitting from the Bloodwatch Network's care packages for years now.'

Judith narrowed her eyes. 'We don't take your bribe crates. And you would know that, because despite destroying every camera we find, I know you have satellites on us. Eyes in the sky, right?'

Wow. Some people said Judith was paranoid, but Hild always said that just because someone is paranoid doesn't mean they're wrong.

'The Burgh has been of particular interest to the Bloodwatch Network in recent years, yes,' Nova laughed, but it sounded hollow.

Recent years? I thought about the label on the package. Oh. She means since I got here. I pursed my lips together. Just another clown for Bloodwatch's viewers to gawk over. Some days I couldn't decide who I hated more: the people putting on the show, or the people that let them.

Overhead, one of the guards shouted, followed by the soft *whoosh* of several bolts being loosed. Just because we weren't still out there didn't mean the Pyres wouldn't try it on.

'Perhaps we could have a proper chat?' Nova continued, plastic smile back on her face.

Judith sighed, then nodded once and turned to walk back to the town hall. The council followed her, and we fell into step behind them. As we crossed the yard, several people had come out to see what was going on. Tonight, all eyes were on me for the first time in two years, and their stares bore through me like a bolt through a Pyre's heart.

We entered the main chamber of the town hall in silence. There was a long wooden table in the centre of the space where the council sat, and they took up their chairs, lining either side with Judith at the head. When Griff, Hild and I came in, we waited along the left wall to be addressed. The council rules were strict inside the town hall. You didn't speak until you were spoken to.

Clearly, Nova didn't get that on her camera feeds, because she walked right across the room. Her cameramen and guards spread out to either side, both lenses and guns making sure they had good coverage.

'Lovely space; love what you've done with it. We can only see the roof from overhead,' Nova said. She leaned on the back of Judith's chair with one elbow as she gazed around the room, and Judith looked as if she was about to strangle her.

'Let's skip the pleasantries. Clearly you are here for a purpose, and we don't need you here any longer than you have to be. What do you want with Ms Fireside?'

I gulped. I knew things were bad when Judith called us by our last names, and she wouldn't even look at me. Someone must have filled her in about the label on the crate.

'A woman who knows what she wants – right after my own heart,' Nova said, and Judith scowled. 'Right, straight to it – Astrid, dear, would you like to come up here?'

I blinked. This was the first time it was confirmed that she knew me. Or at least that my reputation preceded me.

My feet stuck to the floor and Hild had to nudge me forward. Somehow I managed to make my way over without my knees giving out.

'That's right, good.' Nova was speaking to me but looking at her device. 'Filly, a little tighter on that close-up for me. Great.'

As she spoke, I heard the whir of a camera on my left, and the man holding it stepped forward. I'd seen the lenses many times but I'd never felt so exposed.

'OK. Firstly, to you all here – apologies for the theatrics. The pyrotechnics guy told me it would be a small fire at most, so we didn't mean to cause such a stir. But I think you'll agree it made for a rather riveting showpiece, and no one got hurt, so we can take that as a win.'

'No one got hurt?' Hild spat. 'Astrid was nearly a blood bag. We could have been overrun by those things.'

Nova waved her hand in the air as if Hild was a child. 'We had enough ammo to make sure that wouldn't happen. We scanned the area beforehand so we knew there were minimal Pyres nearby.'

'Oh well, that's OK, then,' Hild grumbled.

'Would be nice if you shared some of that technology with us,' Wilf, another council member with a bald head and long dark beard, piped up.

A murmur went round the other members at the table. Jud, Judith's right-hand man, nudged Wilf. The council had their own secret language sometimes, and despite the vote rotating leadership, most of the same faces made it back to the table after every election.

'Oh, sorry. We aren't allowed to interfere too much in the natural environment. The nature channel we sell footage to like to keep the island preserved as much as possible,' Nova said with a smile.

No one had the strength to respond. There was nothing natural about the Pyres, but we had been abandoned since day one. We didn't expect that to change now.

'I think what we need to know,' I said quietly, trying to rein us back to the point, 'is why now. We haven't seen anyone from the mainland since I was a kid, not in eight years of the fall. The government keeps away even the most persistent adrenaline junkies and curious idiots with the patrol boats. No one is allowed to come even if for some bizarre reason they want to, right? So why are you here?'

Nova grinned again. 'I'm so glad you asked, Astrid. I prepared a presentation for you all. Can we dim these candle thingies?'

Nobody moved.

Nova adjusted her top impatiently. 'I'm sure it's dark enough for the projector anyway. Lief?'

One of the men stepped forward, a new device in his hand. We had screens and electronics before the fall, but they had clearly come on in leaps and bounds since then. The devices in these people's hands were little more than a fuzzy memory. Lief pressed a button on the top of his gadget and a ray of light shone out of the end and cast an image on the wall behind us.

'Here we are. So, as you correctly deduced, we're here from the Bloodwatch Network. We're the ones that have been sending the cameras and Influencer crates for the last eight years,' Nova said. The image on-screen was the same as on their shirts, the logo for the Bloodwatch Network: TBN.

'We essentially film the happenings on the island and try to learn from them,' she continued. 'You have to understand, when the Pyres first attacked and took down society here so quickly, the world was both amazed and horrified.'

'Oh yeah? Try living through it,' Hild muttered.

'Obviously, our first thoughts were to send care packages and aid to those still alive,' Nova said, ignoring Hild. The image switched to one of a care package, not on the island but back on the mainland, surrounded by people helping to pack it up with food, medicine, clothes and blankets.

'But unfortunately, after the first few years, people started to lose interest,' Nova said.

'I guess being hunted by bloodsucking monsters every night is one of those experiences where you had to be there,' I said.

'I'm just getting to that,' Nova said with another smile.

I raised an eyebrow at Hild and she shook her head.

The next image was a chart. The bottom axis was labelled AUDIENCE VIEWING FIGURES and the left-most axis was labelled TIME. You didn't have to be great at maths to see that over the last eight years the viewing figures had gone from the millions in the first couple of years after the cameras landed to a little under a hundred thousand last year. A hundred thousand people. I couldn't even imagine it.

'So, as you can see, around two years after the island fell is when we introduced the cameras. That worked for a while, and we even had a twenty-four-hour channel dedicated to live footage from the island. But once the aid packages stopped, viewing got a little gloomy. No one likes to watch sad television,' Nova said.

I bit my tongue so hard, the metallic taste of blood filled my mouth.

'That was when we introduced the Influencer deals. A little advertising, a few bits and bobs for you guys, win–win,' Nova continued. She pointed at a small rise in figures in the middle of the chart, before another decline.

'But to be honest, the network has been struggling recently. Corporate partnerships are down, viewing figures are down – even the nature documentary network has been buying less footage.' Nova sighed, like this was an actual problem. 'The network has sunk millions into Bloodwatch, and we need a way to recoup our loses or we might have to shut down entirely.'

That made me think. We struggled, sure, but if there were no crates at all? A lot of those that took Influencer deals came to trade with us. No medicine was manufactured on the island. If we lost that, it could be the end of us.

'Luckily, that's where I came to the rescue,' Nova gushed.

The image on her presentation moved again, on to a new picture with a photograph of an island at night. Across the centre were the words *Escape from Blood Island*.

'I don't get it,' Hild said. 'There is no escaping from here; you quarantined us years ago. I've seen you blow a raft in the water sky high for trying to escape with the big ships you have patrolling the sea.'

Nova shook her head. 'This won't be documentary footage. *Escape from Blood Island* is a game show. And we're hoping Astrid will be a contestant.'

Game show. Contestant. Footage. Documentary. These almost foreign words swirled around my head while I tried to understand what Nova was saying.

The Bloodwatch Network had come here to recruit me into my worst nightmare.

CHAPTER FOUR

'A game-show contestant? What planet are you living on?' Griff asked.

'I think you might be interested when I tell you what the prize is.' Nova spoke in a sing-song voice. 'The winners of *Escape from Blood Island* get . . . to, uh, escape from Blood Island!'

'But we aren't allowed to leave,' I said. All the guilt from earlier was quickly turning to anger. 'Why are you playing with us?'

Nova grinned. 'That's the beauty. I've been given special dispensation from the prime minister to bring one lucky resident of Modi-Morde to the mainland of Nosferra.'

It was weird hearing someone use the proper names for the mainland and the island. On the island, or Modi-Morde as it was technically called, there was nothing *but* our land, and their land. Hence it was known as simply 'the island' now. And as for the mainland, Nosferra was a long-forgotten name for the place that abandoned us, the place that carried on with life as normal as we grew used to our nocturnal, monstrous inhabitants.

'The winner gets to leave here, no strings attached. There will obviously be checks to see you aren't infected but,'

Nova continued, waving her hands, because yeah, *that* was the unimportant part, 'apart from that, you get to leave.'

'Really?' Griff asked, his mouth twitching. 'So can any of us sign up? The chance to leave this place, I mean . . . you'll have volunteers lined up from one side of the island to the other.'

Nova pursed her lips. 'Ah, now, that's the catch. This is sort of a last-chance-type scenario for the network, so we had to make sure we picked the spiciest of contestants. And we're sort of on a deadline, so we ran a vote back at home so the viewers could choose their favourite characters for the show. It's a done deal.'

'Characters?' Hild scoffed.

Nova waved her hand again. 'Right, sorry, yes. To your adoring fans, you're like characters, but of course you're real people. Don't you see? That's what will bring in the viewing figures. People love reality television. It's just so much more . . .'

'Real?' I suggested, so deadpan that Hild almost laughed.

'Right. See, Astrid, you get it! That's why you're so popular. You got a big chunk of the vote, you know. People miss you since you left our screens two years ago.'

Was this even *real*? Screens, fans, popularity contests. I knew there must be some morbid curiosity after what I did. But after all this time? I couldn't think straight.

Nova took the silence as her sign to continue. 'OK, so let's go over the rules. We have created a series of tasks for you to complete – I won't spoil the fun by telling you those now – over the course of a week. These tasks will take you all over the island, places we've scoped out to be the most filmic locations, obviously. And your job is to keep yourself alive and play nicely with your partner until the finale. Simples.'

'Wait. Partner? You didn't say anything about a partner,' I said, crossing my arms. This was getting more outrageous by the minute.

'Ah, yes. Turns out a lot of people on the mainland *are* total adrenaline junkies. After eight years of watching the island on television, they want to come and take on the challenge. You'll be partnered up with a brave soul from the mainland, who is playing for a huge cash prize – one hundred thousand credits, do you remember those? Anyway, we still use that currency, if you were wondering.' Nova finished and looked around as if we should all be impressed.

Instead, all hell broke loose.

'Excuse me, are you calling our life here an adrenaline trip?'

'We remember your dirty money, all right. We just don't have a use for it any more.'

'Who cares about money? Anyone who wants to come here for some sort of sick holiday is a psychopath. Why should Astrid play nice with them?'

'Brave soul? Stupid, more like.'

'And what if Astrid doesn't want to leave?'

That last one came from Hild, and everyone quietened down. I smiled at her: she always knew me best. My family were gone. Hild, the Burgh, they were my life now. I had never known anything but the island; I couldn't leave.

And who would willingly come *here* in return for something as worthless as money?

Nova clasped her hands together. 'I get it. Truly, I do. But I think you may struggle to say no when you see what I'm offering to this quaint little town—'

'The Burgh,' Judith corrected her.

'Right, yes, the Burgh. I think when you see what we have to offer you'll be biting our hand off. Just a figure of speech, of course . . . Let me show you.'

Nova clicked her fingers and the next image appeared on the wall projection. My mouth dropped open.

It was a survivalist's dream. On the screen was a huge pile of stuff, so much it was hard to take it all in. Dried-food rations. Guns. Ammo crates. Medicine packages. Clothes. Tarps. Tools like saws and drills and new hammers. Sheets of metal. The more I looked, the more I saw. It was enough to keep the Burgh going for months, years even.

'If Astrid joins the cast of *Escape from Blood Island* – and, Astrid, sweetie, it's totally your choice – a plane will drop off all of this in crates tomorrow morning. If not, well, let's just say that there are more fire crates where yours came from, and this little Burgh really lights up on camera,' Nova said with a wink.

Never mind thinly veiled, that threat was out there. Nobody moved. Judith said nothing, jaw set. This wasn't a choice, or even a debate. In one photograph, Nova had cut off my old life and forced me into a new one. One that I would be lucky to live through.

'So Astrid has to join your TV show, complete some tasks you set, play nice with some idiot mainlander partner, and if she makes it to the end, you'll let her live on the mainland? And no matter what the outcome, you'll leave the Burgh alone?' Wilf asked, his eyes on Judith.

'Correct,' said Nova.

'And in the meantime she has to fight off broods of Pyres, night after night?' Hild said.

'I wouldn't put it like that, but it wouldn't be a very good show if we didn't have any Pyres . . . participating,' Nova said, setting her jaw.

'I'll do it,' I said.

'Astrid, no.' Hild reached for my arm.

I turned to Nova. 'Can I have a second with my friend?' I asked. One of the men with a camera swivelled their lens on to us. 'Not on film?' I said through gritted teeth.

Nova chewed her lip for a moment, then nodded. 'Boys? Cameras off. We probably need to clean the lenses anyway before any blood gets under the rubber seals.'

Hild didn't let go of my arm until we were in the far corner of the room. A few council members looked over at us, but most were in deep discussion about what they could do with the goodies on the projection already.

'Astrid, you don't have to go,' Hild said, her voice cracking slightly.

'I think you know I do. Look at what they can do for us, Hild. And before you say that we don't need that stuff,' I said, cutting her off as she opened her mouth to protest, 'we absolutely do. Besides, they're not going to leave us alone now. And Nova's threats against the Burgh aren't exactly subtle. Bloodwatch own this island. I've got to go.'

'But what about when you win?' Hild asked in a whisper.

I laughed. 'Here I am worrying about dying, and you're worried about me leaving?'

'Oh, you'll win,' said Hild. She grabbed me by the shoulders, her blue eyes boring into my muddy hazel ones. 'Even if they give you the scrawniest, most idiotic mainlander there is as a partner, you'll win. You've always run from your nickname, but it's a part of who you are. They call you the Executioner for a reason, Astrid. Use it.'

I blinked. Apart from odd times people called me that when I first arrived, I hadn't told Hild much about how I'd earned my nickname. Rumours spread fast, but she never asked me about it, never pushed. And now I wouldn't have a chance to talk to her properly about it.

No, I couldn't think like that.

'You're right,' I said. 'I'm gonna win this thing and then you know what? I'm not going to leave. I'll just come home. My tourist partner can collect their money, but I'll stay here. I didn't hear anything in the rules saying I couldn't.'

Hild grinned and a tear spilled down her cheek. 'That's my Astrid. You'll smash this and be back home before you know it.'

'Exactly.' I swallowed a hard lump in my throat. I'd been on my own before, for two whole years after what happened to Wynn and Dad and before I was old enough to enter the Burgh, and it had almost broken me. This was only a few days. And I'd killed more Pyres than I could count.

This was my punishment, for what I'd let happen to Dad and Wynn.

Hild and I walked back over to Nova. 'All right, so you promise that the supplies will be here tomorrow?'

'First thing,' Nova said. 'We've offered all the contestants something. We won't go back on our word – it's on camera, after all.'

Right. The other contestants. They were voted for too, nominated to take part in this twisted game for a ticket off the island and something precious that their family or friends needed. The people I had to outlive.

'Then we have a—'

'Wait – Lief, cameras in position.' Nova held up a hand in front of my face while the people with cameras reholstered them on their shoulders. Lief had packed the projector away and was looking at his own rectangular device. Eventually he nodded.

'Sorry, Astrid, mind saying that again? Cameras are rolling now. This isn't live like the other static cams, so we can easily edit it together later.'

I wasn't a hundred per cent, and repeating myself felt sticky and dishonest, but I did it anyway. 'Uh, we have a deal?'

'Great,' Nova squealed. 'You know, they told me that you would say no. But I told them I could get you. What a coup!' She wasn't looking at me any more, instead tapping away on her device. 'The producers will be thrilled. You'll see when we get to HQ. Come on.'

'Sorry – what?' I asked, panic closing my throat. I knew I had to do this, but hadn't thought it would be so soon. 'Shouldn't we wait until morning to travel? And I need to pack a bag, right?'

Nova raised an eyebrow at me. 'You're fine as you are. We'll provide you with everything you need when we get there. Besides, I've messaged the logistics team and they've already set off ground charges to distract the Pyres and scatter them away from here. We need to land the helicopter now.'

'Helicopter?' Hild asked. We had seen helicopters since the fall, just like we had seen cars and old trucks and even small planes, grounded relics of when the island was still considered a part of the mainland, when they actually tried to save it. But it had been years since the mainland sent over anything not stamped with the Bloodwatch insignia. And it was nearly eight years since I'd seen a helicopter in the sky.

Nova put her device in her backpack. 'They're coming in. We need to go. If we hang around too long with the noise of the helicopter, more Pyres will come, and we've troubled you good people long enough.' She flashed another smile at Judith, who said nothing.

I half hoped Judith would jump up, say something, beg me not to go. But that wasn't Judith. I was surprised enough when she grabbed my wrist as we turned to leave.

'Thank you,' she said. And then she let go, and I was being swept out the door.

Outside, a fierce wind had sprung up. A helicopter, blades turning fast enough to kick up a storm, was coming in to land just outside the front gate. Someone had told the guards to open the gates. Nova was right, if we didn't leave soon a whole brood would be beating down on our heads in minutes.

Hild was running alongside me, but we didn't say anything. We'd said our goodbyes already. I gave Griff a smile, a small thank you for helping and an apology for getting caught up in everything.

I took one last look at Hild and reached out, grazing her fingers before I was through the gate. I watched her stern face until the gates closed behind us and the field came into view.

The helicopter was more terrifying than staring down a dozen Pyres. Close up, it was huge and noisy, the blades still turning at the top, and the wind was so strong I nearly fell backwards. One of Nova's people had to practically drag me, head down, inside. Partly because of the wind, partly because I couldn't believe I was voluntarily getting into a metal bird with swords for wings and then flying into the sky.

Once I was in the helicopter someone put a pair of earmuffs over my head and that helped with the noise. Now all I could hear was my own heart hammering against my ribcage, desperate to get out.

I knew how it felt.

Lief shut the door and we took off. The first tilt into the air made my stomach drop, but then we were lifting, faster and faster, and there was nothing I could do but stare out of the dark window in awe.

I'd never seen the Burgh from above. It had always seemed so big when we were climbing the ladder for wall drills or running around the yard, but from up here it looked so small, like a toy castle that Wynn used to have. Then we moved forward, and the Burgh disappeared out of sight.

As we flew, I spotted glimmers of light, fires and some walls built up around the edge of the forest. I knew the Burgh wasn't all there was, but I hadn't left in two years. Seeing signs of life outside the Burgh felt like a dream. I knew from the lay of the land that if it was daylight I might be able to see my old house on the left.

I didn't look.

What I did see, though, was the ocean. In the distance, on the horizon where the sky met the water, there were tiny floating lights. The ships with missiles and guns and whatever else the mainland used to make sure we stayed on this side of the channel.

I'd gone down to the beach once to find one of the rafts that people built to get away, right after what happened with Wynn and Dad. There were always a few along the coastline – whether people built them and then changed their minds when they saw the ships, or whether there were other reasons for the rafts floating back to shore, I didn't know. I pushed one of them into the cold, choppy sea, the water right up to my waist, and willed myself to get on, to get as far away from what had happened as possible.

I never pushed off, obviously. But I knew what would have happened if I'd tried.

The helicopter banked right and I tried not to throw up as I slid across my seat. As we turned away from the ocean, another sight came into view. This one didn't have the soft orange glow of fire, it had the bright white luminosity of electric lights. I couldn't imagine how they weren't being constantly bombarded by Pyres, but as we flew over, I could just make out the hard line of a huge wall, taller than the trees and the beams of the lights, which would make the Pyres pretty much oblivious to them. We couldn't hope to build anything like it ourselves in a hundred years.

And in the centre, overlooking the huge wall, was a tall metal tower with a flashing red light on the top, the only structure I recognised. Everyone knew that was the broadcast tower, the one Bloodwatch, or whatever they were called back then, built to transmit the footage from every part of the island. Some travellers said that dozens of mainlanders died trying to finish it. They even tried to rope in some islanders, those desperate enough to work in exchange for food. But they'd retrofitted an old radio tower, and clearly it was working. It was the highest point on the island and visible from almost anywhere. And it's not like the Pyres ever went for it; there was no blood in those red lights and impenetrable concrete walls.

This was Bloodwatch Network HQ and, from the tilt of the helicopter, we were coming in to land.

CHAPTER FIVE

I couldn't remember the last time I'd slept in a bed with fresh sheets and actual pillows. We had a rota to make sure things were clean enough in the Burgh, but it was more to keep out bedbugs than to make sheets smell like lavender.

When I woke up, it took a second for my eyes to adjust to the dark. I was alone, in my own room, another thing I hadn't had in a long time. In the Burgh, we slept in a barracks. We were each other's family. I'd never felt so lonely in my life, and I pushed down the lump in my throat when I thought about Hild.

I sat up and switched on the small light next to my bed. An actual electrical light. I had used one once or twice after the fall, but it was always battery powered or wound up with a crank, and the light wasn't as bright as this one. After the dark, it was almost blinding.

When we got out of the helicopter last night, Nova's camera crew – I was picking up some of the terminology now – were ushered into a squat building in the middle of what I could only describe as a compound. It was at least ten times the size of the Burgh, with dozens of buildings scattered behind the huge walls. Nova had mentioned with pride that they managed to get it built in only three days by flying everything in prefabricated. I hadn't had a chance to take it in, though, because more people dressed in the same Bloodwatch uniforms had appeared to take me to my bedroom for the night.

The room I was in was small, windowless, with a single bed, a wardrobe and a bedside table. I got up to have a look in the wardrobe and found hanger after hanger of the same Bloodwatch uniform I'd seen on the production crew. The only difference being that the T-shirts were red instead of black, and each one had my name across the back in bold letters. Under that was a string of numbers that made no sense to me.

I put one on and was about to leave the room when I noticed an extra door. I turned the handle and let it swing open.

It was a bathroom. An actual bathroom, attached to my room. I'd seen them since the fall but they never worked. Running water was a luxury. At the Burgh, you went in a latrine that was cleared out twice a day by the poor sod who was on bog duty. As for a shower, we used a jug from the well in the courtyard once a week, as water was rationed for drinking, especially during dry months.

I reached out and twisted the knob on the tap, and out flowed cool, clear water. I hadn't seen water so clean since I lived by the river in the woods. I turned it off, not used to having free rein.

And obviously I used the loo before I left. There was even actual toilet roll, not the recycled paper we used in the Burgh. And it was softer than any we had ever traded for from the Influencer crates. Bliss.

I stepped out of my room feeling fresh. I hadn't dared use the shower, but I did wash my hands, and the soap smelled strongly of strawberries. My palms were silky soft too. Last night the production assistant lady had pointed out where breakfast would be served the next day. I had no idea what time it was, but there were windows in the corridor and the sun was already high in the sky. Shit. I'd slept in.

I hurried down the corridor past other doors that were identical to mine. Were these the bedrooms of the other contestants? I didn't stop, but it did make me curious. Nova said all the contestants from the island were chosen by a vote on the mainland. A popularity contest.

I reached the end of the corridor where a set of double doors led to the cafeteria. The smell of cooked meat permeated through and made my mouth water. We hadn't had meat in weeks at the Burgh.

I pushed the door open to the noise of chatter, so yeah, I was late. Great. The cafeteria was big enough to seat maybe fifty, and most of the long tables were taken up with people wearing black shirts – production crew and staff. The smell was coming from a metal counter nearby, laden with steaming piles of sausage and bacon and eggs. And at the far end of the room, I could see where I was supposed to sit: a table with nine red shirts already tucking into trays of food.

I grabbed a tray of my own and got one of everything. There were fresh pancakes the like of which I hadn't seen since I was a kid, and I smothered them in maple syrup. When you live on the island, you eat when you can, everyone knew that. And right now I could eat a *lot*.

I walked across the room with my tray and approached the red-shirt table.

'Erm, hello,' I said. My voice cracked when I spoke. I gripped the sides of my tray so tightly my knuckles went white.

The table fell silent immediately. Every pair of eyes swivelled to look at me, and nobody moved. After what felt like the longest silence in the world, someone finally spoke.

'Hey, Executioner. Come sit down next to me.' A man with grey hair and a full beard patted the seat next to him, and everyone else on the bench scooched over to accommodate me.

I put my tray down in the empty space and swung my legs over the bench. 'Um, yeah, hi. It's just Astrid, though,' I said.

'Well, shit. You get a bad-ass nickname like that and you settle with something as pussyfooted as Astrid? You have to start thinking about your life choices, girly,' the grey-haired man said. He held out a hand to shake. 'I'm Noon, by the way.'

'Hey, Noon. Erm, can I ask, does everyone here know who I am or . . . ?' I trailed off, addressing the whole table again.

'Oh, yeah. Everyone knows,' said a girl opposite. She was tiny, with neat features and a nose ring. Her hair was bleached white with a pink tinge and she had a full face of make-up. She didn't look much older than me either. 'I'm Cinta. I'd shake your hand but I just did my nails and I'm not, like, a hundred years old.' She went back to her breakfast, which was an apple cut up into pieces.

'Real peach, that one,' Noon said, but he looked more amused than annoyed.

'Ignore her,' said someone from the end of the table. He was a huge guy, at least twice as big as me, and he'd already ripped the sleeves off his T-shirt so his biceps would be on show. Next to him was an almost carbon copy of himself, a little smaller but with the same ripped sleeves and heavy brow. 'She's an Influencer kid, doesn't know she's born.'

Cinta didn't flinch, dissecting her apple bit by bit. I hadn't seen her eat any of it yet.

'Name's Mills, and this is my brother Decke. Welcome to the tourist smashers' table.'

'Tourist smashers?' I asked.

The only other younger girl at the table except for Cinta and me, dark-skinned with tight black curls, leaned across and waved to get Mills's attention.

'You have to stop with that shit,' she said, but not out loud. Her hands moved fast, forming words with her fingers and her facial expressions in sign language. 'The mainlanders already know we call them tourists behind their backs. Stop riling them up. It's going to get you killed before we even start.'

'Whatever,' Mills signed back. 'These people suck. Most of them don't even know how to sign. They have no bleedin' clue what we're talking about right now.'

Whoa. On the island, sign language is something you grow up using. Before any of the big settlements were formed, a lot of us still lived in old houses or in the woods and if you made a sound, you were dead. So we all used sign language to communicate at night, but it obviously only worked if it was light enough to see. I wasn't sure where it started, but Dad taught Wynn and me when we were little. Signing was one of the most important life skills you could have. I guess there was little use for it for hearing people on the mainland.

'And that makes them nervous. So maybe we should talk out loud for a little bit, while we can.' Another lad around my age, who was sitting next to the girl, signed while he spoke. He had jet-black hair, close shaven, and olive skin that brought out the green in his eyes. He turned to me. 'I'm Glaed, and this is Cass,' he said, pointing to the girl next to him.

Cass waved hello. 'By the way, I'm Deaf, so if you could face me when talking or use sign, I'd appreciate it. I can lip-read a little,' she signed.

'Got it,' I said out loud, and signed, back.

'So cosy,' Mills said. 'We're all pretending that the Deaf girl here won't be the first to go as soon as this bleedin' game show kicks off.'

'No, I'll be second. Because my first move will be to rip your big ugly head off,' Cass signed in reply.

Everyone laughed except Mills, who ignored her and went back to his food.

The only other people who hadn't introduced themselves were Aldred, who had a metal arm finished with a knife at the end; Morrigan, a quiet soul with tanned skin and a bald head who barely grunted his name over his breakfast; and Rhegar, a lantern-jawed guy with a shadow of stubble who looked about ten years older than me. None of them were as rude as Mills, and his brother stayed silent for the whole exchange.

'So, Astrid-not-Executioner,' Noon said, once introductions were finished. 'You ready for this? We all got here two days ago, so they must have paid a pretty penny to persuade you to come here.'

'Shit, sorry for keeping you waiting,' I said, and everyone burst out laughing. Even Mills cracked a smile.

'That's OK, we've just been waiting to meet our tourist partners,' Cass signed.

'Did they explain that to you? About the mainlander we have to bring along with us?' asked Rhegar.

'Yes, I got the full presentation,' I said.

The whole table groaned.

'The presentation, shit me, that was something else. But I couldn't say no. A ticket off this piece-of-shit island of the dead? Sign me up,' Cinta said, pushing her half-eaten apple away.

'See, Executioner? Don't get too cocky,' Mills said, more confident than earlier. 'Because only one bleeder is getting out of here, and that's gonna be me or my brother.'

Decke nodded in agreement. While his brother was all mouth, Decke said nothing. Then again, it was hard to read his face through his curtain of greasy hair.

'Bleeders. Interesting way to describe us, Mills. Tell

me, is it you or your brother who will bleed out first to a Pyre?' Cinta said.

Mills stood up so fast, the whole table moved. Some of the black shirts in the cafeteria looked over, and one was talking into one of those earpieces they all wore.

'Listen, painted princess, you take that back,' Mills started, reaching across the table for Cinta with one meaty fist. Decke didn't move, despite his breakfast being scattered everywhere.

But Mills didn't get far. Morrigan, who so far had said nothing either, jumped up and grabbed Mills's fist from the air. He pulled back, and in one fell movement that took less than three seconds he had Mills's hand twisted behind his back and his huge body down on the table.

'Get off me,' Mills protested, his face squashed into the remains of his eggs.

'I'll let go when you've calmed down,' Morrigan said. His voice was hypnotic, calming, which contradicted everything he was doing.

'Piss off,' Mills spat.

'Then we stay here. I can do this all day,' Morrigan said. He didn't even look like he was struggling to keep Mills down, despite being shorter and skinner than him.

Rhegar leaned into Mills's face at the table, so close that he was almost nose to nose with him. 'Listen up, friend. There are no pretty princesses in this life. There aren't any idiot meatheads either. There's us, and the Pyres. The living and the half dead. You understand? So you need to stop fighting us and focus on that prize you say you want so much.'

Rhegar stopped talking, and in the silence that followed I half expected Mills to keep struggling, try and get to him, but he didn't. Instead, he slowly nodded, and Morrigan finally let go of him. Mills stumbled back, rage still on his face, then nudged his brother and they both stormed out of the cafeteria, throwing open the double doors so they smashed into the walls as they went.

'That guy is going to get himself and his brother killed,' Aldred said.

A black shirt approached the table. 'OK, islanders. Please follow me so we can record you and the mainlanders for the show.'

He flashed us a smile but none of us returned the favour. I'd almost forgotten about the tourists, the ones stupid enough to want to be here, so new to the threat of the Pyres they would probably get us killed.

Well, not me. I was living through this thing, and no green mainlander was going to stop me.

CHAPTER SIX

The black shirt led us through the maze of the building and out into the open air. Mills and Decke were already outside. Mills was smoking a cigarette, something you rarely saw nowadays, as they didn't tend to put them into Influencer crates. He winked at me before stubbing it out under his boot and a wave of revulsion washed through me.

As we walked, two armed guards followed behind us. There was no danger of Pyres in broad sunlight – especially with the huge walls that surrounded us – so I quickly realised they weren't protection for us. They were protection *from* us.

Eventually we reached a building on the other side of the compound and the black shirt waved a plastic card next to the door, which then swung open.

'Here we are,' they said, rushing into another long corridor. 'Now, Nova wanted to make sure we recorded your reactions, so be aware that the cameras will be on and try not to swear. Editing out swearing slows the production team right down.' The black shirt glared directly at Noon.

Because sure. You can show us blowing the brains out of Pyres' skulls all day, every day, but curse words? Out of the fucking question. Made as much sense as everything else Bloodwatch did.

'How long is this going to take?' Mills asked. 'I'm already jonesing for another ciggy.'

'Sorry, it will probably take all day. We have to introduce you all, then answer the audience-participation questions and finally introduce the mainlanders. It'll be a long one.'

'Sorry, audience-participation questions?' I asked. 'There are other people here, in the audience?'

The black shirt laughed. 'No, sweetheart. Questions have been sent in online from viewers, and Nova picked out the ones that she thinks are the juiciest for your introductions.'

Juicy questions?

'Damn, did you just call the Executioner *sweetheart*? I hope you sleep with one eye open, sunshine,' Noon said, and that made me feel a little better.

'Sometimes Noon can use his arseholery for good as well as evil,' Cass signed at me, and I smiled.

'OK, ready?' the black shirt asked with one nervous look in my direction. He held open a door at the end of the corridor.

We stepped through to a room lined with mirrors and soft lights, the smell of sweet powder in the air.

'Finally,' Cinta sighed, flopping into the nearest chair set facing the mirror on our left. 'I'd run out of setting spray and had no idea how long this would hold under those hot studio lights you have. Sort me out, stat.'

There were more black shirts in the room, all bearing the same TBN logo. Two stepped forward and started pinning back Cinta's bright hair from her face with clips.

The original black shirt that led us in sorted us all out with our own chair and mirror and left us to it.

I tried not to move much as they took the bun out of my hair and scrubbed my face with something that burned my skin, the tension in my shoulders aching with the effort. Was this what Cinta had to go through for her Influencer deals? I hoped they paid up.

'When was the last time you washed your hair?' one black shirt asked, pulling at my roots until my eyes pricked.

'I wash it whenever we can spare the water,' I said.

'Shampoo and conditioner or just shampoo?'

'We haven't had a shipment of shampoo for years. We have a big block of soap that one of the council members makes from animal fat, though. I use that.'

He wrinkled his nose. 'Full wash and blow, got you,' he said.

Over the next hour we were poked and prodded within an inch of our lives. The only red shirt who was enjoying it was Cinta, who asked for her make-up to be done over and over again, until she had the exact look she was going for.

Finally I was done, so they spun me round so I could see my reflection. My hair was in the same bun it always was, and despite having had my face painted with products for over an hour, my skin looked like it always did.

'I look exactly the same,' I said, raising an eyebrow.

'Exactly,' the black shirt said, clasping his hands together. 'You're you, but camera friendly. The studio lighting was only going to make that greasy hair and skin shiny. Trust me, hon, we did you a favour.'

'Um . . . thank you?' I said, more of a question than a nicety.

'You're so welcome,' he said, grinning at me.

Next, another black shirt came over and asked for the 'girls' to follow him. I exchanged a look with Cinta and Cass, the only other female contestants, but we didn't have much choice, so we trailed the black shirt through a side door.

We entered a small room with a bench on one side and a swivel chair on the other.

'I have to ask you, girls,' he began, once we'd sat down. 'Are any of you on your period?'

'Why would you need to know that, you little perv?' Cinta said, inspecting her nails.

The black shirt at least had the decency to blush. 'Because, you know, we were worried about the impact it would have on the Pyres. All our mainlander contestants have been on preventatives to make sure they wouldn't be, um, you know, which we can give to you too, if you'd like. We don't want you to be at an unfair disadvantage from the boys, after all. We're feminists here at Bloodwatch.'

I'm not sure who laughed first, me, Cinta or Cass.

'Thanks so much for the concern,' I said, 'but we're fine. Pyres can smell blood coursing through veins from up to half a mile away. Period blood doesn't attract them any more than the eight pints already pumping around my body.'

The black shirt paled. 'Fair enough. I'll, um, take you through for interviews now.'

'Besides,' Cinta said, once the black shirt got up and was out of earshot, 'you *girls* have a few more issues than just cramps and tampons. My god, one of you can't hear and you, Astrid, well, you don't exactly scream fan favourite. Don't worry, if a Pyre doesn't put you out of your misery early, I will. That ticket is mine. Don't get in my way.'

She made the threat casually, even signing it at the same time so Cass could follow along. Cinta radiated the confidence of someone that not only thought they deserved to win, but that anyone around her equally deserved to lose. She flounced off behind the black shirt before we could respond, skipping down the corridor. I turned to Cass, but we didn't need words, our jaws set.

Cinta was an arsehole, and as untrustworthy as any black shirt. Somehow she had to go.

We followed the black shirt to the filming studio. Everyone else was already there. I tried to ignore my stomach doing somersaults at the thought of the questions from the viewers. Nova would only pick the ones that would draw the biggest reaction from me, so I just . . . wouldn't react. I had to get it together if I was to have a chance of ever seeing Hild and the Burgh again.

The studio consisted of a stage set up along the far wall, with a stiff-looking armchair under three studio lights, and a dozen black shirts milling about. But all our eyes were on the bench behind the cameras, where ten total strangers sat in a row, each of them wearing a green shirt instead of a red one. The mainlanders. One of these people was going to be my partner for the show, and either help me win, or possibly get me killed.

'Welcome, islanders.' Nova stepped out from the shadows and addressed us. 'It's showtime. Now, don't be nervous. I always find that these things are better if we crack on and don't think about it. Do we have a volunteer?'

For the first time, I agreed with Nova. 'Me. I'll start,' I said. Better get this over with.

Whispers sprang up from the bench where the mainlanders were sat. It was hard to see them from here, with the bright studio lights, but they were definitely turning to each other to talk.

'Astrid, lovely. Come and sit down,' Nova said.

Within a minute, I had what was apparently a microphone clipped to my shirt and I was practically pushed into the chair by another of the production team. They were as keen to get this over with as I was, which suited me.

Three tiny red dots appeared below each camera.

'OK, Astrid. This isn't live and we will be editing it later, but try not to swear? I'm going to ask you a few questions about yourself and then we'll launch into the top-three audience questions that I've picked out. This is your chance to introduce yourself to the viewers, so make it count.'

I shuffled in my chair and nodded.

'And three . . . two . . . one . . . action,' Nova said. 'Now, Astrid, if you could tell us your name, how old you are, and where you're from. First name only, please; last names make it trickier for viewers in the opening stages of a new show.'

I gulped. 'Uh, so I'm Astrid, I'm eighteen and I'm from a place called the Burgh.' Even saying it out loud made my heart ache for it.

'Great. See, that wasn't so hard. On to the viewer questions,' Nova gushed. 'Question one: after what happened to your dad and sister, why didn't you stay in the house instead of going to live in the woods? Weren't you afraid you would die?'

Shit, straight for the jugular. I tried to swallow but my mouth was dry. I shuffled in my seat, the leather of the armchair sticking to my sweaty hands under the heat of the lights. 'OK. Well, erm . . .'

'If you could answer a little more directly, please, Astrid,' Nova said, fake smile plastered across her face.

I dug my nails into the palms of my hands. 'Yep, sure. So I went into the woods because the thought of spending another second in that house made me want to claw my own eyes out with rusty spoons. Is that direct enough for you?'

More whispers from the bench, and even some from the islanders, this time. The same anger that built inside me the night Dad and Wynn died rose again. The one that clouded my vision in a red fog and earned me the nickname of the Executioner, a monster stirring from its slumber. The anger I promised to push down forever, and, shit, they were making it difficult.

'Quiet in the gallery,' Nova said. The whispers died down and she smiled again, as if I hadn't just said something completely horrific. 'Lovely. Next question: do you ever regret going out the night you lost your dad and sister?'

I blinked. Who was asking these questions? Some mainlander who's never had a bad night's sleep in their lives, watching me from the safety of their home? Because of what happened, they thought they knew me. But they didn't. I hardly knew myself. There it was, that angry monster again, looking for a small valve in my resolve to escape through.

'I will regret leaving them every day for the rest of my life,' I said. 'I saw the cameras that night, so I know you all heard the last words I said to them. When you're fourteen, you always hate someone, most of all yourself. So yes, I regret fighting with my sister and telling my dad I hate him. But I think you probably knew that already, because who wouldn't feel like that?'

No whispering this time. I took a deep breath through my nose and out through my mouth, pushing the monster back down into the box I'd created in my head, the defence mechanism I'd spent two years in the woods cultivating.

'Of course.' Nova nodded with a fake frown. 'Third and final question: why didn't you put down your sister and dad when they turned, and does it not bother you that they're still out there living a half-life as Pyres?'

The other questions were rough, nothing that people hadn't tried to ask me before. But this one knocked the air from my lungs. I was expecting more about that night, the gang I found. The torture. The Pyre attack. But the aftermath? That was a place I never wanted to revisit.

'Wynn and Dad are still out there?' I croaked, my voice barely a whisper.

'Focus on answering the question, Astrid,' Nova said. 'Our viewers want a simple answer.'

'A simple answer?' I repeated, dumbstruck. The anger wasn't in the box any more. It was pouring out of my mouth like word vomit. 'There is nothing simple about watching your sister get tortured by other survivors through your dining-room window. There isn't anything *simple* about those barbarians setting a Pyre on your father and letting a Bloodwatch camera record it.'

I stood up. A black shirt stepped forward but I threw him one look and he backed away, wide eyed. Sometimes being called the Executioner had its perks.

I turned back to Nova and the camera. She had paled, but held her ground. 'You want simple? Maybe, after watching my only family turn in front of me while those absolute monsters laughed and drank our rations, something inside me broke. Maybe I hate Bloodwatch too, for promising some sort of prize to the scumbags who murdered my family on camera. Maybe I was a coward, hiding outside the house while it happened because I was the one lucky enough not to be in when they attacked. Maybe I wanted to step out of my skin so badly, I did it. I became another person when I killed those men. I wasn't Astrid any more. Maybe you, everyone at home, you're right. I became the Executioner. And after all that, to also put a knife through my sister and dad's hearts? Maybe that was too much even for me.'

The silence in the studio was deafening. The only sound was my own heavy breathing as spots danced in front of my eyes.

I looked at Nova. She lifted a single finger and gestured to another black shirt.

The backdrop behind me lit up, and I didn't need to watch, but I couldn't look away. I watched as someone who looked like me, but four years younger, walked through the front door of our old house. I watched the close-ups of the men sitting on my living-room furniture, drinking my water and eating my food, and how they started to laugh. It didn't matter who they were or what they looked like. They were more monstrous than the Pyres.

I watched as the girl on the video jumped at the nearest one, grabbing him round the shoulders like an actual Pyre. The blood than ran down her face as she bit his ear off, eyes wild. Soul destroyed.

I watched as she pulled a knife from the waistband of her jeans and jabbed and slashed at the screaming men until she was covered head to toe in their blood. And I watched as she fell to her knees in front of the Pyre versions of Dad and Wynn, their dead eyes bulging, their fanged mouths snapping, unable to move because the men had tied them together on the blood-soaked floor.

Imagine if your worst moment was caught on camera and played to the entire world for millions of people to watch over and over again. And then imagine someone forced you to watch it, just so they could record your reaction.

That was when I turned and launched myself at Nova.

CHAPTER SEVEN

After half an hour of sitting in the make-up studio with my hands zip-tied behind my back, I was starting to regret my actions.

Sort of.

I only managed to get in one punch on Nova before I was swarmed by black shirts, the ones that usually carried guns and wore armoured vests. See, those were for us, because islanders were feral.

And to be fair, I wasn't proving them wrong. Within seconds I was cuffed and carried away, always with a camera on me, of course. Even Nova was muttering something to her crew while massaging her bruised jaw as I left. The last thing I saw was Noon, laughing and giving me a thumbs up before I was pushed through the door to the other room.

I leaned back on the make-up chair and tried to move my weight so my fists weren't digging into my back. This was my own fault, as per usual. It was like there were two versions of me, struggling to live inside the same body. There was Astrid Before: the teenage girl that lived a fairly quiet life, all things considered, with her sister and dad. Astrid that shoved straws up her nose and made faces to make Wynn laugh. Astrid that would go hunting with her dad in the forest around the house on Saturdays.

And then there was Astrid After: Afterstrid. The girl who spent two years in the woods, trying to avoid cameras and Pyres and survivors alike. The girl who always slept in a tree and never for more than an hour at a time, knife always in hand. Who hunted at night and barely saw daylight because she was so scared of Pyres and humans. There's the monster, the one I just saw on the TV screen. The monster that broke free when teenage Astrid saw what those men did to her family. Maybe a monster that was always there. Perhaps that was what happened when you turned Pyre. You were you, just with the monster unchained.

I shifted in my restraints. I wasn't unchained now, and I was calmer. Calmer than I had been in a long time, which was more than terrifying in its own way.

In the make-up room there was a TV screen where I could watch the rest of the interviews. They resumed pretty quickly after I was put in here, and they left one black shirt to keep an eye on me, so I had nothing else to do but watch.

Each interview was short, like mine, with three questions and a brief video clip of the islander's background. Although it must be said, no one else had the urge to batter their producer at the end.

I did learn a lot about what makes a person popular enough for a viewer to vote them into a deadly game show. Rhegar was in the army that the mainland sent across to help contain the Pyres. Morrigan was a hermit living in the woods after his wife and daughter were killed by Pyres in the early days. Aldred became a firm favourite after he got bitten on his arm by a Pyre fighting to save his boyfriend from an attack, which they showed in his video clip. He chopped it off above the bite site without even thinking, one fast slice caught on camera.

Cinta had been taking make-up Influencer parcels for the last five years. All her video clips were of her doing what were apparently called 'make-up tutorials' in front of cameras at various times of day, and her spiky attitude combined with her good looks made her a fan favourite. They showed she'd had a partner, Badda, a stunning androgynous person with a real flair for eyeliner. But Cinta got mad when more packages arrived for them than for her, and she left a blood-smeared blanket next to their sleeping bag after they fell asleep one night, then she climbed a tree to watch them be eaten alive.

'Survival of the fittest, right, Nova?' Cinta laughed, her tooth gem catching the overhead lights. My stomach rolled at the sound of her voice. She was already a stone-cold killer and apparently the audience loved it.

Decke and Mills insisted on being interviewed together. According to Nova, they got the bulk of the male vote for the show. Mills made some crude comments about how he felt pretty confident they could get the female vote too, once they won, which made no sense at all, and Decke mostly grunted. Their clip was a compilation of their best Pyre kills, including a slow-motion shot of Decke blowing up a whole nest of Pyres with a grenade they'd found.

Noon swore so much in his interview that Nova had to restart a few times. One of his questions referred to him as a 'housewife favourite' and a 'silver fox'. I asked the guard what both terms meant and he rolled his eyes. Noon loved it, though. The only time his smile faltered was when they showed his clip, which was of him and a bald woman that Nova referred to as his wife. Over the course of thirty seconds her health deteriorated until the final shot was of Noon burying her. A lump rose in my throat.

Cass asked Glaed to translate for her in her segment, so they did theirs together. Cass was twelve the night that the island fell and lost her hearing after the hospital she was holing up in was shelled by the mainland military, killing her family and burning her throat to the extent that she could no longer talk. A nurse rescued her and she was lucky to be alive. Glaed was a travelling salesman, and he often narrated his journeys and what he found to the cameras around him, earning him a bunch of Influencer crates and a huge following on the mainland. Both their clips were full of courageous rescues and near misses with Pyres.

It was bizarre, watching these people through a screen. I had only met them that morning and yet I was rooting for most of them. Not Cinta or Mills, they were more bloodthirsty than the Pyres, but everyone else. Is this what it was like, watching on the mainland? Did they condense our lives into a series of emotional video clips that would make them root for us and, in turn, get them watching?

Television was a weird sort of magic.

A few minutes later, Nova came in through the doors that led to the studio. She looked sombre and the shadow of a bruise was forming on her jaw.

'Well, have we calmed down now?' she asked.

'Um, yes. And, erm, sorry about, you know, punching you in the face,' I said, shrugging.

Nova flipped her braids over one shoulder. 'It's fine. At least we got it on camera, and the medic says nothing is broken.'

I winced. Great.

The black shirt snipped off the zip ties and I rubbed my wrists where the plastic had been.

'All right, you can come back in. We're still recording, though, so no funny business,' Nova said.

I trundled back into the studio between two strong-looking black shirts and kept my eyes on the floor as they led me over to the bench. The green shirts had been replaced with red ones, and I perched next to Cass.

'You OK?' Cass gestured, concern etched in her facial expression as part of her signing.

Behind her, Noon blew a chef's kiss and laughed, while Mills flipped me his middle finger.

'I'll be fine,' I signed back, then sat on my hands. Quicker this was over, quicker I could go back to my room and maybe the ground would be kind enough to swallow me whole.

'OK, time to learn some essential survival techniques,' Nova called. 'Mainlanders, if you could stand on the stage, an assistant will line you up. That's right, there you go. Now, a member of our security team is going to take you through some basic skills for how to take down a Pyre, what to expect, that sort of stuff. And we're going to record you as part of your VTs. Are we ready?'

Mills snorted. 'They'll never be ready,' he said out loud, not even bothering to sign.

'Silence on set, please,' Nova said, throwing Mills a look. 'OK. I'm going to hand over to Captain Stern now. And cameras rolling in three, two, one.'

A black shirt stepped out of the shadows and into the bright studio lights, and all the cameras swivelled towards him. He was built like a brick shithouse, as Hild would say, maybe two metres tall and muscles so big they were straining under the fabric of his shirt. He had a military fade and a face that matched his last name.

'That's right. My name is Captain Stern and what I'm about to say to you could save your life, so listen carefully,' Stern said.

'I don't remember ever seeing this guy when fighting off broods for the last however many years,' Noon signed down the line. 'Can't wait to hear this.'

'Through the head or through the chest is the only surefire way to know you've killed one. Heart or the brain. If you're a bad shot, try for the chest to slow it down,' Stern said. 'You may have seen on television that most islanders use wooden bolts when attacking the Pyres. This is down to the simple fact that wooden crossbow bolts are more easily manufactured here than bullets and guns. Use whatever you have to hand that is sharp enough to pierce through tissue and bone, and you'll do fine. Remember, while Pyres are alive, they don't feel pain the same way we do, and they have enhanced strength, but hit one badly enough and they'll succumb to their wounds eventually. A hit and a good hiding place is better than no hit at all. Got it?'

The mainlanders nodded. A nerdy-looking guy with skin paler than a Pyre was writing notes on his hand.

Mills leaned forward to catch our attention and started signing. 'Thank you, Captain Obvious. Maybe if the mainland airdropped more ammo and less nail varnish, we could use real weapons instead of makeshift ones.'

'Hey, I'll have you know that my nail varnish Influencer deal paid for six months' worth of food,' Cinta signed, stopping to show off her own painted nails. 'Scratch-proof and Pyre-proof. I heard from a black shirt that it's the leading brand on the mainland, thanks to me.'

Noon rolled his eyes.

'And don't forget Pyres,' Stern continued. 'They ain't people. Some of them will be wearing cute little dresses and shirts and what have you. Those are the ones that haven't been turned for long. Don't underestimate them, though. They're easily as deadly as the older ones. But eventually they turn into the ones you've all seen on TV. Naked as the day they were born, all their hair fallen out. Pale as moonlight. Those ones are as feral as wild animals, sometimes run on all fours to get to you. Watch out if they're in a group too. They'll never get tired, and never give up the hunt for blood. Keep your wits about you or lose your head, that's all I'm saying. One bite and you're infected. If you're lucky, you might not turn for a few hours. But some strains we've studied have people turning in minutes. I know you're thinking you've seen some people on Bloodwatch cut off infected limbs and survive, but even if you have the slower strain, that's a risky strategy. Don't let them get near enough to bite you in the first place, all right?'

He held up three fingers and counted them down as he

spoke. 'One, don't let them get their hands on you. A brood will rip you apart in seconds. Two, aim for the head if you're close enough to get leverage through the eye socket, but skulls are tough. Aim for the chest if you're unsure and keep stabbing or firing until they stop moving. And three, if you *are* bitten on an extremity, like a limb, cut it off as fast as you can and pray like hell to whatever god you believe in. You'll feel the change coming if you're infected. Know when you're beaten.'

'I volunteer Aldred for any slicing and dicing,' Mills called out. 'He has first-hand experience and I wanna see that arm machete in action.'

Even though Mills was a total dickhead, the panicked looks on the mainlanders' faces at his suggestion did pull at the corners of my mouth, and several of us on the bench started laughing. It's not that the idea of anyone getting bitten was funny, but you had to laugh at such basic instructions. This Stern guy had less experience with Pyres than Cinta, who fought them off daily and still had time to dye her hair.

Plus, I didn't miss what Stern told them about different strains of the Pyre virus. Hild and I always assumed they knew more than us, but having it confirmed, especially when we were struggling so much for any scrap of information on the island, made me hate the mainlanders and Bloodwatch even more.

'I said no talking in the gallery,' Nova said, crossing her arms. She held a finger to her earpiece. 'Did we get it? Can you cut off the shouting at the end? Great.' She threw one last glare at us and turned back to the stage. 'Thank you,

Captain Stern. Your helicopter is waiting outside to take you back to the mainland. And, mainlanders, your turn for individual interviews now. My assistant will get you in order.'

The mainlanders were swarmed by black shirts and Captain Stern was led out the way we came in without a backward glance.

I gritted my teeth and leaned back against the wall while the mainlanders began recording their own VTs. They didn't have audience questions, because they weren't 'celebrities' like us, so they gave their names and told Nova why they had applied. It was the first time I looked at them properly, and they were beautiful.

Their hair was shiny in a way you never saw on anyone except an Influencer with a shampoo deal. Their skin glowed in a way that screamed *well fed*. On the island, we had to scramble for food.

The majority of the mainlanders were young; some around the same age as me. Only one of them looked physically older as he struggled to sit in the chair. His name was Herrod and he was in his seventies. His grey beard and receding hairline gave him away. I'd never met anyone that old in the Burgh, and he fascinated me. He told Nova he was here because he had a terminal illness and wanted to see the island at least once before he died.

'I bet they'll pair one of us with the old guy,' Mills signed to his brother. 'Just our bleedin' luck.'

Glaed kicked him under the bench and received a glare for his trouble.

Weirdly, as each of the mainlanders stepped up, none of them mentioned the prize fund. Money didn't have much use on the island; we bartered with what we could make. But surely mainlanders still used money, so it must be important otherwise why would they be *here*?

The next two mainlanders to be interviewed, Reeta and Marg, were both only a year older than me. Reeta was all muscle. She was here because she wanted to prove the army wrong for not recruiting her when she applied last year. Marg, on the other hand, said she had entered for her little boy, who was back on the mainland, as she needed the money to make a better life for him.

That threw me. The mainland had it all. What could be better than living there?

The next bloke was a lot taller than me and the camera had to adjust its height when he sat in the chair. He had a genuine, warm smile that made it obvious his huge frame didn't match his personality. His name was Jupiter, and he said he was here because his family were from the island originally. His mother and father left for the mainland a month before the first Pyre attack, when Jupiter was only a kid.

'Mum passed away not too long ago, and her dream was always to have her ashes scattered on the island where we were all born, alongside Dad,' Jupiter said. 'So I've brought them with me.' He reached into the pocket of his regulation trousers and pulled out two small yellow gemstones, which he held out to Nova.

'And, sorry, Jupiter, but these are . . . ?' Nova asked, peering at the gems over the camera.

'Mum and Dad. Ashes were a little too big, so I found a company on the mainland that compresses them into gemstones. This way I could still bring them and maybe while I'm here I'll have a chance to bury them. Together, just like they always wanted.'

'That is so sweet,' a black shirt ahead of us whispered to their partner on a camera.

'We're killing Pyres, and on the mainland they're making Mum and Dad into wearable trinkets,' Noon signed. 'Now I've heard it all.'

'It's a little over the top, but I think it's nice that they wanted to come back here. At least it's a better reason to be here than being an adrenaline junkie,' Cass replied, and I couldn't help but agree with her. I didn't want to trust the mainlanders, but Jupiter seemed so earnest and genuine. Plus, it was too bizarre a story to make up.

'I needed to be here, to see where I come from, and to lay them to rest,' Jupiter continued.

'He wanted to see where he came from? He can see it any time he wants on Bloodwatch from the comfort of his own sofa,' Cinta signed.

The more these mainlanders spoke, the more it was obvious that they had lost their minds. Who voluntarily came to the most dangerous place on earth, no matter how much money they were getting paid or what they had to do? Were these people so bored of being comfortable that they needed to put themselves in grave danger?

The other mainlanders had similarly wild reasons for wanting to be here. Grayson was a forty-five-year-old pale guy with unbelievable muscles who told Nova he wanted to test his mettle after losing over ten stone. Godric, a dark-skinned guy wearing robes over his uniform, was apparently here to test his faith, whatever that meant. Edric flipped his dreds over his shoulder and confidently told Nova that he wanted to be an actor, and this would be his best opportunity to break into it.

One of these people would be my partner. The person that I would be shackled to for the entirety of the contest. What happened if they didn't make it, or they slowed us down?

Next up was Esmond, a sweaty guy whose pale skin was beetroot red under the lights of the studio. The guy who had been writing notes during the chat with Captain Stern.

'I'm a scientist by trade,' he said, wiping sweat from his brow. 'I wanted to study these Pyre creatures up close.'

Good luck with that one, buddy.

Maeva was a dark-skinned woman covered in tattoos with a shaved head, who introduced herself as being thirty-nine years old. 'I'm here to win,' was all she said after that, and Nova looked annoyed. I liked her.

Then the very last mainlander stepped up into the light of the stage. He had a smile that rivalled Nova's, all perfect white teeth and full lips, and there was a hint of stubble along his jawline. He had dark floppy hair that came down to just above his deep-brown eyes.

My stomach flipped and I folded my arms across it, mortified, as if anyone around me could know what I was feeling. My life was on the line and I was eyeing up a pretty boy. Hild would have a field day. Maybe that's how a desperate Influencer felt when promised food in exchange for completing a suicide mission. Too hungry to care. The island wasn't exactly somewhere it was easy to meet new people, especially when I was living with Dad and Wynn.

Pathetic, the monster deep inside said.

Then the guilt hit – born from the loneliness of never having had these feelings in my life. I hadn't even seen anyone my own age until they let me into the Burgh.

Get a grip, the monster said. *You loved your dad and sister and look what a mess you were when you lost them. We don't have time for this.*

I felt sick. Hild was the closest thing I had to family left and she could handle herself. But there was no more room for the pain of losing someone, especially some ditzy mainlander that had no idea what he had got himself into. People you got close to only broke your heart by leaving or, worse, getting killed when you tried to keep them safe.

'My name is Luke, I'm nineteen and I'm from a coastal town on the mainland called Outlook,' he said, his voice as smooth as honey.

'And what made you apply to *Escape from Blood Island*, Luke?' Nova asked. Was she blushing?

'Well, on a clear day we can see the island from the top window of our house. I've seen the boats that land on the shore. I work with the coastguard sometimes to pull people out of the water before they're inevitably sent back,' he started.

'I'm sorry, what did you just say?' Cinta said, her voice catching between a whisper and a shout.

'Quiet during filming or you'll all be out on your ear,' hissed a black shirt.

Everyone on the bench exchanged a silent glance. Cinta and Mills looked livid, their necks flushed purple, but they stayed quiet. Not every boat was blown out of the water? Some people made it to the mainland? I swallowed my disbelief and willed myself to pay attention, because Luke was talking again.

'I came because I couldn't sit at home feeling helpless any more,' Luke said. He looked over to our bench and our eyes connected across the room. 'I knew I needed to be here. To see what the island is like with my own eyes and to find out if I could help.'

'What a load of shite,' Cinta signed, and some of the others nodded.

I knew that if Luke wasn't part of the solution, as a mainlander who tuned in to Bloodwatch he was part of the problem, not to be trusted. Bloodwatch were the ones with all the power, and we were the abandoned, the entertainment for the higher-ups, I knew that. But that unbroken person I was before losing Dad and Wynn? She wanted to believe him. Of all the reasons the mainlanders gave today, at least this one gave us something real. There was no way that Bloodwatch would be happy about Luke dropping the bombshell about boats sneaking through, and surely he would know that, but he said it anyway.

'Maybe he's telling the truth,' I signed back to the bench. 'I still don't trust him, he's a mainlander, but maybe he's trying to tell us something with that thing about the boats, I don't know.'

'Or maybe he's blinding us with his chiselled jaw and baby-doll eyelashes,' Aldred signed. 'We can't trust outsiders. There would be no Bloodwatch if no one watched their stupid show, and these people do. They're part of the problem, and that makes them just as bad as Bloodwatch themselves.'

'Agreed,' Rhegar said. 'Until they've lived our lives on the island, they have no idea. They're here for the money, for fame. We're here for freedom. Big difference.'

I sighed. We were forced to be here. They weren't. Whatever Luke's game was, I couldn't trust him; none of us could. Maybe this was his plan working already, getting me to try and like him, but I couldn't fall for it. I had to focus all my energy on staying alive, not on working out why mainlanders would come on some stupid, dangerous TV show.

I glanced back at Luke and he was still looking at us instead of at Nova, so she was waving to catch his attention.

'Well, OK, thank you, Luke,' she said eventually, giving up.

Luke finally turned his attention back to the camera. 'I have a question, actually,' he said. 'Can we pick our teammates, or are they predetermined some other way? Because I want to win and I can only do that with Astrid.'

CHAPTER EIGHT

No. *Why* would Luke say that?

Aldred was right: all of these mainlanders were here for some distorted shot at fame and fortune. Luke was saying stuff to cause a scene, and he was succeeding. All that did was put me in the spotlight. If he wanted to make me look weak, mission achieved.

The monster deep down growled a warning: *You can't trust what you don't know. And Luke is an outsider.*

Nova shut that one down immediately, stating that the viewers were going to be given a chance to vote on pairings based on the video interviews. Which ruled me out with someone as calm as Luke, surely. I couldn't even imagine who they would put me with after my outburst. I had my fingers crossed for Maeva.

'I think they'll pair that fit one, Luke, with me,' Cinta said later at dinner.

That would make sense. Luke was saying all the right things because he wanted to win something as trivial as money on a stupid TV show. Of course they would pair him with someone as flawless as they were ruthless, like Cinta.

After the green shirts had finished recording we'd been separated again and sent straight back to our living quarters. Apparently, the mainlanders weren't allowed to be in the same building as us, so we didn't even have a chance to say anything to them. That made sense, though: Nova needed everything on camera, so she would want our first meetings recorded for the show.

'What makes you say that?' Aldred asked Cinta.

'Because the viewers love to put pretty people together. Me and Badda were like that, you know, until I had to boot them,' Cinta said, like she had fired them as opposed to killing them in cold blood.

'You're something else,' Noon chuckled, spearing a potato with his fork. 'You'll eat that poor son-of-a-bitch alive.'

'No. Pyres will eat him alive. Because none of those green shirts are even surviving the first night,' Cinta replied.

'Can't argue with that,' Morrigan replied.

We finished eating and a black shirt appeared. 'Islanders? Nova would like to take you through some rules and regulations before we let you go tonight.'

Mills kicked off, but he and his brother still followed us to what the black shirt told us was the 'briefing room'. We opened a door to a small square room with two rows of five chairs. Nova was there.

'Do sit down, islanders,' she said, smiling and gesturing to the chairs. Clearly the make-up artists had been at her face, because you could barely see the bruise any more.

'Will this take long?' Mills asked, plonking himself down on the back row and spreading his knees so wide apart it was difficult for his brother to squeeze in next to him. 'I signed up to this thing because I was told I could fight some bastard bloodsuckers and get a ticket off this bleedin' island. And so far I've had make-up thrown at me, cameras pointed in my face and had to wait two days for some girl to arrive before we could even begin. I'm starting to wonder why exactly I'm still here.'

Mills got louder and louder as he ranted and was now standing up, leaning on the back of the chair in front of him.

'This may be the last time I ever say this, but Mills has a point,' Rhegar said. 'Are we starting this game show of yours or not?'

'That's why I called you here,' Nova replied, smoothing down her shirt. 'We're starting recording tomorrow, so I have to go over the ground rules before we begin.'

Tomorrow? Tomorrow some of us might not still be alive. By next week, maybe one of us would be crowned the winner.

'Ground rules? What sort of ground rules?' Noon asked.

'OK. Tomorrow you will have one last breakfast and then will be transported to the filming area. There will be a presenter from the mainland there, Cresta, and she will explain the rules of the first challenge to you. You will not know the rules in advance, and you will not know which mainlander you have been paired with. The interviews went out tonight, so we're giving the public time to cast their votes,' Nova said.

'Will the mainlanders be told any different?' Glaed asked.

'They are told the same as you are. Nothing in advance, not even their partners. Once you are in the show, you will be given tasks to complete at intervals. These tasks will be communicated to you via Cresta, or by one of the production team. But apart from that, you'll be on your own. This is where we say goodbye,' Nova said, deadpan.

All I could think about was what sort of dangerous task they were going to throw at us tomorrow. I wouldn't sleep a wink, but I would use that shower once before I left. It would probably be my last chance, because even if I won I wasn't taking the ticket to the mainland, I couldn't. Not only did I not deserve it, I could also never leave knowing that Dad and Wynn might still be out there, never mind the Burgh. I should have cut them down when I had the chance. Now I had to live with the guilt of their half-life until I could find them and free them of it.

If I could find the courage, second time around.

After Nova finished, we went silently back to our rooms. There was a knot in my stomach I couldn't shift. In order to survive this, I might have to rely on the monster I let loose today, the one that had saved me before. And I wasn't sure I could do that. I didn't know what it would do to me.

After I'd showered – which was hard to work out – I crawled into bed and tried to fall asleep. I lay there for hours, tossing and turning as my stomach cramped with stress, but at some point I must have drifted off, because I woke up to a knock at the door.

Without waiting for an answer, a black shirt popped his head in. 'Astrid? You've got five minutes, then it's breakfast and straight to make-up, OK?'

He shut the door before I could reply.

I pulled on my uniform and made my way to the cafeteria. The table where we sat yesterday was empty. I wondered if they wanted to keep us apart until we got there, to make the most of the footage.

I'd barely been sitting for five minutes when the make-up team came to collect me. They did the same routine again, putting on layer after layer of make-up before spinning me round to the mirror where I looked exactly the same, then they sent me off with another black shirt who hurried me to the helicopter pad.

I had to focus on not throwing up my breakfast, so much so that I kept my eyes closed the whole flight. Luckily, we were only in the air for a few minutes before the gut-falling tug that meant we were dipping down to land.

Once I stepped off the helicopter, I took a minute to see where we were. There were dozens of black shirts, carrying spotlights and cameras, all busy with things that didn't concern me.

I hadn't been to this part of the island. I would remember if I'd seen a ruined castle before.

I knew we were at the northernmost tip of the island, not just because I could see the sea on three sides of the castle, but because I recognised the place from old maps of the island that Dad had. This was Dolby Castle, named after some bloke a thousand years ago who built it to defend the island from invaders. I'd always wanted to come and see it but knew I never would.

Because this is where the Pyres came from.

During the fall, the government tried to section off the most badly affected part of the island, and they built chain-link fences across the top third of the land. We had met travellers who claimed to have seen them and could describe the signs they had seen on the road.

TURN BACK. DO NOT ENTER. CONTAMINATED ZONE.

There were no settlements here, no living people. It was the perfect place to film. No distractions for the Pyres.

I tried to remember Dad's old map. There were cliffs on all sides of the castle, no gentle sandy beaches like there were on our part of the island. The cliffs had a bunch of those little triangle symbols on them. Dad said that meant there were caves. The perfect hiding place for whole broods of Pyres to sleep during the day.

I looked up at the sun. It was lower than it should be for after breakfast. There was no clock in my room – what time did they wake me? It would be dark soon and I knew the black shirts would be out of here before then. They wouldn't want to risk becoming Pyre food.

'So we're starting at night? With no body armour?' I asked the black shirt who had been assigned to me. My throat felt like it was closing in on itself.

The black shirt shrugged. 'People are tuning in for the Pyres. The Pyres like the night? I didn't know, I'm not paid enough for this,' he said, wandering off to chat with a camera guy.

Eventually I was taken to what someone called a 'green room', which ended up being a converted camper van with leather seats. There was a hot-drinks machine that spewed out a black liquid I recognised from the smell as coffee, but when I tried some it tasted bitter, so I left it.

Dad used to drink coffee, when he could find some on

raids or by trading out by the roadside near our house in the woods. And even further back it was the smell that filled the house on a Sunday morning when I woke up. It reminded me of him, which in turn wrenched my heart out of my chest. I could remember how Sunday mornings smelled, but most of my memories from before the fall were a blur. Bloodwatch did that. My life now was in ultra-high-definition, pumped out to millions of television screens day and night. My face in every home. Dad's memory reduced to the smell of cheap coffee.

In the hours they left me in that van, I'd never missed Wynn and Dad more. The monster deep down growled hungrily, feeding on the sadness until it gave way to anger and, eventually, quiet rage.

I don't even know what I did to pass the time, lost in their memory and the thought of what was coming next. If I didn't die, I'd see Hild again; but if I did, I'd see Dad and Wynn again. That was weirdly comforting. I loved Hild, and even Griff was OK when we were all hanging out, but it wasn't my life before. It wasn't coffees on Sunday morning. Maybe that's what it was like on the mainland, but that wouldn't fit either, because I didn't want the smell of coffee without Dad and Wynn, and I couldn't imagine living a comfortable life knowing Hild and Griff and the Burgh were suffering here. I wasn't a monster like the mainlanders were; this was my home.

Maybe they were doing this on purpose. Maybe they knew that, by separating us and keeping us in the dark, it would scare us, make us more feral by the time night fell. I could imagine it would work on some of us. Mills must be out of his mind by now, especially as I'd never seen him separated from Decke.

Eventually, as I was wondering whether it might be worth sleeping, the van doors opened. I stepped out and saw that I wasn't the only red shirt out here: the other nine islanders were ready and waiting on the grass near the castle ruins.

I also noticed how low the sun was in the sky, almost touching the horizon.

I went up to greet everyone, like the first time we met. Everyone nodded, but they were clearly trying to get their heads in the game. This was it; we were about to begin.

'Oh, look, the reluctant star of the show is here. Nice of you to join us,' Cinta said, her fake smile not reaching her eyes.

'Excuse me?' I asked. The monster prowled deep inside, heating my blood instantly. 'No one is the star in this. We all just want to get out of here alive.'

'Oh, OK, hun, you keep telling yourself that. You know, when you're punching producers in the face and making eyes at the mainlander contestants so they'll fancy you. Totally low-profile stuff. Keep it up, shy girl,' Cinta said, her voice piercing.

'I didn't . . . That wasn't . . .' I stumbled over my words.

Most of the others looked away. Glaed and Cass shrugged empathetically, which I took as a sign to ignore Cinta. Mills cackled and drew a line under his chin with his finger.

'Princess Perfect is right. I'll get a lot of votes if I take you out. The man who defeated the great Executioner, woo-wee. You're a regular power vacuum,' he laughed.

That did it. Any trace of embarrassment melted away and the monster inside grinned, drunk with power. I hated what she said, but I couldn't let them think I was easy prey.

'No need to be jealous that I'm better at this TV thing than you. I've been off-screen for what, two years, and you've been doing this for . . . almost your whole life? But sure, take it out on me, not on the fact that you won't even win a single vote pretending to be something you're not. You can't paint on popularity, Cinta.' I spoke evenly but loudly, and the whole group heard. Morrigan even let out a small laugh.

Cinta's face flashed beetroot. She looked up from her nails and pressed one into my chest, as pointy as a knife. 'I need this ticket more than any of you idiots. And you have no idea how far I'll go to get it. You just made an enemy, hun,' she spat.

I was about to ask her what she was talking about when a black shirt came over to collect us, oblivious to the tension. We stepped apart and he led us to a semicircle of chairs in front of the castle ruins with several cameras and bright lights pointed at them. All the helicopters had gone and in their place were a few black Jeeps. Even the vans that held us for hours sped off as soon as we were let free. They were getting ready to ship out.

A woman dressed in a neon jumpsuit stepped out from the crowd of black shirts. Dressed like that, I had to assume that this was the host Nova had mentioned.

'Hello, darlings,' Cresta said, all blond hair and red lipstick. 'How are we all feeling? Excited, I expect.' She didn't wait for answers, and Mills worked his jaw in response. 'Let's get your make-up touched up and we can get rolling.'

We walked over to the chairs and sat down. Cresta called out a countdown.

'Sixty seconds,' she said.

Time slowed. Some more make-up artists buzzed around, patting our faces with powder. I couldn't think straight. All I could do was try to swallow down the lump of panic that threatened to block my throat.

Cresta winked at me before turning to face the sea of cameras and lights.

'And three . . . two . . . Hello, world! My name is Cresta Golding and welcome to the first-ever episode of *Escape from Blood Island*.'

None of us moved. The camera lights all blinked with the same red light. On air.

'By now, you've seen our introductory videos of our fabulous contestants,' Cresta continued. She paced the grass in front of us, a camera following her every move. 'And you've voted for your favourite pairings. As you know, the rules are simple. Each mainlander has the chance to win one hundred thousand credits, as well as one ticket off the island for their lucky islander. And don't forget: if one contestant from a pairing dies, they're both fed to the Pyres. This is a fight to the death.'

My head whipped round to look at everyone. From the others' faces, they had been as much in the dark as I was.

That's how they stopped us just offing the tourists. They died, we died.

CHAPTER NINE

'During the next few days, our contestants will take on five challenges, testing their skills in courage, survival, cunning, endurance and teamwork.' Cresta counted off each skill on her fingers as the cameras zoomed in.

I was trying to pay attention, but I couldn't look away from the fast-disappearing sun.

'First up: teamwork,' Cresta said. She pulled out a shiny piece of paper. 'Hidden around these castle ruins are ten golden envelopes, each with one contestant's name written on it. Inside, they will find the name of the intrepid teammate that you, the viewers at home, voted to pair them with.'

Screw my partner, all I could think about was how much I felt like a caged animal.

'And don't forget to vote! Contestants have their names and numbers on their shirts, and they will appear at the bottom of your screens. During each trial, you will have a chance to vote for your favourite team from that challenge. The winners of each challenge will be those who finish first, and the runners-up will be those who win the public vote. Winners and runners-up will each gain an advantage to take into the next task, so choose wisely.'

So that explained the number on the back of my shirt. Another way for me to fail on broadcast television: via a popularity contest. Great.

The sky was painted orange and pink. The Pyres would be waking any minute.

'Each contestant must find their envelope and then save their teammate from certain death.' Cresta said 'certain death' like she was announcing we were all about to get ice cream.

More floodlights lit up the castle ruins behind us, illuminating the tallest tower left standing, and something innate told me to look up. At the very top of the patchwork turret, ten silhouettes cast long shadows on to the stone wall behind them. I squinted; it was hard to tell, but it looked like each one had their hands folded in front of them.

No, not folded. Tied. With the rope stretched down to the floor they were stood on. They were sitting ducks.

There could only be one winning team, I knew that, but every fibre of my being was fighting against what Cinta said to me and Cass earlier, what she said about getting in her way. It didn't have to be a bloodbath; we had lost enough people already on the island. But if push came to shove, did I have it in me to throw someone under the bus? Someone like Cinta, maybe. But what about Cass or Glaed? And these mainlanders were idiots for coming here, but that didn't mean I wanted to kill them. Was my partner one of the smart ones who could survive?

As these thoughts made my vision swim, one of the mainlanders high above screamed.

Cresta clapped her hands together and turned back to camera. 'Exciting, right?'

The last of the pinks and the oranges had faded from the sky now. It was properly dark. My palms were slick with sweat despite the cold. Somewhere in the distance a shriek pierced the twilight. The Pyres had heard the screaming from up on the tower. We had just called them to breakfast.

No time to think about what I might have to do later. One challenge at a time.

Cresta looked over her shoulder at a producer, who drew a line under their chin. Even from her side profile, I didn't miss the small crease in her brow, despite her painted-on smile. She was scared.

She had no idea.

'And that's our cue to leave,' she laughed, and the cameramen backed up. Within thirty seconds, the whole crew packed into the backs of the trucks and drove off into the night without so much as a goodbye. None of us had even moved, frozen in shock.

They left the bloody lights on, though. And the cameras.

'OK, get up. We have to move,' I said, leaping out of my chair.

'Don't need to tell me twice,' Mills grunted. He and Decke were up at the same time as me, running off towards the rocky outcrops of rubble outside what used to be the castle gates.

It was like a switch had been activated in all of us. We were terrified, but you don't live long if you freeze when caught outside after dark. Noon leaped up and smashed one of the floodlights before running off towards the castle. Glaed and Cass stuck together. Rhegar, Morrigan and Aldred ran off in different directions.

Cinta stood up and applied another layer of lip gloss that she had stashed in her pocket. 'Break a leg. Literally,' she said, and ran off into the fray.

I followed behind them. The air was now filled with screaming, but whether it was coming from the tower of terrified tourists or the Pyres that were bound to be running in our direction, I couldn't be sure. What I did know was that neither was a good thing.

I ran to the nearest pile of rocks and dug through them. A golden envelope, Cresta said. That would have the name of my partner inside. The rocks were heavy, but did move with a little persuasion. After only a minute, I saw a glimmer of gold amongst them.

I couldn't believe my luck. I pulled at the rocks faster, ignoring the stinging as I inevitably sliced my skin on the hard edges. Finally, I grasped at the paper and pulled it free.

The name on the front read: CASS.

I looked up, scanning the field for her. There were even more floodlights than I first realised, lighting up the castle and casting long shadows over the piles of rubble. I could spot five of us still in the courtyard looking, mostly people bent over as they pulled up rock after rock from the ground. Then I spotted a flash of dark curls and the fast hand signs of her partner. Glaed and Cass, on the opposite side of the courtyard.

I sprinted over, jumping over Mills as he took a swipe

at my legs with one meaty arm from his spot on the ground. Dick.

I tapped Cass on the shoulder. 'Here,' I signed, handing her the envelope. 'Found yours over there.'

Cass grabbed the envelope and grinned. 'Thank you,' she signed back.

'I think we should make a run for the tower, then,' Glaed said, holding up an envelope with his name printed across the front.

Cass shook her head. 'Astrid helped me. We should help her find her own envelope.'

'No. I think you guys should go. Someone has to win. Besides, someone needs to stop whoever it is screaming up there,' I told them. I was also worried for Cass. It was really dark out here, and that made signing and lip-reading harder. The quicker she could save her partner and get to safety, the better. 'I'll be fine.'

Glaed chewed his lip. 'OK, but if we finish early and can come back, we'll help you.'

I tried to smile. 'Like it'll take me that long. I'll see you up there.'

'I hope so,' Glaed said, looking over his shoulder. 'I know this is an obvious thing to say, but I don't like this. The Pyres should be here by now with the racket we're making. Unless they're here already, waiting.'

I raised an eyebrow at him, following his gaze to a pile of rocks nearby. 'You think the Pyres might be, what? Hiding?'

Glaed shrugged.

Cass shook her head. 'That would require them to have

any willpower at all,' she signed. 'They'd jump at us as soon as they scented us. Bloodwatch is probably keeping them back for dramatic effect.'

Glaed gulped. 'Well, watch your backs. I've heard stories on the road of Pyres holding back, stalking their prey. Don't underestimate them. Once one came at me with a knife. An actual knife, like they were going to stab me. I ran and didn't look back.'

Cass raised an eyebrow. 'A Pyre doesn't need a knife, and they wouldn't even remember how to hold one. That was probably someone who covered themselves with Pyre entrails. Some people think it hides the smell, but I don't think it works. You got unlucky with some poor sod who attacked you, and thank god you survived, right?' she signed.

'You sound like my friend Hild. You live here long enough, you hear some story about some sort of superpowered Pyre. Let's focus on the task, yeah?' I said, giving Glaed's shoulder a squeeze. His eyes stayed wide but he nodded. Even for an experienced islander, the dark held a certain type of nightmare.

Cass gave me a hug and they ran for the broken steps that led up to the tower. Her cold embrace lingered on my shirt.

No time for feelings. I had to find that envelope.

Most people were searching in the courtyard with no luck, so I headed inside and started digging around near the bottom of the staircase. The castle itself seemed smaller in here. There was no roof, the only proper structure left being the tower, which was around five storeys high. All the inner walls had fallen long ago, and the grass was up to my knees. Cinta was the only one in here with me, busy reaching into cubbyholes set into the far wall.

'You find anything yet?' I called across to her. Who knows, maybe she saw my envelope and left it somewhere.

Another shriek pierced the night, and it didn't sound human. We both froze and stared at each other.

'That's close,' Cinta said.

We stood in silence for a few seconds, the only sound being the screams up in the tower.

Something caught my eye and I saw Mills and Decke running towards us.

'Move!' Mills screamed at me as he shouldered me out of the way to the staircase. Decke followed close behind with two golden envelopes in hand. He did at least have the decency to nod to me as he ran after his brother.

'Shit. Come on, we're wasting time,' Cinta said, pulling moss out of holes in the crumbling walls.

I turned and carried on looking under the stairs, along the low walls, under piles of rubble. Nothing. After a minute or so, Cinta gasped.

'What?' I called out. 'Find something?' I was still mad at her about earlier, but every drop of adrenaline was aimed squarely at staying alive. There was none left for grudges right now.

'Nope. Just a spider,' Cinta called back, sugar sweet. I raised an eyebrow. Cinta didn't seem like a girl who would be afraid of spiders. She didn't seem afraid of anything, but I didn't have time for her games.

The sound of footsteps made me run out from under the stairs to check for Pyres, but it was only Rhegar. He nodded at me as he dashed up the staircase with his envelope, closely followed by Morrigan. After a few more seconds, Aldred and Noon ran in through the half-door that led out to the courtyard.

'Time's ticking, Executioner,' he said, tapping his left wrist, where in another life a watch might have been. He headed up and their footsteps echoed away from us.

'Yes,' Cinta screamed. She raised her arm into the air and she held a golden envelope with her name printed across it. She jogged over to me and shrugged. 'Sorry, Astrid. Good luck, babe.' She smiled, and had the audacity to skip up the first couple of stairs.

Shit. I was the only one left. Where else was there to look? The castle didn't have many hiding places left. I rubbed my eyes, the panic welling up in my chest. Any minute this place would be swarmed by Pyres. Hild was wrong. I wasn't going to win this thing. I was going to die on the very first night.

'Whoa!' I heard Cinta's voice echo on the staircase.

'Cinta, you all right? You took a tumble and I think you dropped something.' Was that Aldred replying? It was hard to make out.

'No, no, I'm good. Keep moving,' Cinta replied.

But Cinta had dropped something. Because down the centre of the winding staircase, a golden square of paper flitted down to the ground.

I picked it up. Printed across the front was one word: ASTRID.

My mind raced back to the gasp I'd heard minutes earlier, when Cinta said she had seen a spider. Spider my arse. She thought she found her envelope, but it was mine. And she pocketed it so I wouldn't have a chance. She said she wanted me gone, and she was willing to kill me to do it.

She left me here to die.

And just like that, there it was. The monster I kept squashed down inside, broken out of its box. Rage built up inside me until it was almost a physical pain.

A branch snapped on my right and I whipped my head round. All the other red shirts were on the stairs. There were no wild animals on the island, not any more. There was only one thing that could make a noise like that, and it wasn't human.

Through the gate to the courtyard were at least twenty Pyres. A large brood. Most of them had turned long ago, because they were completely naked and almost bald, their fangs glistening in the artificial floodlights as they stared at me.

'Shit.' I turned on my heel and jumped the stairs two at a time. On the first turn of the spiral staircase, the group moved towards me as one giant swarm of death. I couldn't freeze with fear. And besides, Cinta was ahead of me and if I was fast, maybe I could push her off the stairs.

'Pyres!' I screamed, running up the staircase. Ahead, I could make out a couple of red shirts, maybe one floor up. 'They're here – move! Move!'

I chanced a look back and my eyes widened as one Pyre swung wildly, long fingernails grabbing thin air. I spun round and aimed a kick squarely at its chest. It fell backwards, screaming, colliding with another behind it. The two Pyres fell off the staircase into the well in the middle of the tower, landing head first on to the stone pile below. They didn't get back up.

More Pyres climbed up after them, scrambling over each other to get up the stairs.

Cinta screamed and shouted up my warning to the next person.

Soon the tower was an echo chamber of chaos: human shouts and Pyre screeches melding together into a terrifying cacophony that made it impossible to think.

My thighs burned as I climbed, but I couldn't slow down, couldn't risk looking back again. At one point I lost my footing badly enough that my whole right leg hung out over the void, but the glimpse of pale faces and glistening teeth only ten or so steps behind me was enough to get me back on my feet and running again. Finally, I reached the top, where a group of red shirts stood waiting.

'Move your arse!' Noon shouted.

My eyes adjusted to the floodlights and I saw him holding open an old wooden door at the top of the staircase, blocking it from the room beyond. I was barely through the gap before Noon slammed it shut, he and Rhegar piling themselves on to the other side to hold it.

The Pyres were on it in seconds, their claws scrabbling through the gaps in the wood, Rhegar and Noon struggling to keep the door on its hinges.

I took a second to catch my breath. Set into the stone floor were ten metal rings, and tied to each was a thick rope. From the top of the castle the looming red light of the distant broadcast tower was more ominous than ever. Several green shirts were still tied up, and islanders were rushing to untie them. Some of the ropes lay limp on the ground, and I looked around for Glaed and Cass. They came up here ages ago, so where were they?

'You wanna save your partner or you too busy enjoying the view, Executioner?' Noon asked.

Right. Focus. I pulled the envelope out from where I'd stuffed it down my bra and ripped it open.

ASTRID,

CONGRATULATIONS ON FINDING YOUR ENVELOPE!
PLEASE CLIMB THE STEPS OF THE TOWER, FIND YOUR
TEAMMATE AND FREE THEM FROM THEIR BONDS.
YOUR TEAMMATE HAS A WRISTBAND WITH A FOB
THAT WILL LET YOU INTO THE SAFE ROOM.
PARTICIPANTS WILL BE RELEASED FROM
THE SAFE ROOM COME MORNING.

Safe room? I craned my neck and spotted a solid metal door set into one side of the tower. I could see from here that it was a huge metal box, with enough room to fit all of us. There was a light next to the door that flashed red.

That explained where Cass, Glaed and their partners were. Morrigan pulled the last knot free on his partner and practically carried her to the door. What was her name again? It would be on the back of her shirt, but I didn't have time to read it.

Partner. Shit, I forgot to check mine. I turned over the paper and read the final line.

YOUR PARTNER IS . . . LUKE.

I scanned the letters of his name again to be sure. There would be time to work out why the public did this later, but for now I had to be sure. I looked up and found him immediately, his floppy hair hanging loose over his dark eyes. My traitorous heart stuttered as he blinked at me.

'Little help, partner?' Luke asked, gesturing at the ropes around his wrist.

'And preferably some time before this door caves in,' Rhegar shouted.

As he spoke, the soles of his boots scraped against the stone with the effort of keeping the door shut. It was like everything had gone into slow motion. It had taken me precious seconds to read the card and take in the carnage around me. Luke was my partner and I needed him alive, so it was time for action before I overthought us all into the mouths of the waiting Pyres.

'I'm coming.'

CHAPTER TEN

The only tourists left were mine, Rhegar's and Noon's, so I went for Luke first.

'No, I'm good, we can help them.' A voice I didn't recognise made me look up and I saw Morrigan and his partner having what looked like an argument by the safe-room door. She had her back to me and her hair hovered just above her collar so I could read the name on the back of her shirt. Marg, that was it.

Morrigan, keeping his reputation as a man of few words, nodded, and without having to say anything they both ran to help Noon and Rhegar hold the door shut.

'Oh my god, ohmygod, we're going to die, we're going to die,' one of the other two green shirts screamed. Esmond, was it? The scientist.

'Have faith, friend,' the guy with the dreds, Edric, said. 'This is but the first battle of many. This is the life we so bravely signed up for.'

'Bugger this, I want out,' Esmond said. He was actively sobbing now.

'Does Edric always talk like that?' I asked Luke as I made my way through the intricately tied knots in his rope.

'I think it's the thespian in him. Guy really wants to be an actor,' Luke said.

I looked up at him and he smiled at me like I was down here tying his shoelace, not trying to free him before he became Pyre food. It was unnerving, if anything. An unpredictable partner was something I could do without.

'How are you so calm?' I asked through gritted teeth, turning my attention back to the ropes. I also didn't want him to spot how red my cheeks were after seeing that smile, which felt wrong given the situation we were in. Everything about him set me on edge. This wasn't the time to be thinking about how soft those lips were, and yet here I was, dedicating precious seconds to that instead of survival.

'I guess I know what I signed up for. But trust me, I'm doing a very good impression of calm,' Luke said.

Yeah, I bet he was pretty good at impressions. He already said Edric was an actor. What was Luke, a model? Probably, with those cheekbones. I untied the last knot and he freed his hands.

'Oh god, don't leave us, please help us,' Esmond begged.

I turned to Noon and Rhegar. 'We'll free yours and then we'll find something to block the door so we all have a chance at the safe room. Sound good?'

'Good? Oh yeah, sounds just peachy,' Noon said, his voice straining, and he leaned against the door. It rattled again and a piece of rusted metal from the frame hit the floor with a loud clang, making the screeches of the Pyres louder.

'Where do you want me?' Luke asked, his hand on my forearm. At least he was listening to me but – why? Why put himself in danger like this? Surely he'd want us to get to the safe room as quickly as possible?

Those were questions for when we all got out of here – hopefully alive.

'You get Esmond, I'll do Edric,' I said.

Luke nodded and ran over to Esmond, so I got started on Edric.

'Don't worry, I'll have you out of here in no time,' I said.

'Never fear, courageous young lady,' Edric said. 'I have full trust that you will prevail. And if not, 'tis a beautiful night to die.'

'Can you please make him stop saying that?' Esmond shouted. 'It is not a good night to die. If he says that one more time I'll kill him myself.'

I exchanged a look with Luke as we kept working on our knots. If Esmond wanted to kill someone, I'd love to see him try. Luke smirked his crooked smile.

He needed to stop with that.

I got through the knots faster this time, and Edric massaged his wrists as the last ones fell. That's when I noticed the rubber bracelet there, black with a small bulge where a watch face might usually sit.

'The fob thing to unlock the safe room?' I asked, pointing at his wrist.

'Indeed,' Edric said. 'But first we must help our comrades. Do you have a plan, fair maiden?'

'Yeah, I think I do,' I said, ignoring the fair maiden comment. In the few seconds we had been talking, Luke had got Esmond free of the last knot and he was frantically pulling at the rope to get his wrists free. 'I think we need to— Wait, stop.'

Esmond was running for the safe room. He slammed his wrist frantically down on the sensor, which flashed from red to green, and threw the door open when it clicked. He was inside before I could see what was beyond it.

'Who had Esmond?' I shouted to Aldred and Rhegar.

'Unfortunately, Mr Shit-His-Pants is on my bingo card,' Noon replied.

'Good luck with that one,' Marg scoffed, her voice breathy as she forced her weight against the door. I was kind of amazed she was still here. Apart from Luke and Edric, she was the only one of the tourists who had offered to help. Maybe mainlanders had some humanity in them, after all – or maybe they wanted to look good in front of the cameras.

The only one who didn't look out of breath was Morrigan, but he never gave anything away. We had maybe minutes until the door was pulled apart by the Pyres.

'Listen – Edric, right? Grab some of your rope and tie it round that stone on the left of the door. Then secure it on the other side, on to that rusted metal pole thing. The rope will stop the door opening long enough for all of us to get through the safe room. Luke, you go and stand next to the door and get ready to open it so we can all run through at once. The rest of us will hold it until Edric can tie the rope. Everybody happy?' I asked.

'Having the time of my life,' Rhegar replied, his voice strained.

We got to work. Luke went and hovered by the door, ready to open it as soon as we could move. Edric collected up lengths of rope and I helped him tie them together until they were strong enough to go across the door and hold it.

Edric hooked them around the ruined stone on one side of the door while I secured them to the metal rod on the other. Marg, Morrigan, Rhegar and Noon kept their weight on the door until we were done.

'OK, we ready to run?' I said, raising my voice to be heard over the screams of the Pyres on the other side of the rotten door.

Everyone nodded.

'I'll count down and we'll all come off the door. Three, two—'

But I never got to one. A cracking sound split across me and we all looked down. Between Noon's legs, through a gap in the wood, a Pyre's head appeared. Its face was purple with rage, a network of black veins crisscrossing its cheeks. And its teeth narrowly missed chomping down on Noon's ankle.

'Oh shit.' Marg was the first to panic. She was unmovable in her bravery when she volunteered to come back with Morrigan, but this was probably the first time she had seen a Pyre up close. She stumbled away from the door and the wood she had been holding began to buckle despite the rope.

'Leg it, we have to bloody leg it!' Noon shouted, and we all sprang away from the door just as it shattered into splinters.

Body after body poured through the doorway, trampling one another to get to us. A few Pyres even fell off the open sides either side of the door, down the staircase or off the edge of the building towards the ground below.

Noon, Rhegar, Edric and I stumbled to the left of the door, to the side with the safe room. Luke ran forward, all thoughts of the door forgotten, and grabbed my arm. We watched wordlessly as the Pyres raced in, sniffing the air as they sought us out, like a pack of rabid dogs. Morrigan and Marg were not as lucky. They had fallen to the right of the door, and now there was a brood of Pyres between them and the safe-room door.

One of the Pyres turned in our direction, bared its teeth and screamed.

'We have to help them,' Luke said.

He picked up a discarded wooden beam from the ground, one with nails sticking out of it, and ran out in front of us. If this was another theatrical performance for the cameras, to win himself fame and fortune, it was a very good one. Luke was putting himself in the firing line for this, which was either incredibly stupid or insanely brave. He swung in a semicircle and hit the first Pyre in the chest, sending it backwards with a sickening thud on to the stone floor.

The noise drew more. I grabbed a stone off the floor that was light enough for me to wield but heavy enough to do some damage, and Rhegar and Noon found some bits of old metal pipe to use.

There were a few Pyres who, after watching their friend take a tumble, were a bit more cautious about approaching us. Noon swung out with his pipe, a warning shot, and the Pyres paused. Did they look at each other, or was I imagining it? Hild's story about the Pyre who went for the corpse outside the walls of the Burgh popped into my head. We battled Pyres, sure, but in small doses and we never travelled out far. But Hild's story was wild. There was no way they were communicating with each other.

'Get back, you ugly bastard!' Marg's scream snapped me back into the present. Even the Pyres in front of us turned round to get a good look. Marg and Morrigan had found makeshift weapons of their own, but it was too little, too late. They were surrounded by at least a dozen Pyres, with more still coming up the stairs. The floodlights and the noise were drawing every bloodsucker for miles around. We had to get into the safe room and hope it would hold until morning. It was now or never.

'Maybe if we create a distraction, I can run through and . . .' Luke trailed off, his eyes wild. It was like he was trying to save them, but surely he knew it was useless at this point. More likely he was creating airtime for himself by still talking.

'It's too late.' Rhegar shook his head.

As if in confirmation, the first Pyre dashed out and reached for Marg, teeth clashing. Marg froze, wooden stick hanging uselessly at her side. Just before the Pyre hit, Morrigan jumped in front of her and swung out with his own metal pipe.

The Pyre missed Marg and sank its teeth into Morrigan's exposed forearm.

'Shit,' Noon hissed under his breath.

Morrigan stumbled backwards, surprised, and the Pyre clung on, blood dripping down its mouth on to the stone floor. At the smell of first blood, all the Pyres lost interest in us and ran at Morrigan. He disappeared in seconds under the writhing mass of pale bodies, his wide eyes turned to us as he succumbed to the brood.

And then he was gone.

'Marg, run for it!' I screamed.

But Marg's eyes were on Morrigan; she was hypnotised by the feeding frenzy. A Pyre at the edge of the group who couldn't get near enough to feed on Morrigan ran at her.

'Marg, watch out!' I yelled.

Marg turned, saw the Pyre and met my eye, all within the same split second. Then she spun on her heel and ran off the side of the tower into the night air.

For a second it seemed as if she would keep going, her momentum carrying her forward into the sky. The Pyre ran after her, as if it too could somehow defy gravity. But then Marg and the Pyre pitched forward and disappeared into the darkness, their screams cut off in a way that made their death final.

'Come on, kid.' Noon grabbed Luke, who was stuck as still as a statue, and pivoted him towards the safe-room door. Luke was totally unreactive, so it took Noon slamming his wrist against the panel and opening the door before we were all inside. Typical. In the end Luke's bravado had melted away when he realised all was lost, and it had taken one of us to save him. I watched through the gap before the door closed as the Pyres continued to swarm

Morrigan, no longer interested in us at all. In the end, we didn't need a rope.

We needed a human sacrifice.

The door slammed shut and the Pyres' feeding frenzy was finally silenced.

We turned round to take in the room. The walls, floor and ceiling were made from reinforced steel. There were no windows, so it felt safe enough from the brood outside. Set into the ceiling were four cameras, one in each corner of the room. The walls were lined with metal benches for us to sit, although the majority of the red and green shirts were on their feet, clearly worried about who – or what – might be trying to get in. In the corner nearest to me was a door labelled w.c. At the other end of the room was a table with a white tablecloth laden with sandwiches, cakes and bottles of water. I was amazed they hadn't all been eaten already, but there was enough to feed us more than twice over.

Plus, we were now two people down.

'You made it.' Glaed grinned, and he and Cass ran over to hug me. 'We were so worried, after you helped us out and everything, but once the door closes you can't open it from the inside.'

'It's cool,' I said, hugging them back. 'I'm glad you got in safe.' Over Glaed's shoulder I caught Cinta's eye, who was trying to look anywhere but at me. I wasn't going to let her get away with signing my death warrant, but I could speak to her later.

Everyone wanted the details. Noon took over, with Edric adding in extra details for dramatic effect. Noon was more matter-of-fact about the whole thing, listing what happened, the plan and who didn't make it. As islanders, we were used to people not making it.

Edric, on the other hand, was using this as an opportunity to show off his acting skills. He described the rope-idea attempt in great detail, and even broke down how difficult it was to untie the ropes of three different people. As he spoke, Esmond wandered off to the buffet table to eat sandwiches. Noon stared at his back until I thought he would bore a hole through it. If looks could kill, that green shirt would be dead.

Once Edric got to the end of his story, everyone sort of peeled off. The first thing Cass wanted to do, naturally, was check us for bites. Glaed told me that she'd already checked everyone else as they came in, so the five of us who arrived last were still up for debate. I went first and then, once Cass was happy I hadn't become Pyre food, she checked Luke.

'Thank you,' he signed, when she had barely started. He was bright red, embarrassed as she pulled up one trouser leg to check his skin, so she held her hands up in surrender and let him go.

'You sign?' Glaed asked, impressed.

Luke shrugged. 'Only a little. We weren't given much notice between them letting us know we'd been picked and getting here, so I learned what I could. I've seen you signing on Bloodwatch sometimes. Thought it might come in useful.' He signed a little as he spoke.

'Clever bastard,' Cass signed.

Clever was right. Must be nice to sit at home on a comfy

sofa, learning all of our ways. Luke had been watching us for years. I hated that.

'What did she say?' Luke asked me, his wide brown eyes fixed on me.

'I'll teach you some time.' I sighed and sagged down on to one of the hard benches.

Luke sat down next to me. 'You OK?' he asked.

I sat up. 'Me? Yeah, Cass checked me. I'll live.'

'No, I mean, how do you feel? Up here.' He reached out and tapped the side of my head. My skin prickled under his touch. 'Morrigan, Marg. That was rough to watch. How are you coping?'

I paused, unsure how to answer. It felt like a trick, him asking me to be vulnerable. There was never time for a mental-health powwow after a full-on night of slaughtering Pyres back in the Burgh. And the last person who checked in on me had been Hild. Hild was my best friend. I'd known her for years, and I didn't trust easily. So how was this boy making me want to open up after only a few hours?

Because he cared. Even as the realisation washed over me, the monster inside growled.

Mainlanders only care about themselves, it argued.

Well, maybe both things could be right. Luke needed me as much as I needed him to survive this. To look after himself, he had to look after me – and I had to do the same. It didn't matter why any of these mainlanders signed up in the first place, not any more – they were in this now, for real, not just on a TV screen. What mattered was that I was getting out of here, and that meant Luke was getting out of here too. Whether I trusted him or not – I just had to trust myself to survive.

I laughed, but it was hollow. 'How am I coping? That's unfortunately a pretty regular sight for me. I hate to say it, but I've seen worse.' I muttered the last bit. We all saw the footage at my interview. 'I should be asking how you're doing. I guess that doesn't happen much on the mainland.'

'Just because it happens a lot, doesn't mean we can't honour them,' Luke said, ignoring my comment. He held up two bottles of water from the buffet table and then handed me one. 'A toast. To Morrigan and Marg. May we never forget their sacrifice.'

I blinked at him. I didn't even have a funeral when I lost Dad and Wynn. We survive or we die, that's how it goes. If you started to dwell on it, on what those absences in life meant, you started to lose yourself. That said, Luke's words, and his earnest eyes, even if they were all fake, wheedled their way under my skin. He was beautiful, all dimples and sun-kissed skin. Beauty that tricked my heart even when I didn't want it to, but Luke's looks weren't what made him dangerous; he was a mainlander and under Bloodwatch's spell. Maybe I could take him at face value, literally in his case, just this once. After seeing him freeze out there, it was possible that he really did want to remember them.

'To Morrigan and Marg,' I said, clinking the plastic tops together.

And then we sat in silence for a moment, the tips of our knees touching.

CHAPTER ELEVEN

Luke crossed the room and grabbed some sandwiches. 'You should eat something,' he said.

'Oh, thanks,' I said, taking one. A few hours ago I probably wouldn't have eaten anything a mainlander tourist gave me, especially from Bloodwatch's table, but if Luke and I were going to survive this show I had to start trusting him a little more. Not with my heart, or my head, or my safety. But a sandwich I could just about handle. I turned it over, inspecting the soft bread and the filling. 'What's in it?'

Luke peered closer at it. 'Looks like egg mayonnaise. Sorry, did you want to swap? I've got ham.'

I smiled. 'No, it's not that,' I said. I turned the sandwich round between my fingers. 'I probably haven't had a sandwich in over eight years.'

'Really?' Luke asked. He bit into his. 'Why?'

'Because sandwiches are the pinnacle of civilisation,' I said. He raised an eyebrow and I laughed. 'Hear me out. Basically, a sandwich used to be this simple meal you'd take to school or have as a snack, right? But actually, a ton of work goes into making a sandwich. The bread, for a start, requires flour, which requires a mill, which requires a power source. And don't even get me started on how hard it is to get the wheat, the mayonnaise, the oil . . . Dozens of people all over a country coming together to make something as seemingly simple as a sandwich.'

'That is the smartest thing anyone has ever said to me,' Luke said. 'And I'm glad to have someone as smart as you on my team. Maybe one day we'll be old friends, sharing a sandwich on the mainland. We're bonded for life after an experience like this, right?'

An experience.

That's all this was for the mainlanders. Disaster tourism, a story to tell, instant money and a path to fame. Annoyingly, though, he was right. If Luke died, I was out, so I had to get on with him. Plus, while I was pretty bad at navigating the cameras, he revelled in it. He always knew what to say at least. His camera-readiness might mean we stayed in this game until the end with help from the viewing public. I could be friends if friends meant survival.

'You're right. We're in this together. Friends,' I said, nodding at him and hoping I sounded more convincing than I felt.

Luke's expression relaxed and he leaned back. 'Excellent. Friends it is.'

My new *friend* placated, I ate my sandwich and marvelled at how soft the bread was. I'd heard a couple of the tourists already complaining about the quality, but to me it tasted like a slice of heaven, and I wasn't the only one. Around the room, red shirts were devouring the sandwiches like the people we were – underfed and malnourished. Everyone had split into groups, mostly with their partner, which made sense. This was the first time we could get to know them, and a good chance for Luke and me to get some screen time so we could win over those viewer votes, and whatever treasures they would bestow upon us. Time to make an effort.

'So I have a question, *friend*. Why did you tell Nova at your interview that you wanted to pair with me?'

Luke blinked. 'Isn't it obvious?'

'Obvious why you would pick a girl who punched someone on a television show? Unless you're unhinged in some way, it's not super obvious, no,' I replied.

Luke raised an eyebrow. 'Do I seem unhinged?'

'Well, you applied to come to the most dangerous place on earth, so the jury is out on that one,' I replied. His laugh made the hairs on the backs of my arms stand on end.

Luke nodded. 'No, that's fair. I picked you because you were the most real person in the room.'

I raised an eyebrow right back at him.

'Everyone else was so calm and collected. But living here, how the mainland abandoned you? You're angry. You should all be angry,' Luke said. He took a swig from his water bottle. It wasn't that he was angry himself as such, but he was definitely riled. It was like, I dunno, like he cared more about us than what Influencer lipstick we were wearing that week. The perfect act for the cameras and I couldn't be mad about it – it was speeches like that that were going to get us more votes.

'From where I was sitting, you were the sanest person on that stage,' Luke finished, setting his water back down.

'I will take that as a compliment,' I said, having a drink from my own water bottle. See? I could say nice things for the cameras too. Maybe this would work out. I pretended to be his friend, he pretended to be mine and we would both get out of this alive. 'Well, they probably broadcast your choice. I was quite surprised that the public put us together.'

Luke grinned. 'I wasn't. The public like to vote attractive people together. I've seen enough reality shows to know how that works.'

Heat rushed up to my cheeks and I almost choked on my water. Luke thought I was attractive?

That threw a very large spanner in the works of my *friends* plan. I didn't have many of them, but I was pretty sure friends didn't call each other attractive. At least Hild and I never had. And their hearts didn't do backflips whenever the other one smiled. I swallowed. This wasn't real, it was for a television show. Luke was playing the game – and shit, he was good at it.

But I'd rather have a partner who was good at the game than a dead one.

Before I could respond, a shadow fell over us. Cinta was standing over me. 'We should probably talk,' she said.

'Oh, you can take my seat,' Luke insisted, standing up.

Cinta shook her head and flashed him her artificially whitened smile. 'No, no, over here would be better.'

I glanced over her shoulder and saw she had cleared a space in front of one of the fixed cameras. I rolled my eyes, but I stood up.

'I'll speak to you in a bit?' I said to Luke, and he nodded.

As soon as I sat down, Cinta started talking.

'Listen. I think there may have been a bit of a mix-up with your golden envelope.'

'A mix-up? You mean how it accidentally found its way into your pocket?' I said, setting my jaw. 'Cinta, I nearly died because of you. It's not even like you were going to win; Cass and Glaed were way ahead of you. What the hell was that?'

'All right, chill. I said I was sorry,' she said, her eyes flicking over to the camera on the right. Did she turn herself more towards the lens?

'Actually, you didn't say "sorry",' I said, folding my arms. She wanted the screen time? She'd have to pay the toll.

Cinta sighed. 'All right, OK, fine. I'm *sorry*. But I knew you would be fine, you're the Executioner. And besides, if I hadn't pulled that stunt you wouldn't have warned us about the Pyres, and you wouldn't have got nearly as much airtime. I did you a favour, if you think about it.'

'Don't push it,' I said, and Cinta shrugged.

'Whatever. Plus, you got Luke, so I wouldn't complain so much if I were you.'

I scoffed a laugh. 'Cinta, this isn't a dating show. It's a life-or-death game.'

'I know. But just because it's life or death doesn't mean the audience don't care. With a smile like his, you'll be swimming in votes. You'll see,' Cinta said. She cocked her head, eyes flitting between me and the camera. 'So are we good?'

I drew in a deep breath, trying to keep the monster inside its box. She was only apologising because she was assuming that Luke would be popular with viewers and, by extension, me. She never in a million years thought I would have Luke on my card, and she didn't have time to check. She still left me for dead.

'I don't forgive you, and I don't trust you,' I said with a sigh. 'But we have to work together because Bloodwatch is the enemy – it's always been the enemy – not us islanders. So, for the sake of staying alive, if Bloodwatch by some miracle allow that, we're good.'

'Keep your friends close, right?' Cinta said, beaming as if the end of that sentence wasn't *and your enemies closer*.

She jumped up and went back to her partner, who had her back to me so I could read her shirt. Reeta, the athletic girl who wanted to be in the army. They were like chalk and cheese, Cinta all lip gloss and powder, Reeta all muscle. But maybe that's what made them interesting to watch.

I needed to understand what viewers wanted to see. While Cass won the foot race to save her partner, Cresta did say that the viewers could vote for their favourite, and that team got an advantage in the next round too. That could be me and Luke. Maybe we *could* win this thing, after all.

I went back to sit with Luke.

'Everything all right?' he asked.

'Yeah, everything's fine,' I said. It was amazing how easy it was to lie with cameras on you. This wasn't real life, inside this safe-room container. Out there was, and when it mattered, Cinta failed, and Luke followed orders. That was what was important. The mind games could wait.

A crackle overhead interrupted us and the room fell silent. A set of speakers started talking to us.

'Congratulations, contestants. Please find supplies under the buffet table. Doors to the safe room will open in the morning. Thank you for your cooperation.' The voice was mechanical.

Rhegar was already by the table so he lifted the cloth.

'Jackpot,' he said, revealing twenty backpacks neatly lined up in a row. We wandered over one by one and collected a pack, each one labelled with our name. At the end there were two left, labelled MARG and MORRIGAN. Cinta strolled forward and grabbed Marg's bag before tipping the contents on the floor.

'Dude, what are you doing?' Jupiter asked, shaking his head in disbelief.

Cinta answered without looking up, digging through various things. 'It's not like they're going to use this stuff. They're dead, get over it,' she said, her voice even.

Jupiter looked around, pleading with his eyes at me and Cass, but we shrugged.

'She doesn't need to be such a bitch about it, but yeah, she's right. Welcome to Blood Island, as that Cresta would say,' I said, just as Mills and Decke grabbed Morrigan's bag. At the bitch comment, Cinta paused briefly to raise her middle finger at me before continuing her pillaging. 'Can't waste anything here. Trust me, Morrigan would have wanted it that way.'

'Marg might have wanted a bit more forethought, though,' Luke murmured, and the green shirts awkwardly shifted their feet.

I stared at him, a sharp pain of betrayal in my chest. Luke didn't get it. He could try, but as a mainlander he'd always be different to us, to me.

After Cinta and Mills had finished taking what they wanted, and the mainlanders had accepted that the rules might be a little different here, we formed a circle on the floor and got to work pulling out the contents of our own bags.

The backpacks were what we had been waiting for. Folded into the top were a fleece and a waterproof jacket, which was a relief in the cold of the safe room. There was also a metal water canteen, a lighter, a silver-foil blanket and even a first-aid kit, although that wouldn't do much good against Pyre bites.

'Why is this in here?' Glaed asked, pulling out a bottle with a plastic cap. I took out my matching one and turned it over.

SUNCREAM. SPF 50.

'I haven't seen one of these in years,' Noon laughed, tossing his own bottle on to the floor.

'Well, come on now,' his partner, Esmond, said. 'Sunburn is one of the leading causes of skin melanomas. Cancer is no joke, sir. It's a killer.'

Noon snorted. 'Listen, Nerdy McGee. If you live long enough to develop cancer on this island, you're one lucky son-of-a-bitch. We don't exactly have a nice little suncream factory down the road pumping this shit out.'

Cass rolled her eyes and started to sign, which Rhegar interpreted for the tourists. 'I think what Noon is trying to say is that we take sun blemishes as a blessing on the island. Sunlight is what protects us. Because the Pyres burn to death in the sun, we love it. A suntan is a precious sign of life.'

'Well, all I'm saying is it's summer and maybe we should take sun protection seriously,' Esmond muttered. Noon cackled and slapped him on the back so hard he nearly fell over. All was forgiven, then.

'Is that true? About the sun?' Luke whispered to me. It was the first time he had said something since the comment about Marg, and I was still bristling a bit, but I also knew I had to follow my own advice. I had to get my head back in the game, and that meant communicating with my partner.

'Oh yeah. I know it's probably not the healthiest, but a sunburn is, like, a badge of honour on the island.' I shrugged. 'Not that you'd have to worry. You're not exactly Pyre-pale yourself.' I pointed to the skin on his forearms, stopping short of touching him. *Friends*, remember?

Luke blinked twice like I'd said something wrong, but then his smile returned and the cloud lifted from his brow. 'Oh yeah, but I have to admit I'm pretty sun-safe myself. Might keep hold of mine. I may rock a tan, but I burn faster than a Pyre in the midday sun.'

'All right, tourist. But don't expect me to protect you from Noon's ribbing,' I said.

'I would never,' Luke said, with a wink that made me need to look away.

There were bedrolls in the packs too, so we all settled down for the night on the hard floor. We naturally split into red shirts and green shirts, despite having our partners, but I didn't mind. Sleeping next to Cass and Glaed felt safer than sleeping next to Luke. I wasn't ready for that. And obviously the islanders slept better than the mainlanders. We were used to the all-night howls of the Pyres as they hunted. One even banged on the door of the safe room at one point, which spooked Esmond, but they left after they realised they couldn't get in. Noon lay with his eyes open, staring at the ceiling, working his jaw. If the Pyres didn't kill Esmond, Noon might.

Eventually I woke up to the low, murmuring voices of the other contestants, all trying to whisper as some of us were still asleep.

I scraped my hair back into a bun and scanned the room until Luke caught my eye. He gave a silent wave and I returned the favour, feeling more than a bit silly. Hild would have had a field day.

Oh, waving! Wow, I hope you were wearing protection!

We ate the rest of the sandwiches for breakfast, and after a few minutes the safe-room door clicked open. Some of the green shirts jumped back, hiding behind their partners, but I knew we would be safe. There was no cover on the top of the castle so any Pyres left would have run back to their caves hours ago. Sunlight spilled through the gap, and stood in the doorway, smiling, was Cresta.

'Hello, contestants,' she said. 'Do come outside. It's time to reveal our winners and their prizes.'

'So no good morning, how are you, glad you survived the bloodbath?' Noon muttered as we walked out into the bright sunlight.

It was warm outside, and I tied my waterproof around my waist, underneath the straps of my backpack. Cresta had stepped back towards the plinths where the tourists had been tied up.

The remnants of last night's battle were fresh on the ground. There was blood, so much blood, soaked into the stone and dyeing the floor a deep red. A couple of Pyres hadn't made it back down the stairs before sunrise, and one was still draped over the half-wall where Marg had jumped, its neck and back bent at an unnatural angle. It was one of the naked ones, and its once-pale skin was covered in blisters and burst ulcers, oozing yellow pus over bright-red burns. It was still alive – I could tell from the quick rise and fall of its chest – but it didn't move.

The worst part, though, was Morrigan's body. He had been eaten alive, that much was clear. White bone poked out from bite holes in his legs, licked clean and glistening in the light. His chest had been ripped open and his lungs dragged out, the contents of his stomach spilled over the flagstones. The skin on his skull had been mostly picked off, but one terrified eyeball hung loose from his right socket.

I'd seen worse.

Esmond vomited.

'Yes, can't say I'm enjoying being here much either.' Cresta tried to laugh but a wave of revulsion made her screw up her nose. Her camera team were equally struggling.

Cresta clasped her hands together. 'All right, congratulations to Cass and her partner, Jupiter! Come up here and take a box. What's inside will help with the next task – no peeking yet, though.' Cresta's false enthusiasm was only bolstered by the obvious fact that the faster she got through this segment, the quicker she could leave.

Cass and Jupiter, the big guy who seemed a bit too happy to be here, stepped up next to Cresta. A member of the production team handed her two small golden boxes and she gave one to Cass.

'And now for our winners of the public vote.' Cresta's eyes scanned the crowd until they fell on me. 'Luke and Astrid, come on up here.'

CHAPTER TWELVE

Well, if there was one thing Cinta would excel at, it was knowing what the mainlanders liked to watch. All those years of Influencer crates had come in clutch in the end – for me and Luke anyway.

She scowled at me as Luke and I took our places on Cresta's left side and she handed me a box. In fact, a few of the others looked miffed. Mills glared like he was going to snatch the box out of my hands. Cass beamed at me and waved her identical package.

Which made us both a target, depending on what was in there.

'OK. For your next challenge, we will be testing your courage. You found your teammate. Can you hold your nerve when faced with true horror?'

'Like we didn't already do that,' Cass signed, her face indicating the snark with her signs, and I smirked.

Cresta looked to each of us. 'Cass and Astrid, please open your boxes.'

I pulled the lid off the golden box and peered inside. It was a stopwatch.

'The next challenge will be timed,' Cresta said, by way of explanation. 'Cass and Jupiter, Astrid and Luke, you will have a five-minute head start on your fellow contestants. How you use this will be up to you, and there will be more instructions once we get you into the crypt.'

'Excuse me, but a crypt?' Cinta put her hand up but spoke anyway. Two cameras swivelled towards her. 'Like a graveyard?'

'I'm glad you asked, Cinta,' Cresta said, smiling. 'The crypt in question is an old burial chamber under this very castle ruin. The ruins may not look big but they do cover a large area, so your first task will be to find the hidden entrance in the woods nearby. The crypt itself is a maze of tunnels that you must navigate to find the exit, where another safe room will be waiting for you. You will have ninety minutes to locate the entrance, go through the maze and be the first team to find the exit. Astrid and Luke, Cass and Jupiter, you lucky ducks will have ninety-five minutes.'

'What if we don't manage it in the time given?' Esmond asked.

'Then the doors will be closed and you will be sealed inside the crypt forever,' Cresta said cheerfully. 'Or worse – but that surprise can wait until later.'

I glanced at Luke and his jaw twitched.

'And let me guess. We won't be alone in there?' Mills said, resting a crooked elbow on his brother's shoulder.

'Well, where would be the fun if you were?' Cresta said, spreading her hands wide. 'Our scans show a couple of Pyre broods live within the crypt itself during the daytime. But if you're very quiet you should be able to tiptoe past them without any issues.'

'So it's super easy, then,' Decke said, and I realised it was one of the few times I'd heard him speak.

'I'm sure for seasoned islanders such as yourself, this will be a piece of cake. And stay with your partners. They are the only ones with keys – aka those snazzy wristbands – to the safe room,' Cresta said. 'OK, contestants. Are you ready to begin?'

'Do we have a choice?' Noon asked.

'Ha-ha, so funny today, Noon,' Cresta said, without a drop of humour in her voice. She turned to Luke, Cass, Jupiter and me. 'Your stopwatches already have your five-minute head start loaded up. After that, everyone will be released at the same time. When I say go, set them off. Got it?'

'We understand,' Luke said, because I was busy interpreting for Cass what was going on.

'Great.' Cresta beamed and turned to camera. 'On your marks, get set, go!'

We didn't waste any time. Luke and Jupiter handled the watches and the four of us took the castle stairs two at a time, racing to the bottom as fast as we trusted ourselves to go. Around the base of the staircase was what was left of any Pyres that fell the night before. Jupiter's eyes got wider as we passed, but none of us said anything. There were more out the front of the castle, in the courtyard, but that wasn't what stopped us in our tracks.

Marg's body was there, her head turned at an impossible angle to face us as we approached. She had died on impact. One of her feet had twisted all the way round, so it faced the opposite way to her knee, and blood spilled over the green of her shirt.

'Oh shit,' Jupiter said, resting his hands on his knees. He turned very pale, which wasn't what I would expect from a guy as big as him, but maybe I should. Maybe the fact that Cass and I were so used to scenes like this should be the weird thing here.

'We should close her eyes,' Luke said. Without waiting for us to respond, he closed the space between him and the body and bent down, muttering something under his breath as he carefully pushed her eyelids shut. Yesterday I would have said it was a little performative, but there was a gentle carefulness in the way that Luke pressed his fingertips over Marg's closed eyes that felt . . . real, somehow. Like he didn't want to rush despite the head start.

'We should go. One minute gone already,' I said awkwardly, checking the stopwatch. Whether it was for the cameras or for his conscience, Marg was gone. We couldn't waste what we had been given here. Cass nodded and Jupiter sucked in a deep breath before straightening up.

'You're right. Let's go,' Luke said, standing up.

'Yes, please. I don't know how you're doing it, man. You see the blood on the TV but my god, the smell is what gets you,' Jupiter said, gagging as he spoke.

I raised an eyebrow. Jupiter was right, Luke was pretty unfazed by the gore so far.

Luke shrugged. 'I hold my breath. The smell of blood isn't something I like to think about. I just . . . block it out.'

There was an edge to his voice, but I pushed it aside. Luke wasn't squeamish and he was my partner in a fight to the death. I wasn't about to look a gift horse in the mouth – he could tell me about his secret life as a serial killer later.

We ran to the edge of the treeline and I had one last look back at the castle before we disappeared into the woods, the only other thing looming above it being the broadcast tower in the far distance, marking Bloodwatch HQ.

'What do you think the entrance will look like?' Cass signed once we were far enough into the forest. I checked the stopwatch. Three minutes gone.

'Probably like a mausoleum or something, if I had to guess,' I said.

She raised an eyebrow.

'I mean, like a stone structure you might find in a graveyard. The crypt has bodies in it, right? It's a sacred place for mourning. The entrance will be in a graveyard,' I explained further.

'See, this is why we need to stick together,' Jupiter said. 'I can't understand a word of sign language, and I don't want to let Cass down. We can't go off on our own.'

I saw the look of fear in his eyes, and it matched mine. He was right, he and Cass wouldn't last five minutes on their own. Besides, there was safety in numbers. Just like my realisation that Luke wanted to survive this as much as I did, so did Cass and Jupiter. We had to watch each other's backs to stay alive.

'Surely that works out for both of us,' Luke said. 'I know a little sign language but nowhere near enough to hold a conversation. And remember what Cresta said? If we can stay quiet in the crypt, we can sneak past the Pyres. It's daytime; they'll be sleeping after the hunt last night. Cass and Astrid can use sign to communicate with each other if there's any light down there, and we follow them.'

'Sounds good to me,' I said. Maybe the viewing public did know what made a good team when they put us together. I checked the stopwatch. Four minutes gone.

We had been half jogging in a straight line from the castle, and in the distance I could see a clearing where the trees weren't quite as dense.

'There.' I pointed, and we sped up towards it.

We emerged into an overgrown graveyard. The sun cast dapples of shadow over the broken tombstones, which were almost completely covered over with long grass. And of course there were cameras. Everywhere.

'Is this what you meant, Astrid?' Jupiter asked, and I nodded.

'Feels right, don't you think?' I replied. 'The entrance has to be here somewhere. We'll spread out, stay where we can see each other. Cass, stay with Jupiter so he can hear me call if we find it first. Me and Luke will take the left side; you go right.'

'Got it,' Cass signed.

'Wait,' Jupiter said. He reached into his pocket and pulled out two small yellow gemstones, the same ones that he had in his interview. 'This is a graveyard, right? And it's kinda peaceful. You guys go ahead if you need to, but this is as good a place as any to leave Mum and Dad, you know?'

Cass and Luke looked at me and I didn't need sign language to know what they were asking.

Should we really waste time on this?

But my heart softened, at least a little. I'd lost my family and had never had a chance to grieve or hold any sort of proper goodbye. If this was what Jupiter needed . . .

'Be fast. We're right here if you need us,' I said.

Cass looked worried and Luke's brow furrowed, but he nodded, deferring to me. They both did. At some point, somehow, I had become the leader of our small group. People do what you want when they're scared of you. But this was different. Cass and Luke weren't tense around me. They seemed to *like* spending time with me. Well, I think Cass did. Jury was out on Luke.

Except that every time he smiled at me I melted into a puddle. That part was pretty distracting.

'No sweat, boss,' Jupiter said with a grin, confirming my suspicion that somehow I was the de facto leader here.

And he was fast. He spun on his heel, knelt in the grass and said, 'God made dirt; dirt won't hurt. Love you.' Then he poked the two gems into the exposed bit of soil between two mounds of knotweed and stood up.

'That was . . . impressively fast,' Luke said, eyes wide.

'Oh, I'm not very good with words,' Jupiter chuckled, like he had made a speech at a wedding, not conducted a ten-second funeral. 'Just something Mum used to say when I fell at the playground a lot. Plus, I'm happy. I've done what I came here to do.'

I raised an eyebrow at him. 'Well, then, I'd say you're better at words than you thought.'

'Thanks, boss. Now, where were we?' Jupiter asked.

In the distance, someone blew a whistle.

'That'll be everyone else,' Luke said. 'So we have five minutes until they catch up.'

'Unless they get lost,' I said hopefully. 'Shout if you find something. Good luck.'

The four of us split off in our agreed directions. Luke and I pushed back the grass, looking for signs of a fallen structure that could be the entrance.

'I'm glad we're teaming up with Cass and Jupiter,' Luke said as we searched behind a taller tombstone that ended up being a dead end. 'They deserve to get to the end of this thing.'

'Yeah. Cass is pretty cool. Jupiter's OK too,' I said, pushing some bramble aside. 'The shortest funeral in history was nice.'

'He's a bit of a gentle giant, Jupiter. On the first night Marg found a spider in her room and wanted to kill it, but Jupiter caught it and put it out the window,' Luke said. 'Made me like him right away. You ever get that? You know, drawn to people?'

I stared at the ground, scared to meet his eye. Sometimes it was like he could read every feeling I had towards him just by looking at me. Like he could see into my soul.

There was a crashing sound and I whipped my head up to see what had happened. Luke was staring at a tombstone, turned over on the ground. The graveyard was old, overgrown, and more than a few of the graves had taken damage, but that same tombstone had been upright a second ago. I was sure of it.

'Did you just . . . ?' I trailed off, pointing at the grave.

Luke blinked for a second, then smiled and looked at me. 'Guess I don't know my own strength. Or more likely, I need to remember not to lean on ancient tombstones that are probably cracked and can't take my weight, right?'

I looked back at the tombstone. There was still thick ivy covering the name and date, and the crack at the base looked fresh. Even if it *was* cracked, would it . . . fall over like that? Luke was tall, but he wasn't huge. And from the damage done to the stone . . . it was like a wrecking ball had knocked it down.

'Come on. Let's keep looking. Don't want to waste our head start,' Luke said, brushing it off.

He started walking and I jogged a few steps to catch up. Whatever happened, for some reason Luke didn't want to talk about it. Maybe he felt awful desecrating a grave, even if it was an accident? Still weird, though.

'Hey, Luke, I wouldn't worry about— Whoa.'

I stumbled over a hidden rock in the grass and Luke caught my arm. I looked up at him, expecting to be embarrassed, but that melted away when I caught his smile.

'Th-thank you,' I stuttered.

'You're my teammate. You fall, I fall,' he said, pulling me back upright.

We were standing so close together that his breath was on my cheek, and a warm feeling sprang up in the pit of my stomach.

'Hey, Bloodwatch's favourite couple.' Jupiter's voice rang through the clearing, causing us to jump apart. 'Cass found the entrance. Come on.'

That broke the tension. Jupiter was waving from the other side of the graveyard and we quickly picked our way over to him. Cass came into view behind what looked like a small stone shed. It had a wooden door.

'Nice one, Cass,' I said, patting her on the back.

I checked the stopwatch. We left eight minutes ago, so we had eighty-seven minutes remaining, and no idea how big this maze was.

'OK, no talking out loud from this point on,' I said, laying out the plan. 'Everyone keep a lookout for clues about how to reach the end.'

'You think there will be clues?' Luke asked.

'Well, they made this bit easy enough. And there are three tasks left. They've spent so much money and time on this thing at this point, I have to assume they want at least some of us to survive until the end. So that must mean that we have enough time, and that they have given us half a chance of reaching the end. Clues, maybe, pointing towards the exit,' I said.

Jupiter grinned. 'Yo, that's smart. I like how you think.'

Luke said nothing, only smiled and nodded. He was trusting me. They all were.

'OK, we ready?' The other three nodded.

Cass pushed open the door to the mausoleum and we followed her inside. It was pitch black, but in the light of the door leading outside we could make out two rows of helmets, neatly laid out on some sort of bench to the left of the entrance. Each one was fitted with a head torch. I signalled to the others and all four of us grabbed one, clicking the torch on at the front until we had four beams of light leading the way. I quickly counted the helmets that were left. Twelve. With our four, that only made sixteen. Whichever team made it to the entrance last would be caught out in the dark.

A loud clatter from behind us made me jump and I spun round to see Jupiter looking sheepish, teeth gritted as he tried to steady two helmets that he had knocked to the floor on the far side of the bench. He was huge, his frame nearly filling the entrance, and he had to stoop a little below the low ceiling. Keeping quiet was going to be trickier than I thought, but maybe if we were fast enough, that's all that would matter.

Time check: eighty-three minutes left. The other teams set off seven minutes ago.

Our headlamps illuminated a tunnel straight ahead, long and with a carved, round ceiling. The crypt. I signalled to Cass to move that way and we arranged ourselves in a line: me at the front followed by Luke, then Jupiter and Cass bringing up the rear. We moved quickly, knowing that the longer we hung around the entrance, the sooner the others could catch up, who might not think to be as quiet as us. Silence was the name of the game here.

A screech echoed in the darkness and I stilled in my tracks. Luke barrelled into me as both Jupiter and Cass shunted him forward. My breath froze in my throat. This wasn't going to be easy, and icy fear slicked through my veins, freezing my limbs.

I blinked, focusing on the monster deep inside, on the box I used to keep it locked away. I could open that if I needed to, I just had to focus more on how angry I was that I was stuck in this situation, put here by Bloodwatch, rather than how scared I was that I'd never get out alive.

It was a delicate balance, fear and anger, but it worked. My breathing slowed and I gestured for us to move again. We had a plan, and they wanted a good show. This was not how we were going to die.

We stepped quickly through the dark tunnel, relying on the head torches to show us the bends and twists of the passage. Finally, we reached our first decision: a fork in the path. The tunnel split left or right. We had to pick a side. I checked the stopwatch and saw there was only sixty minutes remaining. How had we used so much time already?

At least this was simple enough to silently communicate a vote. Left or right?

Cass voted for left at the same time Jupiter pointed right. Luke said nothing, scanning the walls of the two options with squinted eyes. I raised an eyebrow at him. He signed back crudely and disjointedly that he was looking for clues.

I nodded – looking for clues was my idea, after all. I scanned the names of various dead people on the walls of the tunnel.

There. Something caught my eye, a name carved into the stone that looked newer than the others: RUTH TRING

I signalled to the others and pointed. 'Look at this new name,' I signed to Cass. 'It must have been added by Bloodwatch. It's a hint.'

Luke looked at me and his eyes widened. He moved his mouth, then thought better of it and closed it again, frustrated.

'Can you show us?' I signed, not knowing whether he understood or not.

Luke nodded and pointed to the letters in Ruth's name, but out of order, first to the R, and then to the I in TRING. I grinned. I could see where he was going.

'It's an anagram,' I signed to Cass. 'The letters in Ruth Tring can be rearranged to spell TURN RIGHT.'

Some of that must have got through to Luke, because he nodded and pointed to the right tunnel. Poor Jupiter looked confused but determined to follow us anyway. We dashed into the right tunnel.

As we walked, I thought I heard something creak in the distance. Was it Pyres? Or had the first of the other teams caught up to us? We were so deep now, it was impossible to tell. It was so cold, I could see my breath in small puffs. I checked the stopwatch again: forty-eight minutes left. Maybe we could do this, after all. I followed the tunnel round again, and then for the second time that day stopped dead in my tracks.

I held up my hand to signal we needed to stop walking, and I let the others take in what I could see.

An entire brood of Pyres, at least fifty-strong, all curled up asleep on the cold stone floor. And on the other side of the room was the only exit.

We had to go *through* them.

CHAPTER THIRTEEN

'Maybe we misunderstood the clue,' Cass signed. 'We should go back, find another way round.'

I shook my head. 'I don't think so. The clue said to turn right, and besides, what do you think Bloodwatch would rather see us do? Have a safe trip around the maze or have us tiptoe across a room full of sleeping Pyres?'

Cass paused for a moment and then swore.

Jupiter waved to get our attention and knitted his eyebrows together in an expression that pretty clearly said, *I know you can't seriously be asking us to go through that, can you?*

Luke patted him on the back and nodded. Jupiter gulped. All three of them turned to look at me, waiting for my decision.

I took a step forward.

Luke grabbed my arm and shook his head, pointing to his own chest.

'We need to keep formation for communication to flow,' I signed, hoping he was taking some of it in. 'Follow me, step where I step and stay silent.' After that, I put my finger on my lips to highlight the part about silence, to be sure Jupiter understood.

I knew Pyres didn't react to artificial torchlight, but what did concern me was smell. We all knew that, to an extent, Pyres could smell fresh blood and track their prey that way. The cavern in front of us had dozens of Pyres in it, all sleeping in piles like dogs, with a narrow path naturally being formed between each pile. Some of the Pyres at the bottom had their noses to the ground, faced outwards like they were put there specifically to scent us as we tiptoed past. We would have to be careful, sure, but we'd also have to be fast. The longer we lingered, the longer they would have to sense one of us and wake up.

And then there was the noise. We'd done a good job keeping it to a minimum so far, but we couldn't afford a single trip, or stone kicked, or stumble. The only sound currently was the fast snores of the Pyres, their chests rising and falling with superhuman breaths. Even when they were asleep, they were built to be alert.

So we had to move quickly but not too quickly, and completely silently, around a room of killers, and not wake any of them up or we would all die. Perfect.

Time check: forty-one minutes left.

I took a step to my left. I wondered how they even got the cameras in here to watch us, because there was no way they were putting us through all this and not recording it. It must have been when the Pyres were out hunting us at the castle, or maybe even earlier. They probably had more machines that would draw them away. Maybe if we had some of that technology, we'd be able to kill all of the Pyres and retake the island. But that would make Bloodwatch meaningless, so obviously it wasn't an option.

I stood on tiptoe as I moved, weaving my way between the sleeping corpses.

I chanced a look over my shoulder and saw that Luke, Jupiter and Cass were following along behind me, eyes on their feet, stepping in the exact place the person before them had recently vacated. Good. Even Jupiter looked like he was managing. We could do this.

I made it past a pile of sleeping Pyres and approached the part of our path I was most worried about. The gap between two more mounds of corpses ahead wasn't very wide. There was no way round it. A stone pillar holding up the roof of the crypt blocked our path to the right, and on the left was another pile that leaned against the far wall. The exit was straight ahead.

I wiped my sweaty palms on my trousers and walked on, forcing myself through the gap. There was just enough room for us if we tiptoed sideways, our toes and heels between the mouths and noses of the sleeping Pyres on either side. I looked to my right after I turned sideways and saw Luke, Jupiter and Cass do the same.

My toe knocked a small pebble I hadn't spotted. It skittered across the rocks, impossibly loud in the silence, and came to a halt in front of a Pyre's closed eyes, almost touching it.

We froze. Every muscle in my body was ice; I was an immovable thing focused on that stone.

The Pyre took a deep breath, then let it back out. Its eyes stayed closed.

It was only another ten paces until we got past the narrow section of the path, but it felt like a thousand. I was much more careful now, scanning each centimetre of free floor for loose rocks and indicating to Cass to do the same. It took an excruciatingly long time to get past the piles of corpses, but somehow, eventually, I stepped out into another open area of the cavern.

I turned and watched Luke complete the final step then walk to me, followed by Jupiter, and eventually Cass. She stumbled a little on the last one, her arms pinwheeling to keep upright. Soon we were all out in the open space, catching our breath and psyching ourselves up for the last section.

The exit from this part of the crypt was close, a small arched doorway that no doubt led to more tunnels and wall-side graves. The last pile of sleeping Pyres was maybe the largest, but there was a clear path on the left-hand side that curved round to the exit. We just had to hold our nerve.

I turned back to Cass to tell her the plan, but something caught my eye on the other side of the cavern, back to the passage from where we first entered. Standing there were Mills and Decke, bracing themselves against the entrance before they fell on to any Pyres. Behind them were their partners: Herrod, the older tourist, and Godric, the religious guy who was dressed in robes at his interview. This was the slowest part of the trial, and we'd used up our head start on it. They all stopped and looked around the cavern, taking it in, and then their eyes fell on us.

Mills grinned, and my stomach dropped.

'What's that dickhead up to now?' Cass signed.

'I think we have to move,' I signed back.

Cass raised an eyebrow at me and we all swivelled back to Mills, who had picked up a heavy stone brick.

I shook my head, pleading with him. If he waited, we'd be gone and his team could pick their way across. He didn't have to do this. Herrod and Godric looked confused, but Decke didn't. He grabbed his brother's arm and shook his head firmly, but Mills simply lifted his free hand, the one with the brick, even higher.

He launched the stone through the air like a grenade.

I didn't need to sign this time. All four of us turned on our heels and ran.

Somewhere behind us, the stone landed with a soft thud, which told me one thing. It didn't land on the floor and echo as it skittered away. It landed on a pile of sleeping Pyres.

I didn't turn round. I raced for the doorway, past the largest pile of pale corpses, and slid through to the other side of the threshold. Luke, Jupiter and Cass slid in behind me and we piled on top of each other on the far wall a few metres in. In the few seconds it took to pick ourselves up off the floor, I looked at what was happening in the cavern.

Mills's plan, by all accounts, had backfired. Instead of causing a noise that would attract the Pyres to us while his team hid in safety, he had chucked a rock at a bunch of sleeping Pyres and royally pissed them off. The sound of breathy screams echoed around us as the Pyres all woke up at once, like a hive-minded monster on the rampage. All of the Pyres were focused on Mills and the other three blood bags that he was standing with. They were screwed, and the wide-eyed look on Mills's face confirmed it.

Luke's hands on my shoulders brought me upright and Cass stepped into my eyeline.

'Move,' she signed, and that brought me back to the present.

We ran. There was no telling how many Pyres would go for Mills, and how many might smell that we had already come through the room and follow us, so we ran as fast as we could. Being quiet wasn't as much of an issue either, as the screams of the Pyres mixed with the screams of our fellow contestants drowned us out.

After a minute or two of running – and only twenty-seven minutes left according to the stopwatch – we hit another fork in our path, this time with three options: left, right or forward. Because Luke had already worked out that the clues were anagrams, and therefore we knew what to look for, it was much quicker to decide this time. Jupiter found the fresh name in seconds – DHATISHA GREAT – and Cass moved to the right-hand tunnel.

'Look. RIGHT, I see all the letters. Let's go,' Cass signed, already moving off.

I grabbed her arm. 'Wait. The letters that are left don't make sense. It's a bluff; it's not right,' I narrowed my eyes. 'It's STRAIGHT, and then the remaining letters spell AHEAD.'

Cass looked over the words and then nodded, and we moved into the tunnel ahead of us. We ran again, sprinting faster and faster to put as much space between us and the screaming as possible. Finally, we hit another fork in the road, And Cass found the name without a date instantly – REN TULFT.

I grinned. That one was easy – TURN LEFT. Before we continued, I pulled out the stopwatch. Twenty minutes remaining. We must be getting close by now – and apart from Mills and his crew, we hadn't seen a soul. At the end of the tunnel on the left, I thought I could see something.

'Wait – everyone, turn off your headlamps and look down the left tunnel. I think it's a light,' I signed.

Cass obliged and the boys followed suit. The hallway was plunged into darkness and instinctively I reached out and grabbed the first set of fingers I could find, lacing my own firmly through them. Luke. A warmth spread in the pit of my stomach as I squinted in the darkness at the thing that had caught my eye: a blinking red light, like the one we had seen on the room on the castle tower.

The safe room.

Jupiter must have spotted it at the same time, because he let out a small gasp in a high pitch and turned on his light. It took me a second to get accustomed to it after the dark, but I grinned at him and nodded, hoping he understood that I saw it too.

But once my eyes adjusted and I could see him clearly, he wasn't smiling. He was staring over my shoulder at something behind me, mouth frozen in a tiny 'o'.

I dropped Luke's hand and spun round. Running down the tunnel, mostly on all fours, was a tidal wave of Pyres. The echoes of the screams and the pounding of our feet had drowned out their approach, but there they were, maybe ten of them, scrambling towards us.

'Run!' I screamed, because it was too late for silence. We were so close. We couldn't die here.

We sprinted down the tunnel towards the safe room, the only light coming from Jupiter's headlamp. As a result, because Jupiter was behind me, all I could see ahead were long shadows pierced with jerky moments of light.

'Shit.' Luke moved ahead of me, his speed increased not by running, but by gravity as he fell.

'Get up, get up, get up!' I screamed, grabbing his arm as he fell and yanking him upwards. Somehow it worked, because he kept pace with me.

I looked up. The keypad on the door was visible now. We were so close. I still had a grip on Luke's arm as we ran, so I pulled back his coat sleeve to reveal the wristband, the key that would open the door.

We reached the safe room and pain flashed through me as both Jupiter and Cass piled into the back of us, squashing us against the door. The screaming was so loud I couldn't hear myself think as we untangled ourselves and backed up to get it open. The door was wedged into the hallway at an unnatural angle, the stone cut away in corners of the curved roof so that it would fit.

'Hurry!' Jupiter screamed, pushing Luke towards the door, his own key forgotten. Luke fumbled to get the fob to the keypad and I made the mistake of looking back down the hallway.

The Pyres were seconds behind us. The ones on all fours were the fastest, crawling along the stone floor like giant spiders from a nightmare. Several pale, naked bodies followed from behind, their arms pumping at their sides as they tried to reach us faster. One trampled a Pyre on the floor and didn't even look back. Their eyes were wide with hunger, their teeth bared, the saliva of anticipation dripping off their fangs and down their chins.

'Any time today, buddy,' Jupiter said, his voice high pitched again, his eyes on the approaching brood.

'I'm trying,' Luke said. I whipped my head round and watched as he jammed his wrist against the keypad, his voice shaking with panic.

The door light stayed stubbornly red. My mind flashed back to the night before when Esmond ran off to the safe room on his own, leaving Noon out in the cold. The door to the room had let him in with only one wristband. They weren't letting it happen again. For Cass and me to make it past this door, it needed *both* Luke's and Jupiter's wristbands to work. I gritted my teeth at the thought of the Bloodwatch producers coming up with this.

Hey, we can't have just anyone let in with one wristband. How about we only let the islander in if it's their partner's wristband against the door? Either they have to work together or we get a great death shot for the cameras. Win–win.

The first Pyre would be on us in seconds, ripping into our skin, bleeding us dry.

I grabbed Jupiter's wrist and pushed it up against the keypad next to Luke's.

The lock turned green and the door swung open. We all piled in through the open door and turned to slam it shut, just as a pale hand reached out for the space where we were standing seconds before.

We closed the door on the Pyres, their screams still echoing in our ears.

CHAPTER FOURTEEN

'I'm not used to running. Cass and I were first yesterday; I don't fancy another foot race with those things any time soon,' Jupiter said, his hands on his knees as he caught his breath.

'Me neither,' Cass signed.

Despite it all, we laughed. Obviously everything we went through was terrifying, but there was an adrenaline high to surviving that tipped us into hysterical laughter. We'd stayed alive, again. We were unstoppable, even when we cut it fine.

After we recovered, I checked the stopwatch. Still sixteen minutes left. There were around ten Pyres between that door and the others, but they were silent now. Perhaps they had already been distracted and run off.

There was a set of stairs that led up steeply. We must have travelled further underground than I realised. We made our way up the stairs and looked around.

The safe room was less of a room and more of a single-storey building. It was hard to tell if we were still below ground, but it would be difficult even for Bloodwatch to fit a space this size into an old crypt. The stairs opened on to a hallway with a series of doors off to each side. The doors were marked with more red blinking keypads and a pair of teammates' names printed on each. Luke and I were the first door on the left, so Luke used his fob to open the door while Cass and Jupiter ran off to find theirs after Cass checked us all for bites, letting Luke check himself after his embarrassment first time round.

Inside the room was a sink, two bedside tables, a wire hanger attached to the wall for our clothes and something that made my cheeks flush: a double bed.

'Let's drop our bags and see what else we can find,' Luke said, completely ignoring the bed-shaped elephant in the room. I followed him out, glad to be away from *that* situation for a while.

Cass and Jupiter had run straight for the end of the corridor, where there was a living room, small kitchen and large dining table with enough chairs to fit all eighteen of us – if we all made it.

As if he read my mind, Jupiter paused, his hand on a cupboard handle, and turned to look at me. 'The others will make it, right?'

Cass gave me a look that didn't need sign language to interpret. 'You can't think like that,' I told him. 'What will be will be. Come on. Let's see what Bloodwatch has left for us.'

Jupiter didn't like my answer, but he was as hungry and thirsty as the rest of us. It had been hours since the sandwich buffet. The boys opened every cupboard and pulled out packets of biscuits and chocolate and cereal, stuff Cass and I knew as rare but which were probably everyday supplies to Jupiter and Luke. Jupiter was searching through the giant fridge-freezer, pulling out a bottle of water and sinking it in one long series of gulps.

'Do you even remember the last time you saw so much food?' Cass signed, flopping down on the large corner sofa that dominated the opposite side of the room. It was pointed at a huge widescreen TV, and my heartbeat sped up.

How long are we staying here?

A packet of chocolate biscuits hit me squarely in the chest and snapped me out of it. Cass grinned and patted the seat next to her, and I took it. Deep inside, my worry melted away as I pulled open the sides of the packet and the rare smell of cocoa filled my nostrils.

Why can't we enjoy this, even if it's just for now? The monster in the box peeped its head out. *It's been a colossally shit eight years. We deserve this.*

And while I wouldn't usually indulge the angry demon always ready to emerge, I couldn't fault its logic. I bit down on a biscuit and the flavour was so intense, I drooled. Cass laughed. Luke and Jupiter were chatting at the dining table, drinking water and basically not acting like animals that hadn't had chocolate in eight years.

Cass tapped me on the shoulder. 'How long?' she asked, her face suddenly serious.

I knew what she was asking and pulled out the stopwatch. 'Twelve minutes left,' I said.

We both turned and stared at the corridor that led to the staircase. Surely we couldn't be the only ones that made it. Bloodwatch wouldn't allow it. I was sure they had their ways to top up contestants if they needed to. I shuddered at the thought.

Two minutes later, we had our answer. There was a series of shouts and a loud bang as someone piled through the door downstairs and slammed it shut. Mills, Decke, Herrod and Godric finally spilled into the room. Godric looked a little worse for wear, his cheeks bright red from exertion, and Herrod was leaning on his knees trying to catch his breath. Mills and Decke, on the other hand, looked like they had barely broken a sweat. I caught Mills's eye and he grinned at me, a real shit-eating grin that made the monster inside leap out of its box.

'What the hell was that back there?' I yelled, running at Mills.

He didn't have time to react before I was on him, pushing him up against the wall with my forearm across his neck. Decke moved forward and took a swipe at me, but Jupiter and Luke grabbed both his arms before he could get to me. Godric and Herrod simply stared at us.

To my absolute fury, once Mills had composed himself under my arm, he started laughing. 'There she is. The Executioner. Good. That shy-little-girl act doesn't suit you, sweetheart.'

I pushed my forearm harder across his windpipe, making him cough. Decke struggled against Luke and Jupiter, but no one else tried to stop me. Cass was still watching from the sofa. 'See that? Only your brother will follow you. I could kill you right here, right now, and no one would give a shit,' I spat.

All other emotion had left my body, and my limbs were

stiff with pure, unadulterated rage. Mills actively tried to kill all four of us. He had to be punished. The monster inside was dancing, fully out of its box, swinging on my heart to make it beat faster and faster, to pump that anger around my body.

'You're right, Astrid. No one would care.' Luke spoke softly and I turned to look at him. 'He's an arsehole, there's no two ways about it. But Bloodwatch do enough killing for all of us. And you wouldn't only be killing Mills, but you'd kill his partner too. The rules, remember?'

I blinked at him, then looked over at Herrod. He had recovered from the climb and was staring at me, his white beard stark against his red face.

'I wouldn't blame you if you did it,' he said. There was a sad edge to his voice that made my limbs a little looser. 'I wouldn't forgive someone who did that to me either.'

'Do what you need to do, Astrid,' Luke said. 'But do it for you, not for them. Don't let the cameras dictate who you are.'

I blinked. He was right. Losing it on camera all those years ago, knowing it would be immortalised forever, that was part of what broke me. Part of what made the monster so big and scary, I had to create the box deep inside. Decke shifted under Jupiter's and Luke's grip and I recognised the look on his face too. Sheer panic. It was the reflection I saw in the window of my own face when Dad and Wynn were attacked right in front of me.

I couldn't do that to someone else.

I let Mills go and he dropped to the floor, purple faced, gasping for air. The look of terror in his eyes as he pulled at the neckline of his shirt was enough payback for me. Luke and Jupiter let go of Decke and he ran to his brother's side and helped him sit up. Without Mills seeing, Decke looked up at me and gave me his trademark silent nod.

I stepped back, the anger dropping from my limbs. Luke closed the gap between us and pulled me into a hug, which in reality meant he was holding me up as my legs went to jelly. I folded my arms across his back and sank into him. He didn't say anything, just held me for a few seconds and then stepped back, hands on my shoulders.

'Surely the others are right behind you anyway, right?' Jupiter asked. 'You guys all set off at the same time.'

Godric shrugged. 'No one trusted anyone else enough to follow each other. We sort of split up. Everyone had their own ideas on how to find the crypt, and the forest was thick. I'm sure the others found it eventually, but we were just lucky we got to the entrance first.'

'Second,' Mills growled, still massaging his neck as he glared at me. 'Some of us got to cheat.'

'Let's sit down,' Luke said before I could respond, and I let him lead me to the sofa. I bit my cheeks and tried slow, shallow breathing. Not worth it. Not. Worth. It.

Over the next five minutes, six more people joined us in the safe room. Mills and Decke stuck to the kitchen and me, Luke, Jupiter and Cass stayed in the living room, keeping our distance.

The first to arrive were Glaed and his partner, Maeva. I was glad to see both of them, but Cass ran at Glaed with a flying hug that nearly knocked him over. We asked him what happened to the Pyres we escaped from, the ones we left right outside the door and didn't have the chance to ask Mills about, but Glaed said they were gone when he and Maeva got there. Once again, I wondered whether Bloodwatch had interfered. What else would shift them in that narrow tunnel? There was no way any other teams would have got through them.

Cass also checked Glaed and Maeva for bites, as she'd already checked Mills's and Decke's team. We couldn't be too careful, after all.

Next to arrive were Noon and Esmond. They had worked out the anagrams like we did – well, Esmond did – messed up the STRAIGHT AHEAD puzzle and turned right instead of continuing on. They ended up at a dead end and had to retrace their steps back through another brood cavern, which is why it took them so long.

At ten seconds to go, we were all at the top of the stairs, waiting. And then just as it looked like we were it, another team fell through the door, slamming it shut behind them. A panicked flurry of pink hair and a long dark ponytail.

Cinta and Reeta.

Cass quickly checked them for bites.

The last few seconds ticked over on the stopwatch, and then the hands stopped moving. Time's up.

'Did we just lose two teams?' Jupiter said, counting the heads in the room.

'Yeah. Rhegar and Edric, and Aldred and Grayson,' Luke said, his voice heavy.

I hadn't spoken much to Rhegar, but he had been brave enough to help us with the door on the tower. As brave as Edric had been, at least. He'd wanted to be an actor. Now he was Pyre food. Aldred and Grayson were so powerful, especially with Aldred's knife arm and Grayson's give-no-shits attitude.

The TV near the sofa clicked on and a crystal-clear image of Cresta filled the screen. We all automatically drifted over to the sofa quietly and took our seats while Cresta fiddled with her earpiece.

Eventually she smiled at the camera. 'Hello, wonderful viewers! Welcome back to another episode of *Escape from Blood Island*,' she said. 'And hello to our wonderful contestants, who are live and watching alongside us!'

The image switched to a view of the sofa where we sat. It was like looking into an uncanny mirror.

'Do my knees really look that knobbly?' Cinta said, crossing and uncrossing her legs. Reeta nudged her so hard Cinta glared at her, but she stopped fidgeting.

The screen switched back to Cresta. 'First of all, let's recap the sad moment that we lost Aldred and Grayson. Viewers, you saw this earlier in the episode, but let's get the reaction from our contestants.'

The image moved to a view inside a dead end of a tunnel in the crypt. Two head torches bounced into view – Aldred, with his knife hand at the ready, and Grayson, who was holding a thick wooden stick.

Grayson touched the dead-end wall and shook his head at Aldred. Then they both turned to face back the way they came, legs apart and slightly bent, bracing themselves.

The Pyres ran at them so fast, they knocked Grayson clean over and into the wall. There were so many, too many to count, the screen filled with the pale shine of their naked bodies.

The Pyre that rammed into Grayson ripped his chest open through his layers of clothing with one smooth action. The superstrength of a Pyre could never be reckoned with, and he went down without a chance. Grayson didn't even have time to scream. Jupiter leaned over the back of the sofa and vomited on to the floor.

Aldred lasted a few more seconds. Several Pyres leaped at his wrist only to taste metal. He used their confusion to his advantage, slicing forward and catching one through the eye, killing it instantly. But there were too many. They swarmed Aldred, ripping at his clothes until they got to his skin, and then sinking their teeth in deep, the camera zooming in on the Pyre's gullets as they greedily drank. The last image was of Aldred's face, his skin tight over his skull as the blood drained from him like a deflated balloon.

No one spoke. We knew they were filming us, wanting a reaction, but we wanted it to be over. After a few seconds, Cresta reappeared on-screen.

'Goodbye, Aldred and Grayson. But, boy, didn't they go out with a bang, huh?' Cresta laughed like she'd said something funny. 'And we didn't miss the moment that sent them hurtling the wrong way, which I can now reveal is currently the most shared clip of the contest online with over one-point-five million views. Let's watch, shall we?'

The image changed again to a different part of the crypt, showed Cinta and Reeta heading down a tunnel after working out the right way to go. But then Cinta doubled back, staring at the engraved name on the wall.

She bent down, grabbed a handful of mud from the floor and pressed it into the stone, then she followed Reeta. The camera zoomed in on the false name, now completely blended into the filthy walls.

The footage sped up, and a minute or two later Aldred and Grayson appeared, searching the walls frantically with their fingers for the clue. After precious seconds ticked by, Grayson shook his head and pointed over Aldred's shoulder. Whatever they both saw made them run, down the opposite path to Cinta and Reeta, followed closely by a huge brood of Pyres.

'I can't tell who's more bloodthirsty, these contestants or the Pyres!' Cresta's voice tinkled over the shot and eventually gave way to her big stupid face. 'But we sure know that Cinta wants that ticket. Our teams are working hard for your votes, folks. Don't let them down.'

'You're a bloody cheater,' Glaed said, his voice almost too quiet to register.

Cinta unfolded her arms to raise one perfectly manicured middle finger at Glaed. She didn't even flinch. She really was a psychopath.

'She's a survivor, you mean,' Mills said. 'Good on you, I say, girl. Not your fault they were too slow. If they'd been ahead, they would have done the same to you.'

'No. They wouldn't. And that's Glaed's point,' I growled. Cass put a hand on my arm. The cameras were still waiting for our reactions. I wasn't about to give them any more, not tonight.

'As for Rhegar and Edric, they failed to find the safe room within the time limit and headed back to the surface,'

Cresta droned on, drawing my attention back to the screen. 'As the last team to reach the entrance, they were left without head torches and decided they didn't want to go any further. Let's show our contestants what happens to quitters on this show, hmmm?'

The image changed to two people hanging by their wrists from two different pieces of rope. Rhegar was on the left, stoic, with a black eye and his lips pressed into a thin line. Did he try to fight his way out and Bloodwatch dragged him back? Edric was scrambling, swinging from his rope with his eyes focused on something underneath him, off-screen.

The camera zoomed out. Below Rhegar and Edric was a pit of dozens of Pyres. The Pyres were all stood up, some on tiptoe, some on top of others, all reaching for the dinner about to be delivered. The mass of writhing bodies reminded me of the time Dad took me fishing and opened the lid on the bucket of maggots, ready to spear one on the hook of his rod.

The ropes that were holding up Rhegar and Edric jolted, then unravelled from the metal pole that Bloodwatch had suspended above the pit. They fell into the mass and disappeared out of sight.

'And that's *not* how you Escape from Blood Island,' Cresta said, her voiceover like nails down a blackboard in my ears.

CHAPTER FIFTEEN

I wanted to get up, smash the TV and everything else in this stupid place. But what would be the point? I was trapped in here until Bloodwatch let me leave or killed me. It was now crystal clear: the only way to make it out of this hellscape alive was to be the last team left standing. The monster growled deep inside me as rage burned my skin at the thought of Bloodwatch's editors combing over the footage of their deaths, zooming in on the blood splatters and enhancing them like they were actors in a show. Like we were just pretending, and not rats in a maze that they created for entertainment.

And most of all, that thought made me feel useless.

So instead of fighting, and screaming, and burning the world down, I sat on the sofa, numb, as Cresta kept talking.

'And now that's finished, we should get down to the important business of our winners, and the winners of our viewers' vote for this challenge,' Cresta said.

Her voice sounded far away, and I couldn't get my eyes to focus on the screen. Everyone else seemed frozen too. There was something about the way Rhegar and Edric died that had us all stuck in place, watching this ridiculous TV show.

'So our winners are tied. Both Astrid and Luke, and Jupiter and Cass, made it across the threshold of the safe room at the same time. However, if we check the footage in slow motion, we can see which team was technically first through the door.'

I tuned it all out. Did it matter who won? Did anyone win in this game?

'And as you can see, Cass and Jupiter retain their lead with Luke and Astrid mere nanoseconds behind,' Cresta said, filling the screen again.

I looked at Luke and he simply shrugged, as done with it all as I was. Cass and Jupiter didn't exactly celebrate either.

'And now on to the winners of the public vote.' Cresta smiled and held a finger to her earpiece, waiting for the results. 'And the winners, with their grand performance with a rock and a room full of Pyres, are Mills and Herrod. Airtime is airtime, and wow, did you put on a blood-soaked show for us. Congratulations, boys – tomorrow you, together with Cass and Jupiter, will receive a prize that will help you in the next challenge.'

'Victory tastes sweet,' Mills muttered under his breath. He looked at me with that grin again and I held his stare until he looked away.

'That's all we have time for on this episode, folks. See you all back here, same time and place, tomorrow!'

Same time and place. Did she mean the middle of the day? It was morning when we set off. Didn't these mainlanders watching at home have anything better to do?

After the TV snapped off, no one wanted to talk much. We grabbed some food, but most of us were drained. I knew it couldn't be much later than mid-afternoon but all I wanted to do was crawl into bed. I felt heavy, like the air in the safe room was pressing down on me. I made my excuses to Cass and Jupiter and stood up to look for Luke, but I couldn't spot him. Maybe he had already turned in himself.

Then I remembered the double bed.

What was the scariest thing in the world earlier hardly registered now, though. Not after watching that. I dragged my feet down the corridor to our room and knocked to see if Luke was already in there. No wrist fob meant no way of unlocking it.

The door swung open on the first knock, so I poked my head round it. Unlocked. Luke was already in there, moving extra pillows and blankets from the wardrobe on to the hard metal floor.

'What are you doing?' I asked.

'I'm making up my bed. You can have the mattress. I don't expect you've had as many nights as me in a warm bed over the last eight years. Seems only fair.'

'I can't ask you to sleep on the floor,' I said, crossing the room to sit on the bed. What was the game here? Luke said viewers liked to see potential couples together. The only reason I could think of for him sleeping on the floor was to genuinely make sure I was comfortable. And every fibre of my being was working against trusting this man, this mainlander, so I knew that wasn't it.

'You're not asking. I'm offering,' Luke said, putting down the pillow he was holding. 'Look, see? Nice and comfy,' he said, pointing to the flat blanket. It certainly didn't look comfy.

'This is unreal. The bed is huge,' I said, flopping back and holding my arms out as an example. 'We can put down a pillow wall if you want.'

Luke laughed. 'If it makes you more comfortable. Are you sure? I promise not to try and seduce you in the night,' he said, grinning.

I laughed. 'Yeah, I'll try to control myself,' I said, but my cheeks were warming up.

The pillow wall was a good idea for keeping my head straight. I helped Luke move the pillows from the floor to the middle of the bed, and then he excused himself.

'I'm going to go brush my teeth. There are some bathrooms down the hall that you don't need to unlock. No cameras in there either, according to the signs they put up, but I wouldn't trust that. I'll leave you to get changed,' he said. Luke disappeared out of the room.

Luke had a point about the cameras. I ducked under the duvet and got changed, pulling the pyjamas they allocated to us with difficulty over my head. As always, my name and number were printed on the back. Last minute, before I resurfaced to go to the loo, I turned the shirt inside out and slipped it back over my head. It was a small act of defiance but it gave me a boost. The numbers and the vote could piss off. I didn't want any votes from people who would give someone like Mills an extra advantage.

After I'd nipped to the loo and got back to the room, Luke was already in the bed, on the left-hand side, fiddling with his kit bag. He looked up when I came in, his tousled hair almost more attractive than usual. 'Ah, sorry, I assumed sides of the bed. Are you OK on the right?'

'Perfectly,' I squeaked, crossing the room as fast as I could and climbing in the other side.

'You OK for me to turn the light off?' Luke asked, like getting into bed together was something we did every night. Like we hadn't just watched several people get murdered on television. Like I didn't want to scream and shout and smash up everything in the room.

'Sure,' I said.

We were plunged into darkness. I bet the cameras had a view of the whole bed. My stomach rolled at the thought of what might be being broadcast in the other rooms.

'You wanna talk about it?' Luke said, breaking through my thoughts.

'What?' I asked. Clearly he couldn't fall straight to sleep either.

'Anything. All of it. Why Mills of all people won the public vote, maybe,' Luke said.

I blinked. Did he care, or was he just trying to keep me calm before the next challenge? Either way, it *was* nice to be asked, real or not. 'I don't get it. We won the first challenge vote, and we bloody well should have. We were basic human beings and helped out, and we got a reward. Mills threw a rock at a pile of Pyres and tried to murder us, and he got a reward. These viewers are nuts. I don't know what they want.'

'I know. I've lived on the mainland for a long time, but even I struggle to understand the people who watch Bloodwatch so avidly. And Rhegar with that black eye? That wasn't a Pyre injury. He was dragged into that pit kicking and screaming, and I'll give you three guesses who did the dragging,' Luke said, his voice louder with every word. He took a deep breath and his voice softened again. 'Not that I can talk. I've seen enough on TV myself.'

'Is that why you applied? Because you're a fan?' I asked, turning to face him. I could just about make out the outline of his face in the darkness.

Luke shifted on the bed before replying. 'No. I wanted to prove that the people on Bloodwatch aren't celebrities, you know? That this is your real life. Does that make sense?' Luke turned over to face me now. Even in the dark I could tell our faces were close. I could smell toothpaste on his breath. He was very good at playing the *friend* game.

'I think so,' I replied.

Luke sighed. 'It doesn't, I know. I think I . . . felt trapped in my life. I wanted to do something that's meaningful. I feel like there is more we could do to help you guys. This can't be all that comes from the fall, a TV show and a hundred thousand credits,' Luke said.

'I guess it's all I've ever known,' I countered. 'It's hard to imagine there could be anything else. I was ten when the Pyres attacked.'

'You don't have to answer,' Luke said. 'But where were you that night, the night of the fall? Do you remember?'

I swallowed the lump that had formed in my throat. How could I forget? It was the sort of thing that gets burned into your brain forever.

'So we lived in the Fon, the city right in the middle of the island. God knows how bad it is now – I haven't met a traveller from there in years. But we had a semi-detached house in the suburbs. We went to my school. It was the closest refugee centre they opened up, after the first Pyre attacks had been reported. I don't know if you remember but they sent the army over from the mainland and started firebombing the larger towns and cities, so they evacuated civilians to refugee centres.'

'I remember,' Luke whispered.

'Well, we were told that we would be evacuated to the mainland, so we didn't have any stuff with us. And it was dark, so obviously everyone was . . . on edge,' I said. On edge was an understatement, but obviously Dad had tried to keep calm in front of me and Wynn. She was only six at the time. 'It was just the three of us. Dad and his partner Ben used a surrogate for both me and Wynn, but Ben died in a car accident when I was five and Wynn was only a baby, so I don't remember him much. Anyway, the army was there and they were registering everyone, telling them what time their evacuation was the next day, that kind of thing. Then the army told us to stay away from the windows and they were going to turn the lights out so we could get some sleep. We had makeshift bunks, so it was sort of like a massive sleepover. That sounds stupid now.'

'It doesn't sound stupid,' Luke said. 'We didn't get to see any of this. Bloodwatch didn't install the cameras until the government had completely given up on retrieving the island. And that was years after the fall. We never saw what happened, and that's why it's important to talk about it. Let them hear it.'

And I knew who he meant by 'them'. The cameras, the viewers at home. His words gave me a strength I'd never felt before, something that sank into my skin, my bones, making me stronger. *Hope.*

'I woke up in the middle of the night and it was so quiet,' I said. I turned on to my back and stared at the ceiling, having a flashback to the day I'd had nightmares about. 'I sat up and the first thing I noticed was that the soldiers were gone. Three nights we slept in that school hall, and every night the army guarded the doors. But they were gone. And even at ten, I knew something was wrong.'

Luke shifted and I thought he was going to say something, but he didn't. Warm fingers looped their way through my own. He squeezed my hand. This didn't feel like a game any more. It felt real. And I squeezed back.

'I woke up Dad,' I said, my voice steady. 'He then woke up some of our neighbours, who woke up their families, and soon we were all panicking. The talking got louder and louder, and then someone turned on a torch. That was when I saw the first Pyre at the window. I'd never seen one that close before. It was a woman, dressed in jeans and a T-shirt. She still had all her hair, because it was like that in the early days. But her teeth. I remember thinking that her teeth looked like knives sticking out of her mouth.'

I shuddered at the thought and Luke squeezed my hand harder.

'It was chaos when the Pyres got in. The army hadn't even bothered to lock the doors when they left,' I whispered. 'There was no evacuation plan. They sacked that off as soon as they knew it was hopeless to try and fight the Pyres. They had to contain us here, so they left us to die. All I remember after that is running. Dad carried

Wynn and grabbed my hand. He told me to keep my eyes closed and I did. He dragged me when I fell, but I never opened my eyes, not until we got home. But I couldn't block out the screams. The screams I'll never forget.'

Luke leaned across the pillow divide, bringing his mouth to my ear.

'Do you trust me?' he whispered, his breath a tickle on my earlobe.

'Yes,' I replied, my body responding before my brain had time to react.

He pushed down the pillow wall and moved close enough that our hips were touching and our noses brushed together, and then brought the duvet up over our heads.

Under the duvet, he moved even closer, his lips almost brushing my cheek as he spoke. Goosebumps sprang up across my skin and my nerve-endings were on fire. Was this going to be my first kiss, several years too late? Was it stupid to even be thinking about kissing someone at a time like this? Probably, but that didn't stop me leaning in, like a magnet to metal.

'Listen. We have to stay quiet so they don't hear us,' Luke said, his voice barely a breath above a whisper. He wasn't trying to kiss me. He was trying to tell me something. My pulse slowed.

'What do you need to say under here that you couldn't say out there?' I asked. We were lying so closely, our bodies intertwined, that I wasn't even looking at him any more. My mouth was on his ear, and his was on mine. I wondered what this looked like from above, but that was Luke's point. He wanted me to trust him because he knew what this would look like to the cameras: that we were doing more than just talking. The perfect cover.

'I think I can trust you too,' Luke said. He was careful not to rest his weight on me as his head was above mine, and I was glad I brushed my teeth as well as I did. His minty breath was almost heady in the close quarters of the duvet. So, he was playing a game, but this one wasn't for the cameras. And he was letting me in on it.

'I think so too,' I said, not sure where this was going.

'And you feel safe with me?' Luke asked.

All I could think about was his pressure on my hips, his fingers still woven in mine. He gave them a quick squeeze.

'Yes,' I murmured in his ear. Did he tense up for a second when I spoke, or did I imagine it?

'Good,' Luke said. 'Because I'm not here to win this stupid show. I'm not here as some ridiculous exotic tourist either, and I think you know that. Bloodwatch has ruined my life. I can't prove that to you, but trust me, their poison has leaked on to the mainland and I hate them too. I'm here to bring Bloodwatch down, for good. And I think you can help me do it.'

CHAPTER SIXTEEN

I woke up and found Luke's arm round my waist. All part of his master plan, and somehow I had agreed to it.

As I lay in the darkness trying not to move – I'd never slept in the same bed as anyone before – I went over what Luke had said last night and tried to work out whether it was a dream or not.

No, the cuddly sleep position definitely suggested it was real.

Luke was convinced that the fluffy duvet would be enough to block the microphones that Bloodwatch must have stashed around the room. He also wasn't stupid about what the viewing public wanted to see.

'So why do you hate Bloodwatch so much?' I had asked him.

'Honestly? If I told you, you wouldn't believe me. Is it so hard to believe that they might have pissed off some mainlanders too, though?'

I'd thought for a second. Luke hadn't pressured me to talk about my family stuff, so I wasn't about to pressure him to talk about his. He didn't owe me his life story just because I told him mine. Plus, just talking about bringing down Bloodwatch put a target on his back. Maybe at some point he'd tell me, but I believed he hated them – why else say all this, away from the cameras?

'If we pretend that we're a thing,' Luke had said, 'we'll get more votes, and votes mean we stay in longer, because we'll win more challenge head starts.'

'That's a bit more than the friend game, then,' I had muttered.

'The friend game?'

'Cards on the table: when you said you wanted to be friends, I thought that was your strategy for winning votes and getting the cash prize. I thought of it as the friend game. You know, pretending to like each other. And it was working, so I went along with it as I have to win. I need to get home to Hild and the Burgh.'

'I wasn't pretending to be your friend. At least, I hoped we would be friends at some point.'

'But you want to *pretend* to be more than friends, right?'

Luke's breath had caught in his throat. I wished I could see more of his face under the cover, to read him, but it was no use. He was the one to use 'pretend' first, not me, and I couldn't help that it stung a little bit, even if it was something keeping us in the contest.

'Right,' he had sighed eventually. 'As long as you're OK with it. It's like the friend game, but levelled up. It's what we need to do to get to the finale.'

'Yeah, but if what you told me is true, you don't want to win, right? So why bother with the pretence?' I had said, pulling back a little.

Luke had squeezed my hand. 'I don't want to win. But remember, Bloodwatch has a lot to lose here. Viewing figures have been way down. But there's no way the mainland aren't watching *this*. Live executions did pretty well with the public a few hundred years ago.' He had paused and then faced me, barely visible in the gloom under the duvet. 'The show will be picking up viewers every episode. The biggest viewership will be for the finale, when they announce the winner. We need to be on-screen for that. That's when we bring them down.'

'How?' I had asked, my heart pounding. The monster had stirred at the thought of bringing down the people who were profiting from my misery.

'I have a plan to reconnect with the viewers,' Luke had said. 'If we can get to the end, and connect emotionally with the mainlanders, maybe it will spark an interest in rescuing the island again. Not everyone over there is a monster. No one cares what we have to say now, but if we win, it's because we've won their hearts and we'll have celebrity status – they'll pay to listen to us then. And besides, if we lose . . . we won't have a voice at all. You saw what happened to Rhegar and Edric when they tried to bail.' He had squeezed my hand again.

And so here I was, wide awake with a stranger's arm round my waist, hoping that the night-vision cameras were picking up a happy facial expression. It made sense now how Luke always knew the right thing to say – he had a plan and he was focusing his energy into making it work. He had told me that plan in confidence. Did that mean he liked me at all, for real? He must at the very least trust me.

An alarm sounded, a bit like the old digital sound that

Dad's alarm clock used to make before the fall. It woke Luke up and automatically turned on the lights.

'All contestants to gather in the living room immediately.' A tinny computerised voice came over the speaker.

Luke moved his arm from round my waist. 'I'll close my eyes while you get dressed. Let me know when you're done.'

'Nice try – I'm getting dressed under the duvet. It has special camera blocking abilities,' I said, sitting up and trying not to smirk at him.

Luke grinned. 'Oh, really? Well, you do you. I'll close my eyes anyway, just in case.'

We were last to the living room. Cinta threw me a trademark scowl as we entered. Did she know what we'd talked about? No, there was no way, and besides, her opinion was the last thing I cared about. Cinta was always analysing people; she was as bad as the Bloodwatch Network. If I was going to make this work, I had to pull myself together.

The monster in my chest growled, but I pushed it firmly back in its box.

A few seconds after Luke and I entered the living room, a heavy thud sounded, and the wall where the TV was mounted began to slowly open, like an electric garage door. Daylight spilled in from outside, temporarily blinding me, and I raised my hands to negate the effect. The sun was higher than it was when we entered the crypt, so it must have been the next day.

Outside stood dozens of camera crew, the ubiquitous guards with guns, and Cresta. Today she was wearing a pink sequinned jumpsuit and stilettos.

I hated her. I hated everything about this so-called 'show'. And most of all I hated Bloodwatch.

The monster inside growled again.

'Good morning, contestants.' Cresta beamed. 'I hope you slept and ate well because we're about to begin the next challenge. Are you excited?'

Cresta paused like we were supposed to cheer or something, but was instead met with stony silence. Either her autocue was trolling her or she had severely misread her audience.

She let out an awkward laugh and continued. 'Quite, yes. I can see you're all in the zone. Well, good. Let me explain the next challenge and I can get out of your hair. Mills and Herrod, Cass and Jupiter, can you step up here, please?'

Mills shoved my shoulder as he went past, and Luke's nostrils flared, but I shook my head at him. He wasn't worth it.

Cass and Jupiter stood to Cresta's left, and Mills and Herrod stood to the right. As before, Cresta brought out two golden boxes and handed one to each team. This time the boxes were different sizes, and were handed specifically to Mills and Cass. Mills's box was long and thin, and Cass's was a big cube.

'And open them! I think you'll be quite pleased with these,' Cresta cooed.

Mills pulled the lid off to reveal a machete. It wasn't a

new weapon either: this one was pockmarked with rust and blood, and the handle was worn with use. Cass opened her box to reveal a crossbow, like the ones we used at the Burgh. Cass brought the bow up to her eye, testing the sights, like she'd held it before.

And that's when it hit me. She had held it before, they both had. When I had signed in for my first night at the Bloodwatch compound, they took my bolt gun.

These were our weapons.

'So your next challenge is one of endurance. Each team will be dropped off in a small abandoned town not far from here. You will have the full day to find shelter and make it safe for surviving the night. Scattered around the town, islanders, are also your trusted weapons. Cass and Mills have won theirs automatically. Once night falls, an alarm will sound to draw in any Pyre broods in the area. You will have to work with your teammate to stay safe within your base until morning,' Cresta said.

'Do we only stick with our teammate, or can we team up?' Glaed called out, his eyes on Cass.

'The only rules are that you must stay with your teammate, and you must not leave the town. The boundary is marked with a red painted line. You cross that line and you're out.'

She said 'out' like we were playing capture the flag. We knew what *out* meant after watching the TV last night.

'No more questions? Great. Anyone still alive when we arrive back at town in the morning will advance to the next challenge! Now, everyone, into the trucks.'

Cresta stepped back and a convoy of trucks rolled on to

the grass in front of us. There were seven of them, one for each team left.

Luke jumped up into a truck and gave me his hand to help me up, which I accepted, his touch sending tingles up the back of my hand. Once we were seated, the door slammed shut and we took off.

'Where do you think we're going?' Luke asked.

I shrugged. 'Abandoned town could be anywhere this side of the old quarantine fence.' I pulled my bag out from under the seat in front so I could get to my water bottle. I unscrewed the lid as the car went over a pothole and it went spinning out of my grasp.

Luke's hand shot out and caught it, mid-air, before a single drop had spilled.

'Bloody hell,' I said, blinking at the bottle. 'That was superhuman.'

'Not really,' Luke said, pushing the bottle into my outstretched palm. Was it just me, or were his cheeks burning red? 'It's an old road, unkept. It's going to be bumpy, right? My hand was ready in case you dropped it, so, you know, mission complete.'

'OK,' I said slowly, taking a swig of the water and resealing the cap. Luke stared out of the window. He was clearly still hiding things, but I also had something on him now, something not for the cameras.

But I wasn't going to get it out of him by force. Trust was a two-way street, and as much as I hated giving up some element of control, there were real feelings there too. I gave him time before and he told me what was up. Maybe he would again.

'I'm pretty sure we're heading to North Point. It was a seaside resort,' I said, trying to bring the conversation back round. 'The broadcast tower is in the middle of the island and behind us, and the woods are thicker on our left, so we're heading north. My best guess.'

It worked. Luke looked away from the window, his expression back to normal. 'Smart. What's your weapon, so we can keep an eye out for it?'

'It's a bolt gun.' Luke raised an eyebrow. 'It looks a lot like a handgun but it fires a hydraulic bolt instead of bullets. It was used on my grandma's farm to slaughter animals. My dad gave it to me,' I said, trailing off. It was ridiculous, but it was only just hitting me how much I missed that gun, that last piece of my dad.

Luke reached across and laced his fingers through mine. 'I'll find it for you,' he said, and even though it wasn't up to him, I believed him.

We arrived at the site of the next challenge about ten minutes later. As soon as our boots hit the ground, the cars sped off, leaving us to it.

A few seconds of silence followed, only marred by the squawks of the seagulls circling the cliffs. We had been dropped into the town square of a small, totally abandoned town, with a row of buildings on three sides. I recognised it as North Point but I wished I remembered it better. Behind us, painted on to the road about a metre or two back, was a red line disappearing into the foliage of the woods that grew either side. It looked like they wanted us to stay in the square, which made sense. More Pyres in one place, more chances to get a great shot for the show.

I was starting to think like a black shirt all right.

'Come on, old man,' Mills bellowed, grabbing Herrod by the arm. They half jogged towards the nearest ice-cream shop, and the rest of us watched.

The challenge had begun, I guess.

'Hey, Executioner,' Noon called, and jogged over to us. 'Wanna team up this time? At least until we find our weapons. Esmond here is a little antsy. Can't imagine why.'

Esmond's brow was already slick with sweat. I looked over to Cass, who was already walking round the square with Jupiter, and Glaed and his partner Maeva. Cass had her weapon, so I didn't want to hold her back looking for both mine and Glaed's. Besides, if we huddled together and the Pyres went for our building, we'd all be done for. We'd be much better splitting the noise, and the brood, to cut them down when they inevitably came.

'What do you want to do?' Luke asked me.

I nodded. 'Let's do it. Noon's right, we should find our weapons first.'

We walked up to a shop on the left-hand side of the square. It had smashed windows and an old slanted sign hanging above the entrance.

NORTH POINT GIFTS AND SOUVENIRS.

'We should check in here first,' I said, pointing at the shop. 'Everyone else has gone straight for the food mart, but I imagine this is a pretty good staging area for Bloodwatch to hide weapons, given all the junk that will be in here.'

'Well, well, well. More than a nickname now, aren't you, Executioner,' Noon said, grinning. 'Let's do it.'

'Wait,' Esmond said, still sweating. 'There might be Pyres hiding in there. Maybe Luke and I should wait out here until we know the coast is clear.'

Esmond looked hopefully at Luke, who shook his head. 'You heard Cresta. We have to stay with our teammate. Come on, Esmond, I'll look after you.'

Esmond's mouth flapped like a fish gasping for water, but he couldn't find the words to argue. I stepped forward and pushed the door.

The top of the door caught on an old bell, signalling to the long-dead cashier that a customer had arrived. We braced ourselves, Luke, Noon and I taking a bent-knee stance, ready to run, and Esmond ducking behind us, covering his ears. But nothing came.

'Well, it's our lucky day,' Noon said, stepping past me and picking up a shell necklace hanging from a shelf. 'I do love a five-fingered discount.'

I rolled my eyes and walked in behind him, Luke bringing up the rear and practically pushing Esmond through the door. The shop had been thoroughly looted. There was no electricity, and the windows were tiny, the shadows ominous.

We needed to do this quickly, in and out.

'All right, let's assign jobs,' I said, my eye on a particularly dark corner near the counter. 'Noon and I will check the back of the shop and look for our weapons. Luke, you and Esmond search the front. If you find any weapons, call out. They might be ours, but if they're someone else's we should take them into the square and give them back. And hope that they return the favour.'

Noon sighed, but he didn't fight me on it. Luke nodded and Esmond, as usual, sweated.

I smiled at Luke and he smiled back, my stomach flipping in response, then he put an arm round Esmond's shoulders and led him towards the front of the shop.

'After you, Executioner,' Noon said, gesturing to the counter in the darkest part of the room. 'I'll be hiding behind you if anything comes at us. Don't want poor Esmond to lose his shit if I get bitten; you know how it is.'

'Are you ever serious?' I muttered.

I stepped towards the counter, and something moved in the darkness.

CHAPTER SEVENTEEN

I looked around for the nearest thing the shop had to a weapon and grabbed a sad-looking stuffed bear dressed in a raincoat. Noon didn't fare much better; he found a decorative ashtray painted to look like the beach. We raised our 'weapons'.

A cat jumped down from above. An actual tabby-striped domestic cat. It still had its collar on, and the little bell tinkled as it ran past us and darted out the door.

'Everything OK back there?' Luke called.

'Everything's *purrfect* over here,' Noon called back, laughing.

'OK, if you're sure,' Luke replied.

'Shit a brick,' I breathed, lowering the bear.

Noon laughed some more. 'And what were you hoping to kill with that, Executioner? Maybe the vibe of the super-scary apocalypse Bloodwatch are going for?'

I threw the bear at him. 'Like you did much better. An ashtray? What were you going to do, smoke the Pyre to death?'

'At least I'd have a good shot at braining the bastard if it came at me,' Noon said, setting the ashtray back down.

I scowled at him. 'I haven't seen an animal that wasn't,

like, cattle or pigs or birds for the longest time. How has that thing survived so long out here?'

Noon shrugged. 'I've been on the road for a while and seen a few dogs and cats here and there. I once saw this whole brood of Pyres, all curled up in this house in the daytime, right? And there was a dog in there too. Like, an actual pet dog. He even had a little water bowl and some kibble by the door. I swear down.'

I shook my head. 'Must be weird timing. Maybe the brood had just eaten the people that lived there, and they had a dog or something. I'm sure the second they woke up, they drank that poor pooch like an alcoholic sinking a bottle of wine.'

'Maybe. But I'd been staking out that house, looking for supplies. The Pyres were there for at least a few days, and that doggo was well looked after.' Noon shrugged.

'That doesn't make any sense.' I frowned, looking back where the cat had run out. It had a collar on, even after eight years of being homeless on the most dangerous part of the island. I thought all animals, anything outside a compound wall that couldn't fly, were dead.

'Just telling you what I've seen,' Noon said. 'These Pyres aren't as dumb as we think they are. Some of them are kinda smart. Human, almost.'

'Let's not even go there,' I said, swallowing down the anger that rose in my throat, my mind shifting briefly to Dad and Wynn. 'Come on. Let's find our weapons.'

Noon and I hopped over the dusty service counter and started searching. I found nothing but a few rolls of receipt paper and some leaves that had blown in over time, but Noon found a cricket bat in the back.

'Is it yours?' I asked when he brought it out. He turned it round in his hands, admiring the handiwork. It had been modified, with several rusty nails sticking out of it, and bloodstains all around the base.

'No, but I wish it was.' Noon whistled with appreciation and laid it down on the counter. 'Nothing else back there. We should take this bad boy out to the square and see who it belongs to.'

'I'm surprised you're up for that, you know,' I said. Noon pretended to be offended by clutching his chest with his hand. I rolled my eyes. 'You know what I mean. I assumed you'd just take it for yourself.'

'Despite these devilishly handsome good looks, Executioner, I'm not stupid,' he said. 'My Bloodwatch fans know which weapon I use, and they'll expect me to hand this one in. I don't think Cinta did herself any favours when she tried to hide that envelope from you. What Mills did, that was different. He wasn't trying to hide anything or cheat. Even though there aren't rules, somehow the viewers have made some up. I need all the votes me and the human encyclopaedia out there can get.'

Noon pointed to the front of the shop, where Luke and Esmond stood. Esmond was in deep conversation with Luke, gesticulating a lot and getting pretty animated. Luke was nodding along, but he was scanning the shelves, not paying attention.

'Does he talk a lot, then?' I asked, watching them.

'If I tell you I'm amazed we haven't been caught from

his talking alone, Executioner, you'd believe me,' Noon said. 'But he is bloody smart. Like, next level. I told him a few of my stories and he was the one that started piecing it together about the Pyres maybe having a bit more going on up there than bloodlust.' Noon tapped the side of his head. 'You gotta remember that the viewers don't see that deep-level brood shit much. No one is stupid enough to put cameras in there for Bloodwatch, and Esmond has a theory that the smart Pyres tear down any lenses they find. I dunno, but as far as conspiracy theories go, it's a good one.'

I didn't say anything. That was a lot of information, and we had a whole sleepless night ahead to talk to Esmond about it. Plus, there was one thought bouncing around my head, a memory of the question Nova asked me during my disastrous interview:

Why didn't you put down your sister and dad when they turned, and does it not bother you that they're still out there living a half-life as Pyres?

If some Pyres *could* still think, and feel, and might be partly human, what did that mean? I couldn't even begin to entertain the thought when we had so much to do before nightfall. I pushed it to the back of my mind.

We met up with Luke and Esmond and explained that Noon had found a weapon, so we wandered back to the square. Esmond practically ran out the door, relief painted over his face as we headed back into the relatively safe sunshine.

Turned out a few other people had the same idea about the weapons. The fountain in the square was dry, so all the weapons had been placed into the shallow bowl that used to be filled with water. Looked like we were playing nice today – maybe the public executions had the same effect on everyone else. Or maybe the fact that Mills already had his weapon meant he hadn't wasted time looking for, and trying to hide, ours. I was surprised that Cinta hadn't hidden any of them either, but maybe she'd somehow learned her lesson with my envelope.

Whatever the reason, all the weapons were here. And in between a fire axe and a serrated hunting knife was my bolt gun. I picked it up and ran my finger over the barrel, the weight familiar and safe in my hands.

'Now, that's what I'm talking about,' Noon said beside me, reaching into the fountain and pulling out the fire axe. 'Hello, Noony Jr.'

'Your axe has a name?' Luke asked, eyebrow raised.

'And you named it after yourself?' I asked, both eyebrows raised.

Noon grinned and slung Noony Jr over his shoulder. 'Is there any greater connection between one man and his Pyre killer, Executioner? The name maketh the weapon, after all, right?'

'Really wish you would stop calling me that,' I muttered, holstering my gun.

'I'll stop saying it when you stop earning it,' Noon said, still grinning.

Next, we had to choose a building as our safe house for the evening. There were maybe twenty different structures all around the square, all terraced to each other except on the side with the sea view, all in various states of disrepair. Most of the others had disappeared inside, except for

Decke, who stood outside a building with boarded-up windows.

'Look,' I said, pointing to him.

'Decke? Why is he going for that crappy place? There are plenty of options left,' Luke replied.

'And where's that dumbass brother of his?' Noon asked, scanning the square.

'Maybe he teamed up with Cass. Or maybe he's scoping out a different building because he has his weapon already. Either way, that's a good pick for a building, Decke's smart. We should see if we can share for the night,' I said.

'Why? That thing was deserted even before the fall,' Noon said.

'Because it's already boarded up. Less work to do.' All three of us spun round as Esmond entered the conversation. He shrugged at us. 'It's Survival 101. If the windows and doors are already boarded up, that's less attention and fewer Pyres trying to get in. Less fighting means more sleep – in watches – which is beneficial to both tired bodies and tired minds. Miss Astrid is correct. Decke is the smarter brother.'

Noon looked at me. 'All right, smartarse.' He raised a hand to his mouth and shouted, 'Hey, Decke! Need a hand clearing that out?'

We crossed the square to Decke without waiting for a reply. His partner Godric was there, kneeling on the ground, his hands together.

'Uh . . . is he praying?' Noon asked, pointing at Godric with Noony Jr.

'Yes, he is,' Godric replied without opening his eyes. 'Also, he can hear you.'

'Yeah, sorry, Godric,' Luke said, glaring at Noon. Noon shrugged.

'Hey, Decke, you looking at clearing this place?' I asked, changing the subject before the boys could embarrass themselves any more.

Decke nodded. 'Yeah. My brother teamed up with that Deaf girl. Said it would be better if we split up, I dunno,' he grunted.

We all blinked. It was the most I had heard Decke speak ever.

'Mills left you? Are you OK?' Luke asked, reaching out to touch Decke's shoulder.

Decke shrugged him off. 'I'm as good as we all are right now. You gonna help me clear this place or not?'

'Sure, man. Whatever you want,' Noon said, palms raised in surrender.

'Why haven't you gone in yet?' I asked, taking the hint from Decke to focus on the task at hand.

'Listen,' Decke said.

We fell silent and leaned into the structure. We heard a muffled wail.

'It's statistically unusual for Pyre species to be awake during the daylight hours. Perhaps it is injured?' Esmond suggested.

'No way to tell. We should kick open the door, make a noise and wait for it to come to us. Then we can knock it out,' I said, pulling my gun from my waist.

'See? The Executioner has style. I like it,' Noon said, adjusting the grip on his axe.

'Her name is Astrid,' Luke said through gritted teeth.

He pulled out his own makeshift weapon, an old metal spike from the postcard rack back at the souvenir shop.

'Less talking, more slaying,' Decke said.

He waited for us to take up a defensive position next to him – all of us except Esmond and Godric, who moved behind us into the safety of the square – and then with one swift kick he busted open the front door.

We waited. That would usually be enough. Pyres were drawn by three things: sound, light and the smell of dinner, and here were all three.

Nothing happened. Even the wailing had stopped.

'Maybe it was the wind making a weird noise?' Luke suggested, his eyes still on the door. 'That can happen in old buildings.'

'There isn't a breath of it today, though,' I replied.

Noon lowered his axe. 'Well, I have to say, I'm more than a little disappointed. Noony Jr was up for some action—'

Noon's complaint was cut off by a piercing shriek. My blood ran cold. A shadow rushed out of the darkness, one with pale skin and clumps of greasy black hair.

None of us were ready for it. A thought flashed across my brain, that the Pyre was watching us, waiting for us to lower our weapons. Like it was toying with us, preparing itself.

Luke reacted the fastest. He raised his metal pole and swung hard at the thing, smashing it to the ground, so fast that I barely had time to register it coming towards me.

The Pyre was dazed, rolling across the cobbles of the square and out of the shade cast by the building. One of its hands fell into a patch of sunlight and it screamed, the skin on the palm blistering red immediately. And then it was back up, crawling into the shade in front of the building, ready to launch itself at us again. It got up on all fours, knees bent, and jumped.

The rest of us were ready this time. Noon swung his axe and it made contact with the Pyre's arm, slicing it clean off at the elbow. It raged, pain and anger painted across its face, and it turned on Noon, but Luke and Decke were ready. They teamed up, Luke with his metal rod, Decke with his dual knives, and they pinned the Pyre to the wall with all three, impaling it through the chest. The monster was strong, though, and it heaved itself forward, pushing past Decke's knives, fangs snapping at Luke's hand, close enough to cover his fingers in specks of blood.

My heart leaped into my mouth, my gun hanging useless at my side.

Decke shouldered Luke out of the way, pushing his knives together until they made a V shape at the Pyre's throat. Luke stumbled backwards as the Pyre's broken yellow teeth strained for Decke, its mouth smeared in fresh red blood. Luke's? My eyes darted to him as he raised his hand, pushing forward again to help Decke, and it was all a blur, blood and weapons and the constant snarling of the Pyre. No one could check for bites until that thing stopped moving. That was when I stepped forward and touched the barrel of my bolt gun to its head and pulled the trigger.

The Pyre went limp, its eyes dead and glassy as it slumped against Decke's knives and Luke's metal pole, the only things holding it up. Its breathing stilled.

I tried to catch my breath. The first thing I saw was Luke, on his knees, covered in blood.

'Luke.' I dropped down to his level and held his face in my hands, looking for where the blood was coming from. 'Did you get bitten? Are you OK?' Everything inside me was on edge with pure terror. I couldn't think straight.

Luke put a hand to my jaw and smiled. 'I'm fine. The metal on the jagged part of the pole nicked me, but I'm fine. See?' He moved his arm from across his chest to reveal a blood-soaked hole in his shirt. I pulled it open further, searching his skin for bite marks, but I only found a small cut. It was rough, but it wasn't deep.

The relief that flooded through my veins made me light-headed. It was a foreign feeling, wanting to laugh and smile seconds after terror had gripped my heart. I let the corners of my mouth tug upwards and Luke smiled back. The line between reality and our game was drowned out by the loud pounding of my heart.

I leaned in, our foreheads touching, breathing him in. He was alive. We were alive. All I wanted to do was sink into him and forget where we were, just for a second.

And then there was a shout and we broke apart, the spell broken by four words no one ever wants to hear.

'My brother's been bitten!'

CHAPTER EIGHTEEN

I didn't see Mills appear, but he must have run out when he heard us fighting in the square. He was kneeling down next to Decke, who was leaning up against a building.

The electric feeling between me and Luke now seemed so trivial. I couldn't even look at him. What was I thinking? I got swept up in the moment and took my eye off the ball, and now someone was paying the price.

'Decke, are you sure? Lift your shirt.' Noon crouched next to him.

Mills glared at me and Luke, so we held back, standing with the rest of the contestants who had since run out from whichever buildings they were fortifying. Decke winced as he lifted up his shirt. There was a perfect bite mark.

'Shame. Decke was kinda hot. I hate it when the hot ones have to go,' Cinta said, slowly walking up behind us and inspecting the wound. Once she got a good look, she dusted her hands together. 'Oh well. One team down, five to go!'

'Not now, Cinta,' I hissed, my eyes on Mills. Either he hadn't heard her or he was too grief-stricken to respond, but Cinta got away with it. She stalked off, hands held over her head in mock-surrender.

'Maybe we can cut it out,' said Maeva, who had arrived

with everyone else. 'It'll hurt like a bitch but we could try. How deep is it?'

'This isn't some bug bite on his arm, kid,' Noon replied, his hand hovering around the bite site. 'It's drawn blood. The infection can sometimes be caught with amputation, but where it is, I don't think we can do anything.'

'Stop talking about him like he ain't here!' Mills bellowed, pushing Noon away with one meaty arm. Noon jumped up, his hands spread in a sign of peace, and came to stand with me, Luke, Esmond and Godric.

'I suppose that means we're out,' Godric said, like he was announcing he had run out of milk, not that he was about to be sacrificed live on television. Decke was the only one who still hadn't said anything.

Mills got up, pointed at Godric and crossed the cobbles to meet him in three long strides. When he got close enough he grabbed Godric's collar and lifted him off his feet, his face close enough that their noses were touching. Luke moved forward to get between them, but I grabbed his arm. Mills needed to let off some steam.

'You looking forward to meeting your god, or creator, or whatever, are you?' Mills said, covering Godric's face in tiny pieces of spittle. Godric, to his credit, didn't even blink. 'You glad that my brother got infected saving your scared-shitless arse, are you?'

'I am particularly aggrieved that your brother has to suffer at all,' Godric replied, his tone steady. 'But yes, I do believe that the Lord will protect us and greet us with open arms.'

Mills opened his mouth to respond, but his brain wasn't fast enough to catch up. He dropped Godric and turned his attention to me, Luke, Noon and Esmond. 'And where the hell were you cowards? I don't see any of you with a chunk taken out of ya.'

'Listen, Mills, I get that you're upset,' Noon began.

Mills gave a hollow laugh. 'Upset? Upset is what you'll be when I break those useless fingers of yours. I'm not upset. I'm bleedin' fuming.' Mills took a step towards Noon.

Luke dashed out between them before I could stop him. 'Listen, Mills. We haven't talked much before. I'm Luke. And I can't begin to imagine what you're feeling.' His voice was so soft, and his face so sincere, it stopped Mills in his tracks. 'I think the best thing we can do right now is make sure Decke isn't on his own and ask him what he wants to do. It isn't every day you get the chance to say goodbye. Don't waste it on being angry with us. Save that for the Pyres, and Bloodwatch for putting us here in the first place.'

'The kid's right,' Decke muttered. We all turned to look at him. 'Mills, I'm done, man. No point raking over the coals now. We have to make sure you all concentrate on getting secure for when night falls. And maybe, for once, you should ask what I want, instead of talking for me. And Bloodwatch can absolutely get wrecked.'

Nobody moved. Far from being one of the few times Decke spoke up, I couldn't believe he had spoken to Mills like that. Maybe Mills had made Decke come with him to this contest For the first time I saw Mills not as an angry dickhead, but as a scared older sibling.

And I knew how that felt.

'Well, if you aren't gonna say nothing, then can

someone at least help me back to the fountain,' Decke continued. 'I want one last day in the sun.'

Noon and Mills helped lift Decke into the middle of the square, a silent truce unspoken between them. Once they had him safely on the stone seat of the fountain, Mills stayed with him while Noon walked back over to us.

'Decke said we shouldn't waste the building,' Noon said, staring at the floor and rubbing the back of his neck. 'So I say we get it cleared and then we can start fortifying.'

We didn't argue. Even Godric helped for a little while, offering to go into the darkest corners of the building first and check for any other secret Pyres. 'At least let me be helpful before I go,' he said.

It was when Luke, Esmond and I were shoring up the windows with some rusty nails and a hammer we found that we finally spoke, keeping our voices low so Decke and Mills wouldn't hear us from across the yard. It turned out that he had indeed teamed up with Cass, so she, Jupiter and Mills's partner Herrod were working double time to get ready while Mills spent some time with his brother. We'd sent Godric over to help, who was in spookily good spirits despite his fate.

'How long do you think he'll take to turn?' Luke asked.

'Depends. Can be minutes, can be a day or two. Depends on the person, I think. Although with the brood that Bloodwatch promised us, I don't think Decke has days,' I said. I saw Decke leaning against Mills. He looked so pale in the sunlight.

'The average amount of time last year for infections was around six hours,' Esmond said.

'Last year?' I asked. 'Why are the mainlanders measuring by the year?'

'Because the speed of the infection from bite to full-blown blood-seeking missile is getting faster,' Esmond said. 'Didn't you know that?'

'Honestly, Esmond, we don't exactly have the resources to measure it ourselves. So no, I did not know that,' I said, hammering in one of my nails with enough force to shake the irritation from my bones. It wasn't Esmond's fault, and this information was, if anything, useful. I was angry that there was so much Bloodwatch knew and didn't pass on to us. 'What else can you tell me about the monsters I spend every waking minute fighting?'

'Oh, there's lots of things,' Esmond said cheerily, totally missing my tone. Luke tried to stop him by putting a hand on his shoulder but he didn't take that hint either. 'For instance, did you know that there have been instances of Pyres choosing not to attack certain humans? We still don't know why. And there was even a group of Pyres that appeared to honour a body of one of their brood before burying it underground. Fascinating creatures. Terrifying, of course, but fascinating.'

'Hold on, go back,' I said, forgetting my nail and letting the hammer hang loose in my hand. 'When you say honour a body and bury it, do you mean . . . like, they held a funeral?' All I could think about was Hild's story, the one about the Pyre woman who came out of the forest to drag a body back into the treeline.

I'd do anything to hear her tell it again now.

'I think human beings have a tendency to project our

own thoughts and understanding on to the actions of animals, but yes, I suppose it could be described as a funeral of sorts,' said Esmond.

'But they're not animals,' Luke said. 'They were people, human beings, once. Maybe, sometimes, something sticks up there. Maybe they're not all gone,' he said.

Just like Noon's story about the dog, when we saw the cat with the collar. Goosebumps pricked across my arms despite the warm sun. If not all Pyres were murderous monsters, there was a chance I could save Dad and Wynn. Maybe.

'Listen, I'm going to say bye to Decke while I can,' I said. I could see that at some point while we were talking, Mills had left the square and Godric had taken over watching him, so this was my chance without having to deal with Decke's cretin of a brother.

Decke wasn't looking so great. He was sweating, much more so than the rest of us, and we were working. His skin had gone so pale that his veins stood out, a map of blue rivers across his neck and face. He looked like he was about to vomit, and kept swallowing.

'Hey, Decke,' I said, crouching down to his level. Decke didn't look up, so I turned to Godric. 'How's he doing?'

'Well, all things considered,' Godric said. He put a hand on Decke's shoulder. 'I'm praying for him. And I'll keep praying for him until God declares it's time for us to go.'

'Wait, you're staying out here?' I asked. 'Even after dark?' I thought about the broods we had seen so far, how quickly they had torn through anyone unfortunate enough to cross their path. I couldn't think of a worse way to go.

'I won't be leaving Decke here on his own,' Godric said,

his jaw set. 'And let's be honest, is the alternative any better? I want to die here, on my terms, not when Bloodwatch decide they are done with me.'

I nodded.

'My brother isn't happy, but yeah, we're staying put,' Decke said. He was wheezing slightly, his breath shallow. 'We'll attract the brood for a while and it might give you a few hours' peace while they share us out on the all-you-can-drink buffet.'

Decke tried to laugh, but it turned into a dry cough. At one point a chunk of his hair flew forward, leaving an oozing yellow wound in his scalp where it had been. The smell was enough to make me gag. I'd seen people turn before. This wasn't the worst that I'd had to witness.

Godric wasn't as well versed, his eyes wide with fear as he turned to puke in the fountain. Believing in a god was one thing. Hoping he would give you a quick death while Pyres ripped you limb from limb was quite another.

Decke did laugh then, and he wasn't interrupted by coughing this time. 'Man, if my dad could see me now. Took me and Mills to Sunday school every weekend until we were old enough to get out of there. He disowned us when we turned our back on that church. And yet here I am, about to go Pyre, right next to a man of God. He'll be turning in his grave.'

He sighed and leaned on the handle of his knife, the end sheathed so it wouldn't puncture his thigh. 'Do you think you can . . . End things with that, if you want to?' I asked, pointing to the knife. I held up my own gun. 'You can take this if you need it. I can collect it in the morning.'

Decke looked at me with bloodshot eyes and shook his head. 'You're all right, kid. Cass tells my brother that she's a crack shot with that crossbow. She'll put me out of my misery if I give her the sign. I ain't going down without a fight, though. I'll be taking out as many of those bastards as I can.'

'Yes, we will, ahem, try our best to channel God's strength for that one,' Godric said, holding up the twin knife that matched Decke's. He sounded more convinced than he looked.

In that moment, I hated Bloodwatch more than I thought possible. This wasn't fair. Decke was only trying to help us, and Godric should be back on the mainland, watching some stupid sitcom with a laugh track, not a blood sport.

Bloodwatch had to end.

I said goodbye and went back to the boarded-up shop. Decke had been smart to scope it out, because it really didn't need much work. All the windows and doors were now covered and had been reinforced with extra planks we'd found. Noon had spent some time clearing an area downstairs and he'd made a clear path through the debris to the stairs too, in case we had to go up and defend from there.

Not long after that, everyone headed into their buildings and we heard the distant sound of hammering as they sealed themselves inside. The sun was low over the sea, and Decke and Godric cast long shadows over the square. Mills went back out to sit with his brother after I left, and they touched their foreheads together, then Mills nodded once before going into his building on the opposite side of the square. There were no other goodbyes. We'd either see each other in the morning or we wouldn't.

I went into our own building and Noon nailed the door shut behind me. Inside was lit with a couple of candles, the flame kept low and away from the windows. I closed my eyes and took a deep breath, centring myself for what was to come.

'I'm not interrupting you, am I?' Luke's voice cut through my breaths and I opened my eyes. He was perched on another crate opposite me, his eyelashes impossibly long in the low candlelight.

'No. I'm at a bit of a loose end, to be honest. Guess we have to wait now,' I said, hugging my knees. 'It's not as bad for us as it is for Mills. Waiting for his brother to die. I know what that's like, how you blame yourself.'

'It's not your fault that Decke got bitten,' Luke said, reaching across and resting his hands on my knees. 'It's not Mills's either. It's this place, bad luck. Bloodwatch above all. Whoever is to blame, it isn't you. You can't save everyone to make up for what happened to Wynn and your dad. You have to forgive yourself.'

'I don't think I can,' I whispered as tears pricked the back of my eyes. 'There's this . . . monster, deep inside, and I never know when it's going to come out. It won't let me forgive myself, and maybe it shouldn't.'

It was the first time I'd told anyone about the monster, and I wasn't sure Luke would understand. He moved forward and knelt in front of me, his hands on my cheeks now.

'Astrid, you are warm and kind and selfless and brave. You're more than just the monster inside you. You're a survivor. You're alive, so grab your life with both hands and go live it. Don't let your whole life be defined by one moment. We are all more than the monster inside of us.'

And after saying all that, he pulled me into a hug. I melted into him. It was like a huge weight had lifted off my back.

'Thank you. I needed that,' I said into his shoulder.

I leaned back and studied his face, my eyes tracing from the curve of his jaw up to the fan of dark lashes that framed his deep-brown eyes. Neither of us said anything. He looked sincere, the crease of his brow casting a shadow over his face, but it was hard to read any emotion in that look. Whether this was all part of his plan to connect with viewers and gather support for shutting down Bloodwatch, I couldn't tell.

But Luke was different from the other mainlanders. He was hiding something, the real reason he hated Bloodwatch so much, but I wasn't being totally honest either. The friend game, even levelled up, was more than that to me. I knew that as soon as I saw that bite on Decke's skin. That could so easily have been one of us. And the fact I was equally scared whether it was me or Luke made the monster deep inside terrified.

When our gaze connected, Luke's eyes flickered down to my lips and back up again. I leaned forward, just a fraction, and he did the same.

An alarm, similar to the ones we heard during the evacuation in the fall, sounded in the night, low and slow like a lazy Pyre wail.

'Here we go, lovebirds,' Noon said, readying his axe. 'Here we bloody go.'

CHAPTER NINETEEN

The first hour was the worst, because nothing happened.

After the alarm, we pinned up some old blankets on the windows to keep the light from the candles as low as possible. Our strategy was defensive as opposed to offensive: we wanted to stay hidden, all night if we could, rather than have to fight at all. Didn't stop me thumbing the handle of my bolt gun, or Noon from palming his axe.

I wandered over to the front window, where Noon was keeping watch through the smallest gap.

'They still alive?' I asked in a whisper.

Noon moved aside. 'See for yourself.'

I peered through the gap. Decke and Godric were still sitting in the square. The moon was almost full, so it was easy to make out their silhouettes. I noted that there were no floodlights this time. Maybe Bloodwatch wanted to go for a realistic gloom on their manufactured death challenge.

One of the silhouettes slumped forward and the other one pushed him back up.

'Decke is fading fast,' I said, stepping away from the window. I couldn't watch any longer.

'Who was your first?' Noon asked, and I knew exactly what he meant.

'Dad. He hadn't fully changed by the time I got back to the house, but he was nearly there,' I replied, fiddling with my gun. 'It didn't take long for the humanity to slip away, though.'

'It's the eyes that get you, right?' Noon said. I looked at him and he was staring into the distance. 'People think it's the gnarly teeth, but it's the eyes. Dead, but hungry. There's something so uncanny about it. You never forget how their eyes change. She was sick already but that made her slow, and she got bitten.' He looked back and me and gave me a hollow smile. 'My wife.'

'I remember from your interview,' I said. He didn't need to tell me any more. After an apocalypse, survivors have a certain understanding of each other.

'Everything OK?' Luke asked, walking over.

I nodded. 'Coast is clear still. I wanted to keep an eye on Decke.' I glanced at the stairs. 'We can probably watch from up there for a bit if we stay quiet. That OK with you, Noon?'

'I trust you not to be stupid enough to bring a brood of Pyres down on our heads, if that's what you mean,' Noon grinned. He looked over at Esmond and sighed. 'Besides, I'd *love* to get in some quality time with my sparkling personality of a partner.'

Luke and I climbed the stairs carefully and made our way over to the boarded-up windows. We could just about see out of the gaps between the planks. The stupid broadcast tower, red light blinking, came into view in the distance. The all-seeing eye of Bloodwatch, mocking us.

'I don't know how they're doing it,' Luke murmured, staring at Godric and Decke.

'Because there's nothing else to do.' I shrugged. 'That's what it's like, living here. Doing shit you don't want to do, even when you're terrified of what will happen.'

'Doing what needs to be done even when you're scared isn't normal, though, Astrid,' Luke said. 'It's bloody brave.'

I shrugged again, unsure how to reply. Is it brave, living like this, when the only other option is to check out? When this is all you've ever known? Maybe to a mainlander it was.

'What would you do,' Luke asked when I didn't reply, 'if I got bitten?'

'That won't happen,' I replied quickly.

'But what if it did?'

'But it won't.'

'How can you be so sure?' Luke asked. He was watching me in the darkness.

'Because I won't let that happen,' I said.

Luke grinned. 'OK, I believe you. And for the record, I won't let anything happen to you either.'

I suppressed a smile. 'I mean, I'm an islander. I don't need you to protect me, but it's a very sweet sentiment.'

'A sweet sentiment?' Luke asked, his grin spreading wider and catching the moonlight. 'Ouch. I was going for brooding, sexy stranger.'

'Well, I don't know how to tell you this but it's not exactly working. Besides, I'm more brooding than you. Bloodwatch literally showed a video of my monstrous origin story.' The dread of letting him in was submerged under how good it felt to catch his eye when he smiled. This game was keeping us alive, for now. Whatever happened afterwards could wait.

'Hey, it wasn't monstrous. Ask Noon, he's the Executioner's biggest fan,' Luke shot back.

I elbowed him. 'Well, the Executioner has to be here tonight. We could be dead by morning.'

'We could be dead by morning,' Luke repeated it slowly and moved a few centimetres closer, so his hip touched mine. I turned to him and our faces were so close together. All I could smell was him. All I could see was him. All I could feel was him.

'Well, I hope we're not,' I said, and I realised that for the first time in a long time, I meant it. I wanted to live, to see this through, to see Luke's face again.

'You'll live, Astrid,' Luke said, his deep-brown eyes unblinking as he stared into my own. 'You're a survivor. Like you said, you don't need me around to protect you. You can look after yourself.'

'You're right,' I said, leaning in further. I closed my eyes. 'I don't need you to help me survive. But I do want you to help me live.'

Suddenly Luke pulled back.

'Sorry,' I said, humiliation washing through me. 'Sorry, I thought you wanted to—'

'Believe me,' Luke said. 'I want to. But with the importance of tonight, I think we need to keep our wits about us.'

'No, you're right,' I said, pressing my lips together. There was a time to act up for the cameras and there was a time to be alert, to stay alive. And knowing the distinction between the two was the difference between winning and not winning, life and death. 'We need to focus.'

'And there will be plenty of time for *that* when this is

over and there aren't any nosy lenses around,' Luke said, pointing to the ceiling and turning his finger in a circle.

'Because we will see the sun rise,' I said, repeating the mantra Hild and I said to each other almost every day.

'Because we will see the sun rise. Yeah, I like that,' Luke said, grinning. 'And we'll be somewhere a bit nicer than an old shop in an abandoned town.'

Once we were away from here, away from the cameras, that was the only time I would know how he truly felt. When our every move wasn't served up as entertainment for the mainland. But for now, at least I knew he was thinking of when there would be time to explore both his feelings and my own.

I smiled at him and he reached out and squeezed my fingers. For now, even if it was just a game, I was happy to not be alone.

Out of the corner of my eye, something moved in the square.

I whipped my head round and watched as Decke let out a terrifying howl, like an animal in searing pain.

'It's happening,' I whispered, unable to look away. Luke squeezed my hand harder.

Godric backed up as Decke stood up, his neck craned at an unnatural angle as he stared at the sky. Then Godric sank to his knees and waited to die.

But strangely, Decke didn't go straight for the kill. He jerked his head left and right, like he was scenting something in the air.

That's when I saw the first one. A Pyre darted out across

the moonlit square, running on all fours. Its naked body glistened in the moonlight as it ran straight for Godric.

And then Decke leaped forward and smashed the Pyre out of the way with one great sweep of his arm. It hit the fountain with a sickening thud and slid to the ground.

I blinked. Not only had Decke not killed Godric, but he had also protected him. I'd never seen anything like it before. More Pyres slipped into view, a few of the braver ones heading right for Decke and Godric. Godric shrank into a ball, his hands clasped in front of him, and if we had been closer I knew I would have seen his lips moving with rapid prayers.

The next Pyre reached Decke and ducked under his arm to get to Godric, bypassing him entirely, but Decke got his arms around the Pyre's body and squeezed until it fell limp, breaking every rib in seconds with his new-found strength.

Neither Luke nor I said anything as the next Pyres swarmed in. There were at least ten of them now, running in from all directions, leaping across the fountain to get to Godric, mouths chomping.

Decke fought valiantly. He punched another two Pyres out of the air as they jumped at them, and had a third in a headlock, but there were too many. We watched as he went down screaming, his guttural noises blending in with the sound of the Pyres' and Godric's shrieks. Within a minute of the first Pyre turning up, they were swarmed.

Decke stood up, his head and shoulders appearing over the mass of writhing bodies that greedily drank Godric dry, still trying to smash as many Pyres as he could with his bloody fists.

That was when he jolted, a crossbow bolt jutting out neatly from his temple, his arms dropping to his side. I looked across at the first floor of the building opposite and saw movement at the window. Cass. She was a good shot.

I thought about Mills watching that. I had to use that pain and misery and anger to feed the monster, the one I had to let out of the box if I was going to survive this night. Even as we were getting up and moving away from the window, more Pyres flooded the square. There must have been a hundred of them, maybe more, all long turned and naked and bald, all trying to get a piece of the Godric buffet. And once that was finished, they would look for more. They would look for us.

Luke and I crept down the stairs and found Noon and Esmond sat by the candles, Noon turning his axe over in his hands, Esmond with eyes closed rocking back and forth in the foetal position.

'Is it over?' Noon signed to me, resting his axe on his knees.

I nodded.

'Then we better get locked and loaded,' Noon signed back.

'What's going on?' Esmond whispered, so quietly I barely heard him over the Pyres' screaming outside.

'It's time for us to stay out of the way and help however we can,' Luke whispered back, bending down to squeeze Esmond's shoulder.

I took a deep breath. Luke always knew how to handle

people in the best possible way, even when everyone else was losing their head.

I gestured to the front of the building with my gun, indicating we should watch the windows.

He nodded and we made our way over to the front door. Noon very carefully moved the blanket about half a centimetre and peered out, just enough so we could both see what was happening.

The square was chaos. I knew that from what we saw upstairs, but being on street level made it much more real. The square was so full of pale, naked bodies that it reminded me of a news piece I saw when I was younger of a music festival, one where there were so many people all in one small space, some of them were crushed to death. There were Pyres right on the other side of the window, but they were pushed around so quickly that they didn't have time to register me and Noon looking right at them.

I signed to Noon. 'This is the biggest brood I've ever seen.'

'That's because I don't think it's a brood,' Noon signed back, his axe holstered at his waist. 'I think Bloodwatch rounded up every Pyre in the area and launched them at us all at once. I think they waited for Decke to turn too. Maximum emotional impact for the cameras.'

I stared at him, but I couldn't pretend I was surprised. I'd already guessed Bloodwatch were encouraging more Pyres into the area, but holding them back while Decke lost his humanity? There were no boundaries left. Bloodwatch had gone too far.

We turned back to the window and I stumbled

backwards. Luke jumped up, ran to my side to steady me with almost Pyre-like speed and grabbed my elbow.

'What's wrong?' he asked.

I pointed to the gap in the window covering and raised my gun. Luke turned, leaning on his pole, and his eyes widened.

A Pyre, one that had finally stopped moving long enough to see in, was pinned against the window, its bloodshot eye the only thing visible in the gap between the boards and the window frame. It had seen us and its mouth was opening and closing against the timber and the glass, its teeth scratching marks into the wood, its mouth filling with splinters.

Luke ran forward and pulled the blanket over the gap. He indicated in broken sign language that it was secure before coming back to us.

'I don't think they can get in the windows that way, kid,' Noon whispered. 'But I don't know how long the door will last with all those bodies pressed against it.'

Esmond stood up and slowly walked over to us. Silently, we stared at the front door. Noon had done a good job nailing boards over it once we were inside, but the building had been empty for a long time. The wood creaked in place and one of the boards popped off, leaving a gap where the glass in the original door used to be. All we could see were pale bodies, so much skin that it was hard to tell where one Pyre ended and the next began. The haunting noise of their screams was deafening as they were compressed against the door.

'Esmond,' Noon whispered. 'I'm gonna need you to blow the candles out.'

But there was no time, because the door burst inwards.

CHAPTER TWENTY

All four of us raced for the stairs as the door was knocked off its hinges and Pyres flooded in.

As soon as me, Esmond and Luke were on the stairs, Noon turned round, ready for the onslaught. I had precious seconds to look around and assess how screwed we were.

I counted maybe ten Pyres that tumbled inside before we moved to the staircase, and then the door was blocked by a wall of writhing and limp bodies – Pyres that were stuck. A grotesque living installation of pale skin and deadly vein patterns.

Noon swung out with his axe and caught the first raging Pyre a fraction above its eye. It went flying backwards down the stairs and almost knocked another Pyre out.

Almost. The second Pyre launched itself at Noon, using the body of its fallen friend as leverage. Its teeth were already snapping together, eager to find Noon's flesh and taste his blood.

Noon kept it back with his axe and I raised my bolt gun up under its chin and pulled the trigger.

Luke spotted another Pyre on the right, crawling along the wall. He thrust his pole forward like a spear, piercing the Pyre's eye and head, spraying the walls with flecks of blood and brain and skull.

'Keep going. We can clear them and barricade ourselves upstairs,' Noon shouted.

The guttural noise of the Pyres was so loud it made my ears ring. My mind wandered to Cass and Glaed and all the other contestants that were out there. Were they doing as poorly as us?

'Astrid, watch out!' Luke yelled. He put his hand on the top of my head and forced me down out of the way as a Pyre jumped at me. Luke thrust forward with his metal pole, missed and pierced the Pyre through the armpit, pinning one of its arms to its side. That didn't slow it down, though. Dark blood spilled from its mouth and it reached for Luke with the other arm, jaw snapping.

And then something weird happened.

Luke stumbled backwards, and the Pyre's mouth was a hair's breadth from his arm, and I knew I couldn't get to him in time, not from where he had pushed me down on to the step. My breath caught in my throat and I froze.

And just as Luke was a goner, as the Pyre was about to bite into his flesh and suck out every drop of blood from his arm, it stopped. It sniffed Luke's skin and closed its mouth. And then it looked at Luke and seemed to whisper something, and Luke nodded.

Then he pulled the metal pole free and stabbed the Pyre in the heart, killing it instantly.

Time sped up again and I couldn't think, process, even know if what I saw was real or some weird adrenaline-induced hallucination. Luke reached forward to help me up and he pushed the Pyre down the stairs, where it fell on to the pile of corpses Noon was expertly dispatching in front of us.

'You OK?' Luke said, his face creased with concern.

I blinked at him. Did Luke just . . . speak to a Pyre? No. That was impossible. They couldn't communicate. Communication made them human, and they were not human.

But sometimes they kept pet dogs and cats, right? But even with that logic . . . why would they talk to *Luke*?

'I'm good,' I forced out. This wasn't the time for this conversation, and something caught my eye over his left shoulder. 'Duck.'

Luke didn't need telling twice. He hit the deck and I pulled out my gun, threw my hand forward and pulled the trigger. The bolt shot out under the Pyre's nose and travelled up its nostril, twisting my hand with the force of the shot and pushing the bolt up into its brain. It slumped to the ground in front of me.

There was a ringing in my ears from the sudden silence that followed. A pile of pale limbs and lifeless, staring faces was collected at the bottom of the staircase. The walls were dripping with dark Pyre blood. There was a severed hand on the step next to my foot.

'Well, that was a little more playtime than I had scheduled for tonight,' Noon said. I looked up and he was wiping the sharp end of his axe on his regulation trousers. 'At least they gave us red shirts, huh?' He pointed with his axe to Luke and Esmond. 'I'd hate to see the dry-cleaning bill for you boys after all that.'

Luke's shirt was soaked with Pyre blood at the front, but the back was freakishly clean. Esmond had one small splatter of blood on his shirt, topped off with a chunk of something flesh-like on his shoulder. Luke leaned forward, picked up the flesh and threw it to the floor. Esmond took one look at it, turned on his heel and vomited over the landing.

'That was way too close,' I said, ignoring Esmond dry-heaving behind me and keeping my voice low. 'We need to block the door with some furniture or something. Those Pyres are gummed up a treat right now, but if there's a sudden movement in the crowd and something unsticks them, our front door is wide open.'

'I agree with the Executioner,' Noon said, switching to sign. 'We block the front door, move upstairs, wait until morning and try to hold on to our arses.'

Luke caught the gist so he told Esmond to go and wait while the three of us crept back down the stairs. Luke grabbed our packs and bedrolls and took them up to Esmond, while Noon and I looked for a big enough piece of furniture we could use to block the door.

It should have been terrifying being down there with the door wide open, the only thing holding back the tidal wave of Pyres being the dozen or so corpses that had been crushed to death in the entrance.

I was spent. My emotions from earlier had been so intense there was nothing left to give except numbness, which was probably for the best. I ignored the mash-up of teeth and blood and glassy eyes and limbs that made up the entrance to the building and helped Noon move an old display unit into place in front of the doorway. All that was left to do was blow out any candles and make our way upstairs.

I tried the handle on the front bedroom but the door didn't budge. After a few seconds I heard the sound of wood being dragged across the floor and Luke opened the door from the other side. He had pushed a bed up against it; smart. It was very dark up there because we didn't dare risk more candles, but my eyes adjusted to the gloom enough to see Esmond by the window.

Noon and I followed Luke over to where Esmond was hunched, his eyes on whatever was playing out in the square.

The writhing throng of bodies that covered every centimetre of the cobbled square drew my eye immediately. I knew it would be bad from what we saw downstairs, but nothing could prepare me for it.

It was like a moving carpet. Around the edges of the square, nearest to the buildings, nothing much moved, the corpses there already trampled by the moving mass of Pyres still hunting. The closer to the fountain you looked, the faster the mass moved, anticlockwise in a circle like water going down a drain. An undead whirlpool.

And the smell. My god, the smell. It was a mixture of body odour and sweat and metallic blood and sewage. Even with the window closed it was enough to make me gag.

I looked across to the opposite building where I knew Cass, Jupiter, Mills and Herrod were hiding out. I couldn't see anything, even in the bright glow of the moon, so I hoped they were safe. I glanced down at their shopfront and saw that both windows and the door were miraculously intact.

'Oh shit,' Luke whispered. He lifted a finger and pointed to the left of our position, right at the narrow old boarding house where Cinta, Maeva, Glaed and Reeta were holed up.

It looked like they'd had the same idea as us and had moved to the top floor for a better view, but that was the problem.

I could see where they were.

There was a light on, flickering like a candle flame, dim but bright enough to be the only thing attracting attention in the dark night except the moon. As the Pyres had no luck at our place, and clearly hadn't so much as noticed Cass, Mills and their teammates, they became focused on the one thing that they could see as a sign of life: that window. It was like a lighthouse beacon on a stormy night, and the Pyres were heading right for it.

As we watched, the movement of the swirling mass of Pyres began to shift into less of a rotating mechanism and more straining to reach the left-hand side of the square. At the bottom of the building, where the door and windows remained boarded shut, a Pyre hand shot out above the heads of the crowd and gripped on to one of the boards. It climbed up, pulling itself from the masses, its silvery body almost fluorescent in the moonlight.

More Pyres spotted what it was doing and followed suit. Soon several of them had gripped on to parts of the building, climbing up. After a few seconds the first Pyre that began the climb missed its footing, and it tumbled back down into the sea of bodies below. But that didn't stop them. There were at least a dozen of them now, climbing up towards the light.

'We have to warn them,' Esmond said, his voice cracking with tears.

'How, blockhead? We yell, or signal, or anything, and we're Pyre cocktails. They're too far away and there's nothing we can do. Gotta sit tight and hold our shit together,' Noon hissed back.

I chewed the inside of my cheek until I tasted blood. He was right, I knew that, but it didn't make it any easier to sit back and watch people die.

Although that didn't stop the viewers of Bloodwatch.

The light in the window suddenly went out.

The windows opposite weren't boarded up like ours were on the first floor. Nowhere else in the square was. The others were clearly betting that the Pyres wouldn't suddenly decide they enjoyed climbing. Big mistake.

The first of the Pyres reached the window. It leaned across, made it to the ledge, pulled back its head and smashed the glass with its face.

We heard several screams, only muffled by the glazing of our own window. The Pyre climbed into the darkness and disappeared, closely followed by more that had made it up the same way. Within seconds, there were maybe ten Pyres in the upstairs room, with more following behind.

The screams continued until eventually someone appeared at the window, their face lit up in the moonlight.

It was Cinta. I'd know that pink hair anywhere. She started swiping at the Pyres with her knife, managing to push off any that were near enough the window to get caught by the blade. She was on a roll now, slicing and dicing anything that came near her, screaming like a banshee. Blood spattered her face and she looked manic, eyes wide, barely different to the Pyres that snapped their teeth at her before she pushed them to their deaths.

Once she had cleared most of them, she jumped on to the windowsill and stood up, gripping the frame for balance.

'She's going for the roof,' I said, watching as she stood on tiptoe to haul herself up. She took off her pack and reached back down to the window with one hand.

Another face appeared at the window – it was Glaed. He stepped out and tried to climb up the same way Cinta did, but she wasn't getting out of his way.

'I don't like this,' Noon muttered.

Cinta leaned forward, stretching out her hand again. Glaed stood on tiptoe to take it. And then she pulled it away and kicked out with her foot, right in Glaed's face. He flipped over backwards and disappeared into the mass of hungry Pyres below.

My breath caught in my throat. The Pyres swarmed Glaed. The next person out of the window was Reeta, Cinta's partner. She didn't waste any time. Cinta pulled Reeta up and they scooted back on to the roof, makeshift weapons ready for any Pyres that managed to make it up that far.

The last I saw of Glaed was his face as it surged through the bodies once more, like a drowning man in a rough sea, before it disappeared forever below the pale-skinned waves.

CHAPTER TWENTY-ONE

No one spoke a word on the bus to the next challenge.

We'd been picked up once the sun had risen. I don't think any of us had slept, not after what we saw the night before. Everyone looked exhausted. I spent most of the night at the window, watching Cinta, wondering whether looks could kill and if I could manifest one.

Glaed would have pulled Reeta up. Cinta didn't need to kill him, but she did anyway. Another contestant murder and she was one step closer to victory.

The monster shifted. I hated her.

Cinta was checking her make-up in the compact mirror she found somewhere along the way. Super important after killing someone. Reeta sat next to her, staring out of the window.

'If you're staring because you fancy me, get in line,' Cinta said, breaking the silence, pursing her lips before snapping the compact closed and meeting my gaze.

'You really think the world revolves around you, don't you?' I spat, the monster pushing its way out. Luke put a hand on my shoulder and I shrugged it off. The whole bus was staring at us.

'Not around me, hun. Around Bloodwatch,' Cinta said.

She leaned forward, her shiny lip-gloss smile making my blood boil. 'And you know who controls them? The viewing public. Sometimes you have to feed the monster, you know? Put on a show.'

The way she said *monster* felt like she was looking into my soul. I launched myself at Cinta.

My seatbelt and Luke held me back. I struggled but then the fight drained out of me. There was nothing I could do anyway. I tried to calm down. Bloodwatch would surely only punish us for missing a good fight between contestants.

'I'd listen to her, girly. Keep piping up and I might have to get myself a slice of airtime by wringing your dainty little neck,' Mills said, grinning, his teeth somehow stained with red. He was straight back to being a dick after the death of his brother, then. If anything, he was probably more determined to win than ever – which meant pushing any emotion from his mind. I'd been there.

'I think what the Executioner here is trying to say, Princess Cinta,' Noon said from across the aisle, ignoring Mills, 'is that you didn't have to be such a dick to Glaed. He wasn't exactly a threat.'

Cinta raised an eyebrow and laughed, but it was hollow. 'Not a threat? You're all a threat. Every time I take out a team it's another step towards that golden ticket. I've heard you all talking about your cute little settlements with your makeshift weapons and your families and friends. I'm an Influencer; survival is what I do. I live in the woods. Sure, I hook up with others for a little while, have a bit of fun. But I don't have a favourite chair to be getting back to, or a sweet little boyfriend waiting for me. There's nothing left for me on this godforsaken island. Bloodwatch can't hurt me, they can only save me. And the sooner you all realise that these stupid set-ups you have aren't shit compared to what your life could be like on the mainland, you'll get it too.'

Cinta sat back, arms folded, and stared out of the window. Under her freshly applied powder, her cheeks flushed red. Nobody said anything. Noon caught my eye and shrugged. It caused me pain to admit it, but Cinta's speech explained a lot of her behaviour.

That didn't mean I'd ever forgive her. Loneliness wasn't an excuse for being a psychopath; that shit is buried deep before you get to the reason for releasing it. I'm the Executioner and even I'm not as cruel as her.

I'd been worried we might have to watch another execution on the part of Bloodwatch, but Glaed's partner Maeva didn't make it that far. According to Reeta, she was the first one to realise the light was attracting attention, and she had her back to the window blowing the candle out when the first Pyre forced its way in. She cut down as many as she could and pretty much saved Glaed's life, but it didn't matter. She was bitten on the back of her neck.

We found her mangled body hanging out of the window this morning, her entire weight hanging by her broken femur, her flesh dripping blood down the side of the building, her head clinging on by a flap of skin to her neck.

I was pretty sure Cinta would try to claim that Glaed was dead anyway because Maeva was bitten, and that's why she didn't want him on the roof.

Mercifully, that was the last of the live action for the night. I was sure Bloodwatch would be disappointed there wasn't more.

When the first rays of sunlight filled the sky after an impossibly long night, the screams started. They knew that sunlight meant boiled skin and a long, painful death. Those Pyres on the periphery of the square, the ones nearest the road and access to the sea beyond, skulked away, angry they had been left with nothing before having to hide back in the darkness again. The square cleared in minutes. A lot were left behind, but they couldn't run anywhere. They had been crushed in the melee.

There were only ten of us left by the time the Bloodwatch convoy rolled into the square. Me and Luke; Noon and Esmond; Cinta and Reeta; Cass and Jupiter; and Mills and Herrod. We walked past Glaed's remains on the way out of the square. They'd picked his bones clean, and Luke had to support Cass as they walked past.

And then the black shirts arrived and packed us all on to a minibus and handed out more egg mayonnaise sandwiches and water bottles. No fancy cars for each team today. There were so few of us left there hardly seemed any point. They also took our weapons, which made Mills especially salty.

The bus came to a stop around twenty minutes later at the edge of the forest and we all filed off, our feet dragging. I couldn't tell if it was the stress of everything finally getting to me, or the lack of sleep, or both, but I felt like I could crash out any minute. The broadcast tower was just visible through the canopy of trees, but it was tiny, so we were a few miles away from Bloodwatch HQ.

The usual circus had already been set up. Cresta was sitting in a folding chair with her name printed across the back, dressed head to toe in golden Lycra. Several cameras and their operators were dotted about, ready to capture our every move. Same old, same old.

We were lined up in front of the cameras and Cresta sank the last of some slimy-looking drink before heading over to us.

'Welcome back, friends, to *Escape from Blood Island*,' Cresta said, all smiles, into a camera marked number three. 'As you can see, we've now halved the number of contestants and, my, what a pick of the bunch we have left!'

Noon coughed. Mills stared at the ground, all his bravado from the bus gone.

Cresta blinked. 'Well, yes, our contestants are feeling a little jaded after that last challenge. And who can blame them? Endurance was the name of the game and, as you saw, they had to fight for their lives all night long. And so how do we decide a winner among these, the fabulous five?'

That got me. I looked up and saw the others seemed a little curious too. This was the first challenge that wasn't some sort of foot race. What now?

'Well, as you viewers at home are aware, there were no winners in the endurance round,' Cresta said. 'But that doesn't mean we don't have room for a favourite team!'

My eyes met Luke's – he looked as nervous as I did. Only one winner? That meant only one team would get the head start. I glanced down the line at the others. The competition was getting tight, and Bloodwatch were making it even tighter.

'So, without further ado, the winners of the endurance round as voted for by the public were . . . Cinta and Reeta!'

Cresta signalled for them to come and stand next to her, and I seethed. What sort of sick bastard would vote for a performance like Cinta's last night? Reeta might have fought bravely, but that little murderer? I had to hope that it was at least close. With five teams left, it wouldn't take much to swing the vote one way or the other.

'Welcome, ladies. This is your first win, but I'm sure you know the rules by now – I have the golden box, ready to go.' Cresta pulled something out from behind her back – but it wasn't a box, it was an envelope, just like the ones we got during the first challenge at the castle. 'In this envelope is a secret. I'll let you read it, and you can decide whether you'd like to share it with your fellow contestants – or not. Totally up to you! But this secret is a helping hand in passing the next challenge. Cinta, Reeta, take your time.'

She handed them the envelope and clasped her hands together. 'Let round four begin!'

Cinta and Reeta were led away and started reading the folded piece of paper that was inside the envelope. The cameras closed in on them as they read silently.

'What do you think it says?' Noon signed.

'Who gives a shit?' Mills signed back. 'I'm ready to go. What's taking so long?'

He swung his fists at thin air, his jaw clenching. It was the most dangerous I'd ever seen him – he had nothing left to lose. Herrod couldn't follow what we were signing, but Mills's agitation was explanation enough.

'Maybe the next round is more cerebral,' Luke said.

Mills rounded on him, fist poised in mid-air. 'Cerebral, mainlander? Careful, you keep talking dirty and the Executioner here will be rubbing herself all over you.'

'Shut the hell up, Mills,' I said, exasperated.

Luke elaborated. 'Cresta told us on the first day that the five tasks would test courage, survival, cunning, endurance and teamwork. Teamwork was the envelope task, and courage was the crypt. We just did endurance, leaving survival and cunning. If the winning team is being given information as their gift to get ahead, I'm going to assume the next task is cunning.'

'So what you're saying, boy,' Mills said, 'is that we need to force Cinta and her tourist to tell us what they know. I like your style.'

'No, that's not what I meant,' Luke started, but before he could finish, Cinta and Reeta were being led back over. Luke glared at Mills, and Mills grinned back, more of a grimace than an actual smile. Unhinged, as Hild would say.

'OK, everybody, let's move on to the next challenge: a test of cunning!' Cresta announced. Luke and Mills exchanged a glance and Mills stretched out his neck, like he was about to wage war.

A black shirt yelled 'Cut!' No more explanations for this task yet, then. Cresta's smile switched off as soon as the cameras stopped rolling. She was away without saying goodbye, muttering into her headset about coffee and a pay rise while a black shirt held open the door to her chauffeur-driven car.

Some more black shirts appeared and told us to follow them. We walked a little further into the forest until we approached a low, single-storey building. It was covered in ivy and looked like it hadn't been used in years.

The cameras followed us, surrounding us on all sides as we tried to work out what was going on. Cinta and Reeta walked a little faster than the rest of us, whispering to each other. There were so few of us now that we were easily outnumbered by the black shirts, and it made me feel small, insignificant. I was so tired.

'OK, listen up,' a black shirt called, signalling for all of us to come closer. 'The next task you have to take in turns. Cinta and Reeta will go first. The rest of you will follow on a points-based system. Cass and Jupiter, you have won the most challenges so you will be second. Luke and Astrid, and Mills and Herrod, you both have one public vote win each, but due to Astrid and Luke beating Mills and Herrod in the crypt challenge, you will go third and fourth respectively. Noon and Esmond, you'll go last. Are we clear?'

'Well, what can I say,' Noon said, nudging Esmond. 'Everybody loves an underdog.'

'They don't get much more "under" than these dogs,' Esmond muttered, and Noon laughed.

'Esmond, you made a funny. That's the way to win votes, attaboy.'

We lined up. Mills was fuming that he wouldn't get a chance to force any information out of Cinta, and Cinta was revelling in it. Mills peered over my head, craning to see what Cinta's paper said. At the front of the line, Cinta turned round, tore a strip off the information she'd been given and folded it into her mouth, chewing. She swallowed and winked at Mills, which made him grunt with rage.

'OK, first contestants, you're up,' the black shirt said.

Cinta and Reeta stepped forward and another member of the crew opened the entrance to the building, a solid door with a metal bar across it that said FIRE EXIT. We all leaned forward, trying to glean what we could in the small amount of time the door was open, but inside was pitch black. The crew member slammed the door shut behind them.

'I don't like this,' Luke said, chewing his lip.

'I haven't liked any of it,' I said. 'Honestly, I'd say it can't get any worse, but Bloodwatch has a way of plumbing new depths of "worse".'

'I wonder if it's a long task,' Luke mused. 'The producers must know how little sleep we've had. There's no way they can keep us moving at this pace, not if they want a decent finale.'

I glanced around. There were maybe fifteen or twenty black shirts who had been left behind to monitor our progress through the next challenge. On the edge of this new clearing, another ten or so guards milled about, guns in hand. For a second I thought about making a run for it. Just me and Luke. If we were fast, we could reach the old quarantine zone perimeter before nightfall. Maybe we could get back to the Burgh. Hild would die that I'd brought a boy back. And there were no cameras there. We could forget all about Bloodwatch and finally be happy. Or at least safe for a while – but Nova's threat about destroying the Burgh if I didn't compete crept into my mind.

A camera walked past me, cutting off my train of thought. What was I thinking – the cameras were everywhere. Bloodwatch had guns and cars and an eye on every treeline. Luke and I would be Pyre food before the end of today's episode. There was no escaping this, not until we either won the game, or brought down Bloodwatch somehow. Preferably both.

'Next team,' a black shirt called out. Cass and Jupiter stepped forward and Cass turned to look at me before she went in. 'See you on the other side,' she signed.

I hoped my face was doing a better job at putting up a brave front than my body was.

'She'll be fine,' Luke said, reading my mind but not sounding too confident. His fingers found their way into my hand and tickled the centre of my palm, drawing circles there. I laced my own through his and squeezed.

'Ah, how sweet,' Mills drawled from behind us. 'So is that only when the cameras are nearby, or are you getting your end away, Lukey boy?'

'You seem awfully concerned about my dick, Mills,' Luke said. 'I'd be more worried about what that big old machete you had last round is overcompensating for.'

Even Esmond cracked a smile at that. Mills took a step towards us but one of the armed guards moved in front of him.

'Save it for the challenges, OK, buddy?' he said, and Mills grunted but backed down. He'd already lost his brother. This stupid game was all he had left.

I stared at the closed door in front of us and strained to listen for screaming. 'It sounds pretty quiet, right? Maybe no Pyres?' I asked Luke.

Luke shrugged. 'It's a windowless building and the lights are out whenever they open that door. It's possible, but . . . I have a feeling they won't let us off so easy.'

I nodded slowly, tears pricking at the back of my tired eyes.

'We've got this,' Luke said eventually. 'I'll be beside you the whole time.'

'Next,' the black shirt called, signalling for us to step forward.

I tried to suck in a deep breath but struggled. Why was the waiting always so bad?

Because it's in the fight where I come alive, the monster inside me said.

The door opened, and Luke and I stepped into the darkness.

CHAPTER TWENTY-TWO

The door swung shut and it was so dark inside I wouldn't have known Luke was there if he wasn't squeezing my hand so tightly. Then light flooded my senses and I blinked, trying to adjust.

We were standing in a small room with three doors labelled Door 1, 2 and 3, respectively. A small screen was set into a table in front of us, and it lit up when we stepped closer:

WELCOME TO THE CUNNING CHALLENGE!

AHEAD YOU WILL SEE THREE DOORS. YOU WILL HAVE
TO NAVIGATE FURTHER ROOMS, WITH FURTHER DOORS.
IN EACH ROOM WILL BE A MULTIPLE-CHOICE QUESTION.
THE ANSWERS WILL CORRESPOND TO THE DOORS IN
FRONT OF YOU.
IN EACH ROOM IS AN INCORRECT DOOR, AN
IMPROBABLE DOOR AND A CORRECT DOOR.
CORRECT ANSWERS WILL GET YOU THROUGH TO
THE END OF THE CHALLENGE FASTER.
IMPROBABLE ANSWERS WILL RESULT
IN EXTRA CHALLENGES.

INCORRECT ANSWERS WILL RESULT IN DEATH.
THE WINNERS OF THE LAST CHALLENGE WERE TOLD
THE CORRECT ANSWER TO THIS FIRST QUESTION,
AND THE CORRECT ANSWER TO THE LAST QUESTION.
THESE ARE THE ONLY RULES. GOOD LUCK!

TAP THE SCREEN FOR QUESTION ONE.

'Well, that explains why Cinta ate her paper,' Luke said. 'It wasn't just to piss Mills off – that was an added bonus. It was to make sure we didn't see any right answers.'

'To be honest, I wouldn't put anything past her,' I muttered. 'Let's get this over with.'

I tapped the screen and the instructions melted away:

QUESTION ONE:
WHO WON THE FIRST PUBLIC VOTE?
1: ASTRID AND LUKE
2: CASS AND JUPITER
3: MORRIGAN AND MARG

'Is this a trick question?' Luke asked. 'Surely everyone will know that.'

'They won't all be this easy. This is Bloodwatch, after all,' I said. 'But remember what the instructions said. We know that Door 1 is the right answer, correct? So Door 2 is wrong, but they *could* have won the public vote. It was possible. The only people that couldn't have won were Morrigan and Marg, because they never made it to the end of the task.'

'So Door 1 will take us to the next question, and Door 2 will slow us down,' Luke said slowly, cogs turning in his head. 'They'll be rating us on how quickly we get out.'

'Probably. But I'm worried about what happens if we get a question wrong,' I said.

We both looked up at Door 3. The doors themselves were all the same type as the fire exit, meaning that they would automatically swing shut when you went through.

'So don't think about it. Come on, let's get this over with,' Luke said. He walked over to Door 1, took a deep breath and opened it. Beyond was an unlit corridor. In the light from behind us, I could just about make out the outline of two other doors, both with no handles, inset into the walls of the corridor. Doors from other rooms depending on your answer, I'd bet. There was another door at the end of the corridor that we could open. This place was a maze, with questions for clues and no way to check your answers.

'Yep, Bloodwatch won't let us cheat. Come on,' I sighed, and stepped over the threshold, walking through the corridor to get to the door at the end. Luke was so close behind me I could feel his body heat through my uniform.

I turned the handle and we walked through. The door slammed shut behind us and I jumped at the noise. Luke instinctively put his hands on my shoulders and my racing heart slowed a fraction.

After a few seconds the fluorescent lights in the room kicked in and we were . . . in an identical room to the one we had come from.

'Déjà vu,' Luke muttered as we approached the second screen.

A message flashed up:

> CONGRATULATIONS!
> SEE, THAT WASN'T SO HARD, WAS IT?
> BUT THAT WAS JUST THE WARM-UP – LET'S MAKE
> THINGS A LITTLE MORE INTERESTING, SHALL WE?
> TAP THE SCREEN FOR QUESTION TWO

I tapped the screen as soon as I scanned the text, the anger bubbling up inside me at how flippant Bloodwatch were being. Anything to keep the mainland watching, I guess.

> QUESTION TWO:
> MILLS AND HERROD WON THE SECOND PUBLIC VOTE
> WHEN THEY THREW A ROCK INTO A PILE OF SLEEPING
> PYRES. BUT WHO WAS LEADING THE POLLS BEFORE
> THAT INCIDENT?
> 1: CINTA AND REETA
> 2: GLAED AND MAEVA
> 3: ALDRED AND GRAYSON

'How are we supposed to know that?' I said, shaking my head.

Luke looked at the question, then at the doors, then back again. 'We can't. They're making us guess based on what we already know about how the vote works. It's a leap of faith.'

'That is not filling me with confidence.' I took a deep breath to steady my rising heart rate. 'Let's look at what we do know. Aldred and Grayson died when they were still in the crypt, remember? By the time we got to the sleeping brood cavern we were over halfway through the maze. Were Aldred and Grayson already dead by then? Are they the impossible answer?' A shiver passed over me at the thought of their deaths at the hands of Cinta.

'Good point. There was a clock at the top left of the footage they showed us when Aldred and Grayson were killed. I'm pretty sure it said something like ten minutes or so. If that clock started when we entered the maze, it rules them out of the question,' said Luke.

I raised an eyebrow at him. 'You sure you remember that?' I thought back to the footage I never wanted to replay in my mind and tried to think whether there was a clock there. It was possible, but we had nothing else to go on.

Luke nodded. 'And I can't think of any reason why the other two would be impossible answers. So we have to choose between Cinta and Reeta, and Glaed and Maeva. What do you think?'

I stared down at the screen, chewing my lip. 'I want to believe it's Glaed and Maeva. Cinta didn't win anything until recently either. But it's a coin flip.'

'Where you go, I go,' Luke said, giving me a small smile.

I took a deep breath. 'Door 2. Glaed and Maeva. Let's go before I change my mind.'

We walked round the podium and I opened the fire door to another corridor with only one possible exit. We stepped inside and I crossed my fingers behind my back as my heart hammered in my chest. I wanted us to be right, but I was also afraid of the unknown. We shuffled along in the darkness and pushed open the door at the end.

The lights slowly flickered to life and I had my answer.

The room was almost the same as the previous two. There were only two doors at the other end this time instead of the usual three, marked A and B. But that wasn't the only difference.

In the middle of the room, where the podium should be, were two rotting bodies. One was almost all bone, pearly white and licked clean, except for a staring, olive-skinned face that hung loose from its skull, like a mask that had been placed over a rock. The other body was more intact, maggots squirming in the crevices where chunks of flesh had been ripped right out of her. The bone in her leg stuck out at an angle that made it impossible for her left foot to lie straight on the floor. Her head was propped up next to her, her braids still intact, her eyeballs and the bottom of her jaw missing like they had been ripped clean off.

It was Maeva and Glaed.

A sob broke free from my throat and I threw my hands over my mouth. Being confronted like this, so close to Glaed's body, with no warning, after twenty-four hours of no sleep – it was too much. Where the monster usually came out, there were only tears. Exhausted, broken, endlessly sad tears. I dropped to my knees.

Luke swore, stumbling backwards. He slumped to the floor, his hands in his hair. Then he crawled over to me, put both arms around my shoulders and rocked me back and forth.

'Let it out, Astrid. I'm here. Let it out,' he whispered in my ear. It was like all of his own anguish was gone, hidden from me for a moment, and I had never been more grateful to someone for something in my life. I couldn't handle us both falling apart. I needed to be held together so I didn't break into a million tiny pieces all over Glaed and Maeva's bodies, because surely no one person could hold this much pain and carry on. This was reality TV at its most truthful, game or no game.

I don't know how much time passed until I noticed the screen sticking out from Maeva's mangled hands, but it was enough that my tears had dried and my breathing had returned to normal. I nudged out from Luke's arms and reached for the tablet, which switched on at my touch. It was propped between Maeva's remaining six fingers, so I gently unfurled them and pulled it free.

UH-OH! WRONG ANSWER!
IT WAS IN FACT CINTA AND REETA WHO WERE LEADING
THE VOTE BEFORE MILLS AND
HERROD STOLE THE LEAD.
BUT DON'T WORRY – YOU DIDN'T CHOOSE THE
IMPOSSIBLE ANSWER, SO YOU HAVE ONE MORE GUESS,
AND THIS ONE'S AN EASY ONE.
PICK A DOOR. A OR B.
ONE LEADS TO CERTAIN DEATH.

ONE LEADS TO QUESTION THREE.
WHICH WILL IT BE?

'This is messed up,' Luke muttered over my shoulder.

I didn't say anything at first. All the tears and tiredness and grief and trauma and the general unfairness of it all had finally made me snap. And now the tears were finished, everything else was feeding the monster deep inside. Resolve tensed every muscle of my body, getting me ready. We weren't finished yet. We wouldn't be finished until Bloodwatch had been taken down once and for all.

'It is. But we have no choice. We have to play along,' I said, my voice even, tempered.

Luke looked at me and gave me the smallest nod, one that told me he knew what I meant by 'play along'. I had to trust my instincts and hope that he could trust his. We had to play the game until we could shut it down.

'You choose,' I said to Luke. I was delirious with emotion, exhausted with it. I was terrified we would choose wrong, be the next ones thrown to the Pyre pit, but I was also getting too tired to care.

'Screw it, A,' Luke said. He crossed the room, careful of Maeva and Glaed's corpses, and pulled open the door. 'I don't hear any Pyres, but I don't think they would make it that easy. Ready?'

I stepped over the bodies and took his hand. 'Let's do this.'

We stepped over the threshold and the door slammed shut behind us. The darkness was oppressive after the light of the previous room and I waited, knees slightly bent, ready for whatever they would throw at us. I wasn't dying here, not like this. Not today. We moved forward, feeling along the walls, until we came to the exit. We pushed it open and hit another door almost immediately – the corridor for the right answer, I hoped – and stepped through.

CHAPTER TWENTY-THREE

The lights came on and we saw there were three doors again, plus the podium, in this room. I walked forward and checked the tablet.

'Fifty-fifty chance. Luck was on our side, I guess,' Luke said, swinging his head back with relief.

'About time,' I said, and leaned in to read the next question.

QUESTION THREE
CONGRATULATIONS, YOU MADE IT! NOW TO CRANK
THINGS UP A NOTCH.
REMEMBER, PICK AN IMPOSSIBLE ANSWER
AND YOU'RE OUT.
HERE WE GO: WE LOST SEVERAL CONTESTANTS ON THE
ENDURANCE CHALLENGE, BUT WHO DIED LAST?
1. DECKE
2. GLAED
3. MAEVA

I tried to push the images of Glaed and Maeva's bodies out of my mind as I turned back to Luke. 'What do you think?'

'It's Glaed, surely,' Luke said, chewing the inside of his cheek. 'Decke is the impossible answer, because he turned, he didn't strictly die. So it's between Glaed and Maeva, and Glaed wouldn't leave Maeva behind if she wasn't gone already. Door 2.'

'Unless,' I countered, 'Maeva was a goner, but wasn't dead when Glaed left. Reeta said she went down fighting after being bitten on the neck. She knew she was done, so she might have told the others to go while she held them off. And then it's a question of how long she lived after the Pyres piled in.'

I swallowed down the sour taste of bile. Maeva's head had been pulled clean off at some point, and that would have been the end. There wasn't enough time for her to turn either – but as for how long she lasted, whether she was alive after Cinta pushed Glaed? It was impossible to tell.

'Reeta would have known,' I muttered. 'Plus, they have some of the answers. For us it's just a guess.'

We stared at the doors.

'Actually, not just a guess . . . Two guesses,' Luke said slowly.

I shook my head. 'We can't risk going through the wrong door again. We were lucky choosing the safe door last time, and lightning doesn't strike twice.'

'I agree. So we take out the choice. The rules didn't say anything about not splitting up. I'll take Door 3, and you take 2. If you're right, knock hard on the door after it shuts. The hallways from the improbable rooms all loop back via a corridor to the next question, right, like last time? So shout as loud as you can. I'll go for the door where your voice is the loudest. And you do the same if I have the correct room. It's the best chance we have.'

I nodded, his plan sinking in. 'That's too risky. And why are you going through Door 3? I thought you were set on 2?'

Luke smiled. 'I am, and that's why I want you to go through it. I think Glaed is right, but I can't be sure. And I trust you to lead me back. It is risky, but not as risky as putting all our eggs in one basket and going back to a fifty-fifty shot at survival.'

I studied his face. He was right, this was our best chance, even if it made me sick to admit it. 'OK. Let's go.'

We walked hand in hand over to Doors 2 and 3. Then with one last squeeze of our fingers, we nodded and stepped through both doors at the same time.

Darkness. It seemed even darker without Luke there, and I had to steady my breathing. *Don't panic. Brace yourself.* We had a plan, now we needed to see it through. I felt along the wall of the corridor, found the door handle and opened it.

The lights flickered on and I was in another windowless room with a podium and only one – unlabelled – door on the opposite wall.

'Luke?' I called out. When he didn't answer, I went to the podium and tapped the screen.

CONGRATULATIONS, CORRECT ANSWER!
GLAED STAYED WITH MAEVA UNTIL THE VERY END.
THEN REETA AGREED TO COVER HIM WHILE HE WENT
FOR THE ROOF. TURNS OUT THE ROOF WASN'T THE BEST
NEXT MOVE – BAD LUCK, GLAED!

DECKE WAS THE IMPOSSIBLE ANSWER, AS HE TURNED
PYRE BEFORE THE GAME BEGAN.
AND THAT'S IT, WELL DONE! PLEASE MOVE THROUGH
THE NEXT DOOR TO EXIT THE CUNNING CHALLENGE!

I made it.

And that meant Luke hadn't.

'Luke!' I shouted at the top of my lungs, and ran back to the door I had come through, the one that Luke would eventually get to if he chose the right path and followed the corridor. I banged as hard as I could until my palms were numb.

'Luke! Can you hear me? Follow my voice. Luke!'

I screamed until my throat felt like razor blades, panic swarming my vision and seizing my heart. The corridor was long. We hasn't been able to hear any Pyres screeching when we were answering questions, and there must be some in here. Without Luke, I'd be sent to the Pyre pit regardless, but that wasn't the point. I couldn't live with myself anyway if Luke had sacrificed himself for me.

Somewhere outside myself, my screaming, I heard something. I pushed my ear to the door, listening for any sign that Luke was still alive, that he was OK, that he had heard me and picked the right door and he would be in the room any minute.

I closed my eyes and all I heard was screaming.

CHAPTER TWENTY-FOUR

I felt like my heart had stopped beating, like my whole body had simply given up, as I leaned against the door in the silence that followed the screams.

Then I heard *him*.

'Astrid?' It was Luke, muffled through the door but very much alive.

I powered back to life, slamming on the door with both fists. 'Luke, over here! Luke, can you hear me? Please hear me, Luke, please hear me!' I shouted.

I stamped my feet too, trying to make as much noise as possible, only pausing briefly to put my ear to the door.

I could hear quick footsteps. Instinctively I moved back, and Luke burst into the room, panting, running so fast he tripped and fell to his knees as the door slammed shut behind him.

'What happened? Are you OK?' I asked, kneeling down and grasping his head between my hands. 'Look at me, you're safe now. Look at me.'

Luke's eyes were wild, flashing around the room like I wasn't there, but once I started talking, he met my eyes and his breathing began to slow. It was easy to forget with everything going on, and how many days it had been since we'd washed, and how wild and dirty our surroundings were, how beautiful he was. Long lashes framing deep-brown eyes with flecks of gold. Olive skin with a smattering of freckles across his nose. The rough feeling of early stubble under my palms, highlighting his sharp jawline.

The thought of almost losing him, of never seeing that face again, had my chest in a vice grip.

'Astrid,' he whispered. 'Sorry, that was . . . that wasn't my favourite moment from this show so far.'

The hysteria of the moment made me laugh. 'You have favourite moments from this shitshow?'

He grinned.

I leaned in and kissed him on the lips, just for a second, then remembered where we were and pulled back. We did it. Holy shit, we made it. The rush of my panic melting into pure joy that Luke was still alive had made me dizzy, and from the flush of his cheeks he clearly felt the same. I wasn't even embarrassed about the kiss. This was real.

I stood up and offered him a hand. 'Let's get out of here.'

'Excellent idea,' Luke said, taking my hand. We were still holding hands as we opened the door, and this time there wasn't a dark corridor beyond but the bright sunshine of the forest.

'We made it,' Luke breathed. The door slammed shut behind us and he scooped me up and spun me round, making me gasp. After one rotation he placed me back on the ground. 'Sorry. Erm, you know, excited to be alive.'

'Got it,' I said, breathless from spinning.

We hadn't even had a chance to see who was waiting for us to exit. I gathered myself and turned round. The camera crew were there, plus a few guards with guns, just in case. Then there was Cresta, who was standing with Cinta, Reeta, Cass and Jupiter.

They'd set up a widescreen TV on a tripod, huge enough that it could fit a dozen or so tiny squares across its surface. Each square was a bird's-eye view of one of the rooms, showing the podiums and the choice of doors, and they even had cameras that could capture grainy footage of the pitch-black rooms. I took a step towards the screen as the others watched us, and unease crept up my spine.

Why were they all staring at us? I could see that we weren't the last out. Mills and Herrod were clearly visible in one of the question rooms. In one of the night-vision rooms I could see a mass of Pyres, all reaching up into the darkness, banging against each other from being shoved together. They were sunk down into the floor, in some sort of pit, so anyone walking through the door would fall straight in.

Instant death, the podium had said.

I broke my gaze away from the screen and met Cass's eye. Everyone was still staring at us and Cass shook her head as I looked at her, a single tear shaking free from her lashes.

'What is it?' I signed. She didn't answer. Cinta rocked back on her heels, a barely hidden smile playing around her lips.

Cresta stepped forward and gestured at a camera to come closer. Held a hand to her chest.

'Oh, Astrid. You were my favourite, you know, so no one is sadder about this than me. But I'm afraid you and Luke are disqualified.'

'What?' I stuttered. It was like the ground had fallen out from under me and I was floating outside of my body.

'Why?' Luke asked. 'Is it because we took two different routes? Because nothing in the rules stated we had to answer together—'

'It's not that,' Cinta interrupted in a sing-song voice.

'Cinta, please,' Cresta said, clearly annoyed her big moment was being stolen. 'Let's review the footage, shall we? We were watching it live as it happened, after all.'

Cresta tapped the screen and one of the individual squares got bigger, zooming in. It showed me and Luke in the last question room, where we'd split up. I disappeared through one door and Luke the other, and then the camera angle switched to Luke.

The tiny Luke on-screen stepped out into a dark corridor and then into an unlit room at the end. There was something moving in the corner. Then the screen flashed white – the lights coming on – and readjusted to show what Luke was faced with.

It was a single Pyre, curled up in one corner, its arms wrapped round its knees like it was afraid. Luke bent down and his mouth was moving on the footage but no noise came out. It didn't matter what he'd said. The Pyre stood up, paused for half a second, then ran at him. My pulse raced despite me knowing that he was fine, that Luke made it, that he defeats this monster and comes out the other side. I flashed the real Luke beside me a look, but his face was stony, staring at the screen.

TV Luke was grappling with the Pyre now, but with the sound off they could have been dancing. He held it at arm's length, his hands on its shoulders as they spun round and round, the Pyre chomping its teeth with anticipation. After a few moments of that, Luke spotted his chance and pushed forward, ramming the Pyre's head as hard as he could into the wall opposite. It dropped to the ground, startled, leaving a trail of black, gummy blood behind as it slid down the white-painted walls.

Luke took his chance and ran to the doors, putting his ear against one, then the other, clearly listening for my shouts. He had a few precious seconds before the Pyre was back on its feet, dazed but still very much out for blood, and it came at him again. Luke looked over his shoulder and ran to a door. That must be where he could hear me the loudest. He threw it open and pushed through.

But he was a beat too late.

The Pyre caught hold of his T-shirt, pulling him backwards and knocking him off balance. He landed back in the room, winded, the Pyre above him. It made a play for his neck and he rolled out of the way just in time, letting it smash its face into the floor, smearing more black blood on to the polished concrete. He army-crawled towards the door he had chosen, jumped to his feet and pushed it open again. The Pyre, still floored, made one last lunge for him as he disappeared. It caught his ankle, snapping with its teeth, before Luke kicked out and hit it in the face.

The door closed behind him.

'What's the issue?' I said, scanning the screen. 'He made it; what's the issue?'

Luke said nothing.

'I'll zoom and enhance for you . . . There,' Cresta said, tapping the screen.

The image rewound and enlarged, zooming in on Luke's ankle, on the Pyre's teeth as it lunged for him. A crushing weight slammed into my ribs. The Pyre sank its teeth into Luke's leg and drew a single drop of blood.

'Show me,' I whispered, turning to Luke, my arms dropping like dead weights at my sides.

Luke squeezed his eyes shut, took a breath and pulled up the leg of his trousers to reveal one tiny red scrape.

'No,' I said, louder this time. I dropped to my knees and rubbed at the injured skin on Luke's leg, trying to wipe the blood away. At first it worked, and a tiny blossom of hope dared to open in my chest.

Then more blood rushed to the surface. It was a bite. Luke had been bitten.

'I'm sorry,' he said, his voice cracking. 'I thought it missed me. I'm sorry.'

'No,' I repeated, the only word that I could say. I stood up and turned to Cresta. 'No, no, no.'

'Yes, yes, yes,' Cinta said with a smirk on her face that I was desperate to slap off.

'I'm sorry, Astrid and Luke,' Cresta said, shrugging her shoulders in an overly dramatic fashion. 'But it's the end of the game for both of you.'

There was movement from behind me but I didn't have

time to react. A hood was shoved over my head and I screamed, reaching out for Luke, struggling as strong arms lifted me off my feet.

'Astrid? It'll be all right, Astrid!' I heard Luke shout.

Then there was a pinprick in my neck and everything went black.

I woke up on a cold stone floor, the roof of my mouth tasting like sawdust.

At least the sack was off, so I could see again. I pushed myself up, wincing as my aching muscles tried to fight me. There was a low light and I blinked, my eyes adjusting, and scoped out the room. I was in a small cell, with bars on the windows and stark concrete walls. There was a single thin mattress in the corner. On the floor were two plastic trays piled up with sandwiches and pieces of fruit. And on the opposite side of the room, his head resting on his tucked-up knees, was Luke.

His head whipped round at the sound of me stirring and he crawled over. 'Astrid, are you all right?'

'I think so?' I said, my head fuzzy. *What are we doing here?*

I blinked as it hit me. The video, Cresta's fake sad eyes. Luke. The teeth of the Pyre. His ankle. I looked at it now, like maybe the sight would confirm it was all a dream, but I could see a streak of red on his leg. It wasn't a dream, but a nightmare.

'Luke, what are we going to do?' I whispered, meeting his eyes with my own. 'They're going to throw us to the Pyres. I'm amazed they haven't already.'

'It's the grand finale, remember?' Luke said. 'I expect they're waiting until the opening of the show, kill us live on air. Maximum viewing figures.'

I glanced around the cell and let out a hollow laugh. 'And look at that, we're finally alone. No cameras.'

'Yeah, I spotted that,' Luke said. He took my hand in his. 'Listen, I have to tell you something. This is the first time we haven't had the cameras so I can say it. I think I have a way out of this.'

I pressed my lips together, holding back tears. 'Luke, there is no way out. If there was, one of the others would have taken it. And even if I can go by some miracle, I can't just let you . . .' What was I going to end that sentence on? Change? Die? Turn into a monster?

Luke lifted my hand and put it on his chest. 'Nothing is going to happen to me,' he said.

I felt his heart beating underneath his shirt, the warmth of his skin, and it made everything more painful than I thought was even possible. 'Luke, you know how it works. You saw Decke, you must have seen the turn happen before, on Bloodwatch. Esmond said on average it took what, six hours for the change? You're on borrowed time.'

A single tear slid down my face.

Luke wiped it away and smiled. 'Astrid, listen to me. Do I look sick?'

I scanned his face. His skin was still a deep-olive tone; his eyes looked bright. There was no sweat on his brow. He did look impossibly well.

'I don't understand,' I said.

Luke lowered my hand and stood up. 'I'm going to

show you this, and you have to promise not to panic. I won't hurt you.'

I frowned, confusion washing away my sadness. Maybe whatever I was injected with was stronger than I thought.

Luke nodded once and proceeded to pull his shirt off, exposing his torso beneath. He was stunning, his perfect skin pulled taut over strong muscles. He spun round, showing me his back. Then he waited.

I stood up, uncertain what he could possibly show me with his shirt off that would either save us or make me panic. He was taller than me, so his shoulders were at my eyeline. I reached out and touched him, my fingers splayed out over his left shoulder blade.

'What am I looking for?' I asked, tracing the freckles on the back of his neck with my fingertips.

'Middle of my back. Left-hand side,' Luke replied.

I stepped backwards, my eyes sliding down his back until I found the spot. There, dug into his side, was a small imperfection in his otherwise even skin tone. I leaned in, resting a finger on the pale, circular outline. It was a scar, small enough that I could cover it with the palm of my hand, bumpy to my touch.

I gasped and stepped back.

'It's a bite mark,' I whispered.

Luke turned and took me by the shoulders. 'It's four years old. Four *years*, Astrid. That's why I was acting shy when Cass wanted to check me over. Me and my family were helping out a refugee raft that washed up on the beach near our house. There was only one survivor, but they weren't a survivor, they were a Pyre. And my dad took it out, but not before we all got bitten. My sister died from her wounds, and Mum and Dad, they turned. I had to take them out, and I was so scared I would turn and be alone forever, and I waited and waited, but it never came.'

It was his turn to cry now.

'And then the mainland police came and I . . . didn't say anything. The sun came up, and I went home, and I just sat there. And days later, the bite started to scab, and I was . . . alive. I was alive. There's more I need to tell you, but the important thing is that I won't turn. So there has to be a way for us to get back into the contest, so we can bring down those Bloodwatch bastards. They can't kill us, Astrid, not after all that.'

'Is that why . . . Is this why you can speak to the Pyres?' I asked. 'I've seen it.' There was so much information I was dizzy with it. Luke on the stairs. Luke bending down in the video. It didn't always work, but the Pyres, he could understand them somehow.

'All I know is what I found out when I came here — I've not been exposed to them since that day four years ago. I needed to come here to discover more about myself, to see if my immunity could help you islanders in some way, but also to take down Bloodwatch. They are responsible for my family's death — without them putting on a show and keeping the island under the control of the Pyres, they would still be alive. I've discovered that I burn a little more in the sun, and I think I'm a little stronger and faster than before. I hadn't met a Pyre until that first challenge, so I didn't know I could understand them, that they could understand me. And I know you must be terrified of me right now. I wouldn't blame you if you were. But this might be our way back into the contest, to buy some time to finish what we started and take Bloodwatch down. Not to mention put off our public execution,' Luke said, his voice hoarse with held-back tears.

The sun cream. The way he caught my water bottle. The ease with which he turned over the granite tombstone in the graveyard. He never said why he hated Bloodwatch but it made sense now. Bloodwatch could have tried to banish the Pyres, and they didn't. Luke was bitten due to their negligence, and his family died because of it. It wasn't just the islanders they were hurting – Bloodwatch didn't care who they hurt as long as they turned a profit, and if Luke had told me at the time under those covers, he's right – I wouldn't have been ready to believe him. When Bloodwatch strikes, we all bleed.

But I wasn't afraid of him. I traced the tear marks on his face with my fingertips, my heart so full it felt like it might explode. And in that moment, I didn't want to think any more. I wanted to take away Luke's pain.

'This is more than just a game to you,' I whispered. 'This is something real, something that could change the world.'

Luke cupped my face in his hands. 'I was never playing a game, Astrid. It was all real to me. And now you know every part of me, I hope it was real for you too.'

And that's when I stood on my tiptoes and kissed him, long and hard.

CHAPTER TWENTY-FIVE

I looped my hands round the back of his neck, pulling him closer, wanting more of his skin on mine.

Luke withdrew. 'Wait,' he breathed, moving his hands from my waist to my wrists, pausing before letting go altogether and backing up. 'We're vulnerable right now. I don't want to take advantage.'

'Advantage of what? The last possible hours we might have left alive?' I asked. 'Luke, I've never felt safe. I've always been vulnerable. I've been orphaned by this island, I've lived every day of my life in fear. The only place I'm safe right now is with you. Can't you see that?'

Luke stared at me, his brow heavy, his eyes dark and brooding. A muscle in his jaw clenched and my gaze followed it down his neck, to his bare chest and back up to his eyes.

He crossed the room in two long strides, cupped my face in his hands, and brought his lips down to mine.

I pulled him closer, the weight and heat of him on my body making fireworks go off in my head. I forgot everything else. The death sentence, the Pyres, Dad and Wynn, the stupid contest, the evil that was Bloodwatch. I let every fibre of my being be filled with Luke's light, his warmth, his smell, his taste. I stepped backwards and he followed me, two magnets that couldn't separate, until I hit the opposite wall. He leaned right into me then, pushing me up against the concrete, and a deep heat spread in the pit of my stomach.

His lips travelled down my neck and I leaned back, exposing more of the skin beneath my chin, gasping as his lips brushed against my jaw. I felt alive, like there was a fire inside me I had never dared to feel before, like I might explode from the sheer pleasure of his touch.

Luke paused, his limbs stiff, and he brought his mouth up to my ear.

'I haven't kissed someone for a long time,' he whispered, his breath in my ear sending shivers down my spine. 'Not since the bite. Sometimes when I get close to people, it's like I can sense every ounce of blood in their veins, like I can smell it. I don't want to lose control.'

'Have you ever bitten anyone?' I asked, my breath ragged. For some reason, I wasn't afraid. Whether it was the fact we might be dead soon anyway, or that it was Luke, I wasn't sure.

Luke lifted his head and looked into my eyes, the tip of his nose brushing mine. 'Never. But that doesn't mean I haven't had the urge to. I've never explored it, but there's something not the same with me, Astrid. Since I was bitten, I'm different. There's a small part of me that feels like a Pyre waiting to burst out.'

'Like a monster, deep inside, that you have to keep locked away in a box?' I asked, brushing his nose with mine. 'I think I've realised that bitten or not, we all have one of those. And someone very smart once told me we are more than the monster inside of us,' I said, quoting his own words back at him.

He pulled back slightly, scanned me with those dark eyes, and then moved in to kiss me again. I kissed him back, pushing my tongue into his mouth, letting his into mine. He moaned softly and the feeling in my stomach exploded upwards, warming my chest and wrapping itself around my heart. I pushed off the wall and Luke followed my lead, letting me walk him backwards towards the bed.

I pulled away from his kiss and sat on the edge of the bed, taking his hands and pulling him down to sit next to me. He obeyed, his eyes never leaving me, his hands warm in mine.

My entire life had been filled with uncertainty. From the moment I lost my family, something inside me died, too. I lost the ability to trust anyone, to let anyone in. Even with Hild, I tried to hide the monster part of myself. I had never quite let her know what I was thinking. And Luke was the one who put the idea of the fake relationship on the table. I couldn't know for sure whether I could trust him, but that was when it hit me: I could never be sure. I couldn't know what people were thinking. Trust was something you had to give and hope it was returned. And looking at Luke, in this room with no cameras, with every secret he had trusted me with – I was ready to trust him with my heart, even if eventually I got hurt. That was the only way I would find a family again. By learning to love and be loved in return.

*

Eventually, we pulled away from each other, nearly satisfied – but knowing we wouldn't go any further on some old mattress in the middle of a TV studio compound. We lay still for a while, watching as the sun painted the sky through the barred window until those colours finally swirled together into night.

We waited for them to come, for the sound of trainers on squeaky plastic floors, for the black shirts to arrive.

'Why aren't they getting it over with?' I whispered, watching the door from my spot on Luke's chest. 'They killed Rhegar and Edric live on the next episode.'

The words were like poison on my tongue. I didn't want to die, not now, and especially not after what Luke and I had shared. I wanted to live, for us both to live. It wasn't fair, and the biting injustice of it all churned inside me.

'It's getting late for the finale,' Luke murmured into my hair, making a shiver run down my spine. 'And they may have knocked us out, but the other contestants haven't had a chance to sleep yet. I think they're going to do it tomorrow. We should get some sleep.'

'There's no way I can sleep knowing that we need to trust Bloodwatch to let us back into the contest, if we show them your bite,' I said, a single tear escaping from the corner of my eye and dropping on to Luke's chest.

'I know,' he whispered, wrapping me tighter in his arms. 'I know.'

I let myself and he simply held me, letting me be, giving me everything I needed without even realising it. And at some point I must have succumbed to the exhaustion of the drugs they injected into us and the lack of sleep, because the next thing I knew Luke was gently shaking me awake.

'What time is it?' I asked, moving my chin up to his shoulder and staring at the barred window. The sky was in twilight again, streaked with watercolour.

'I woke up a few times and it was day. I think you slept for a long time. It's nearly evening,' Luke said. 'We should get up,' he added. 'They'll be here soon.'

I lifted my head from my spot on his chest, kissed him once on the lips and nodded. Despite sleeping for almost a whole day, I was still emotionally worn out. I didn't cry, or shake with fear, or feel much of anything. I went through the motions, lifting myself up on the bed and taking a deep breath.

We got ready quickly and I smoothed my hair back into its bun before sitting back down on the bed. Luke paced, wringing his hands as he walked.

'What are you going to tell them?' I asked eventually, when we were forcing down some of the soggy sandwiches they'd left for us the night before. 'Luke, if they know about you, they might want to experiment on you. You might never see the light of day and they might kill me anyway.'

'I've got to try,' he said. 'This can't be the end. And if they take me, I'll make it a stipulation that they let you go. It's the only way to try and stay in the game and give us more time to work out how to bring down Bloodwatch, Astrid. There are two choices here. One, we stay here and get offed live on TV like the other losing teams. Or two, we stay in the game and try to use those millions of viewers to our advantage. Maybe there's still a way to get through to the mainland with such a huge platform, I don't know. What I do know is that option two keeps us alive and together long enough to find out.'

He was cut off by the clang of the cell door opening. I leaped off the bed and Luke stepped closer to me, his arm snaking around my waist. In the doorway was another nameless black shirt.

'Time to go,' she said nonchalantly, not at all like she was leading us to our death.

We stepped out into the corridor. There were a couple of camera crew out there, lenses zoomed and focused on our faces.

We were being filmed. And I wouldn't put it past Bloodwatch to live-stream this. An idea sparked.

'Luke, say it now,' I said, grabbing his hand. The black shirt raised an eyebrow. 'We're on camera. Tell them now.'

Luke frowned. 'A camera guy isn't going to know how to handle my ... condition. And they won't have any bargaining power. I need to ask to see a producer or something.'

'I can think of someone with more bargaining power than the producers,' I said, eyeing the cameras. 'Or rather, a few million someones.'

Luke's eyes widened as he cottoned on to what I was suggesting. A grin spread across his face.

He stopped walking and turned to the nearest camera.

'Mate, come on. Don't make this harder than it already is,' the black shirt sighed from behind us. I turned and glared at her and she took a step back. Being the Executioner had its perks.

'Hey, mainlanders,' Luke said to the camera. He turned to his side and lifted up his green shirt. 'You want a close-up? Get a load of this.'

He exposed his bite towards the lens. I grinned and folded my arms, looking at the black shirt.

'That bite looks pretty old,' I said to her. She craned her neck to see around me, her face draining of colour as she took it all in. 'And I'm pretty sure that means Luke is immune. Now, *that's* something that could boost your ratings through the roof.'

The black shirt backed up and pulled a walkie-talkie from her waist. 'Get me Nova. Now.'

Minutes later we were sitting in a small office, me and Luke on one side of the desk, and Nova on the other. Funnily enough, there were no cameras in here.

'Long time no see,' Luke said.

I smirked.

Nova rolled her eyes. 'Enough theatrics. Because of that stunt you pulled I had to go to an early commercial break *and* roll the best bits of the series early. I bought you ten minutes. What are you proposing?'

'OK, I'll get straight to the point,' I said, leaning back in my chair with my arms folded. 'Luke is immune so we should be allowed back into the game.'

Nova scoffed. 'Are you kidding? The science guys were on the phone to me the second we took you off the live stream. They want to study your boyfriend here, to see how Bloodwatch can immunise the mainland, and they said they'll be here in a few hours to take him. This is bigger than the game show now.' She leaned back in her chair. 'Besides, we've already signed an exclusive with them to televise the creation of the cure. I've pitched the name BloodStream but we're still in talks with marketing.'

'Televise what? Like a . . . live stream of mainlander scientists performing experiments on Luke?' I asked, the monster in my belly growling with a mix of fear and anger.

Nova shrugged. 'Probably. With science stuff, we'd get someone like Cresta to explain it all to the audience. They're keen to have a cure on the mainland, you know. Not to share with you unfortunate souls, obviously, but we do get the odd Pyre washing up so it's probably only a matter of time before we have our own outbreak. BloodStream might pull in more viewers than *Escape from Blood Island.*'

'And if you control the screens, you control the watchers, right?' Luke said, his voice deadpan.

'Not just a pretty face,' Nova said, pointing her fingers at him like a loaded gun. 'We already almost have a monopoly on the media on the mainland. Once we have total control, the government will fall in line with whatever we need. Never mind dwindling viewing figures — we'll be untouchable. I'll keep my job, you'll be instant celebrities, bish bash bosh.'

'I thought this was about money?' I asked, thinking back to Nova's pathetic plea at the Burgh.

'It is,' Nova said, eyebrow raised. 'And the person with the most money makes the rules. The economy is in freefall, darling. Why do you think we stream Bloodwatch all day – because people are at work? They're at home, glued to their screens. Completely pliable to whatever marketing we send their way. In everything but name, we'll be in charge soon enough. And as long as we keep the people watching this insignificant island, they'll forget about all the trouble around them on the mainland. Troubled people riot. Bored people stay inside with their headphones in, begging for their next entertainment fix.'

I opened my mouth to say something and just gaped at the air like a fish out of water. Nova and Bloodwatch were insane, but there was one thing Nova was right about: people watched the screens. If we were going to change anything, we needed to get out of this office and back on the show, one last time.

'I'm not even touching what you just said,' Luke said, clearly on the same wavelength. He sighed. 'Fine. I'll go willingly. But they have to let Astrid go too.'

I put a hand on his arm, quieting him. 'Wait. Nova, come on. You can't tell me that the viewers aren't desperate to know what's happening right now. This is the finale. What better way to save the Bloodwatch Network? The scientists can't get here until after the show anyway, right? And Luke and I know we can win this thing and get to the end. If anyone can pull this off, it's you.'

I finished and held Nova's gaze. She blinked and pulled out her tablet.

'I can't lie, viewing figures did go up after your steamy little make-out session in the bedroom in the second challenge,' Nova said, referring to the moment Luke whispered in my ear that he wanted to take Bloodwatch down. So it had worked. They hadn't heard us, and they thought we were together. 'You're a meme, did you know that? And you have your own couple's hashtag. #Lustrid. You were even winning the public vote by miles during the challenge in North Point until Cinta pulled that little stunt. She overtook you by two per cent, last-second stuff. It was so close we broadcast the live tally and it doubled the number of votes and revenue we acquired that episode.'

'Really?' I asked. It didn't matter, but I knew that our relationship was real, and maybe, if we were more popular than I'd realised, we could use it to get to the finale, like Luke had hoped all those days ago.

'You surprised? Real or not, the public loves a romance. And then during the quiz task? You had over fifty per cent of the vote. Pity you were disqualified. One of our corporate partners pulled out of the finale ad breaks because you wouldn't be there. We resold the space in minutes, but still. You two were odds-on favourites to win.' Nova shrugged, tapping at her tablet. There was an urgency in the way she flicked her eyes over the screen, taking in whatever information lay there. We had her on the line; now we had to reel her in.

'Come on, Nova. Think how epic our return would be. You can't tell me that bringing us back wouldn't be the twist of the century. Maybe we could even come back and help host next year, after we win this thing. Because we *will* win this thing.'

Nova looked at us over the top of her tablet, eyebrow raised.

'An interesting thought. Cresta will be thrilled,' Nova murmured, and she went back to her tablet.

Gotcha.

'What are you doing?' Luke whispered to me as she worked. 'We're trying to bring down Bloodwatch, not save it.'

'I'm improvising,' I whispered back. 'Buying us time to think of a way to take them down and keep us together. It was your idea to be a couple in this thing, so if we can use that as leverage, we're using it. You can't help me from a testing lab, right?'

Luke smiled and squeezed my hand.

'That's wild. Our hashtag just doubled in mentions online,' Nova muttered, tapping at the screen. 'And according to this, viewing figures are up forty per cent from the beginning of the show. I hate to say it, but you're right. The viewers are eating this up like that Pyre ate you up, kid.' She addressed that last part to Luke.

'So we get to come back?' I pushed, leaning forward.

Nova chewed her lip. She looked at Luke, then back at her screen, then back at Luke.

'This could make or break my career. But the viewers would remember it for decades to come,' Nova mused. She stood up and put both hands on the table, her fingers flexed on the hard surface. 'Fine. If this show doesn't absolutely spank the other ratings red raw, I'm sacked anyway. Let's get you out to the field. And if anyone asks, this was your idea. Got it?'

'Loud and clear,' Luke said.

I chewed the inside of my cheeks, trying not to smile. I knew Nova wouldn't be able to resist a huge ratings boost. It was the first time Bloodwatch had worked for me, instead of against me.

Nova clicked her fingers and two black shirts entered the room. As they escorted us out, Nova said one last thing.

'Hey, love's young dream? You better win. Don't screw this up for me.'

'Yeah, because the only reason we would want to live is so we don't screw up *your* life,' I muttered as we left the room.

The black shirts led us to a floodlit courtyard outside the building where a car was waiting for us. 'Take these two to the Colosseum, and step on it. We've only got ten more minutes until we're back on air.'

Luke and I climbed inside.

'What did she mean, the Colosseum?' Luke asked once the car was rolling.

I shook my head. 'I don't remember there ever being a colosseum on this side of the island. I assume they're filming the finale in the old quarantine zone again. I remembered the castle and North Point, and the crypt made sense, but a colosseum? I don't know.'

I chewed my lip. We'd be there soon enough, mystery solved. My stomach tied itself in knots at the thought of being out there again, fighting the Pyres, watching the others die. The only thing that kept me going was how pissed off Cinta would be at our reappearance. I didn't even know if Mills and Noon made it through the cunning round. We were knocked out before they finished. My heart panged at the thought of Noon being dead. He was an arsehole sometimes, but he was our arsehole.

The car came to a halt and we climbed out. Beyond the usual camera crew, we were in what looked like a wide-open field. The grass had been cut, which was weird, and there were faint painted lines in the dry dirt. It was dark but huge floodlights lit the field.

Stands. There was tiered seating for fans, stretching far off and up into the middle distance, enough to house tens of thousands of people. The floodlights were original, and somehow had been hooked back up to power by Bloodwatch.

'The Colosseum! It was the name of the multi-use sports field here. My dad took me once to see the Goldstone Gladiators play,' I said to Luke, pointing past the floodlights.

Luke nodded slowly. 'Makes sense. It's the finale, right? They don't want us hiding now. They want us well lit and out in the open. They want to see us fight to the death.'

I swallowed. There was a time that I was afraid of the monster inside me, the one that murdered those creeps in my house, that was born the night Wynn and Dad changed forever. The monster that made me punch Nova and had me beheading Pyres without a care in the world. But that monster also meant that I lived. It meant I got revenge for what happened to Dad and Wynn. It had kept me alive all these years, when Pyres threatened to rip the flesh from my bones and drink me dry.

The monster was a part of me. Luke had one too; he felt it ever since his Pyre bite healed. It thirsted for blood, made him stronger, faster. Gave him the will to fight. Yes, there was a time and a place to embrace the darkest part of yourself. And that time was now.

I reached out and took Luke's hand. 'If they want to see us fight, we can show them how to fight. We're going to keep going until this whole thing is burned to the ground. We fight until Bloodwatch is no more. That's how we win.'

Luke grinned and touched his forehead to mine, closed his eyes.

'And what the actual hell,' a familiar voice said, 'are you two doing here?'

'Lovely to see you too, Cinta,' I said, looking up as she approached us from behind a camera.

And I was right. It was worth coming back to see the scowl on her face.

Game on, bitch.

CHAPTER TWENTY-SIX

'What the actual fu—' Cinta started.

'Cinta, darling, you're live in a few seconds. Please do not swear,' Cresta interrupted.

Cinta kicked a nearby stand. 'Fine. I'll put this nicely. They were disqualified last round. Luke's bitten; he's a dead man walking anyway. Is this why the start of the final challenge was delayed? Were you always finding a way to bring them back?'

'You ask a lot of questions,' Cresta muttered, reading through a bunch of flash cards, her eyes a blur as she skimmed the pages. 'OK, I think I'm caught up. Ready to roll?'

Cinta stormed past, and she wasn't the only one less than pleased to see us. Apparently, for the first time we had a full house after the last challenge. Mills leaned against an old advert at the bottom of the bleachers, smoking a cigarette and staring at us. I put my middle finger up at him and he responded by drawing his finger across his neck. Herrod watched Mills, gulped and then shrugged apologetically at me when he thought Mills wasn't watching.

Cass was much more excited to see us. She ran at me with a flying hug, and Jupiter slapped one giant hand down on Luke's shoulder, congratulating us. Noon and Esmond both shook our hands, grinning, full of questions. Luke started to explain, but Cresta nodded to a black shirt and the cameras crowded back around us. There was organised chaos as more black shirts poured on to the playing field, moving us in our pairs on to invisible spots, making sure they had the best possible lighting for the cameras. Cinta quietly fumed, her eyes on me the entire time.

Cresta stepped forward, her sequinned crop top shimmering in the floodlights.

'Hello and welcome back to *Escape from Blood Island*! Apologies for the delay to the live broadcast, but trust me, it's worth the wait. You'll be staying up way past your bedtime when you hear what we have in store for you tonight.'

Cresta turned and gestured at Luke and me, and half a dozen cameras swivelled to focus on us. Luke smiled and waved, his other arm round my shoulder. I smirked at him. He was good.

'Now, don't adjust your television sets. Your eyes don't deceive you – after a spectacular turn of events Luke and Astrid are back in the competition! As we broadcast earlier, Luke does indeed have an older bite on his back that suggests he might be, dare I say it, immune!'

Cresta paused for effect and I shook my head in disbelief. If Luke was immune, he was the hope that everyone on the island was waiting for. This wasn't some sort of game. But then it hit me. The mainland didn't care. Pyres were a problem that we had to contend with, not them. They dealt with it a long time ago by turning our home into a prison. So, in the context of the show, this *was* still a game. A game we had to see through until the bitter end, whatever that looked like.

Hashtag Team Lustrid, after all.

'Now, you know what that means, folks. If Luke here doesn't turn, there's no point disqualifying Astrid. Then again, if this is an elaborate ruse, and they are lying, he'll turn and tear her open. So we thought, what better way to test Luke's "immunity" than to put them through our final round! We set up a ten-minute poll and you guys delivered – seventy-five per cent wanted them back in the game, and we listened. So welcome back, Luke and Astrid!'

Exactly as Nova had said. The viewing public really were powerful. They came flooding to our aid after Luke confessed all to the cameras, probably because curiosity got the better of them.

Meanwhile, I struggled to avoid the surprised looks of the other players. Clearly they hadn't seen the live footage. Because while Cresta didn't appreciate the gravity of what the existence of someone like Luke meant, the other islanders did. Even Cinta dropped her scowl as her eyes widened at the possibilities.

Cresta clapped. 'Incredible scenes, folks! And obviously we have a science team incoming to explore every possible avenue. Let's hope we have a body to hand over, eh, Luke?'

Cresta laughed and the rest of us stared at her in stony silence. She turned back to the camera.

'Wow, tough crowd, but who can blame them? It's been

a wild few days and it's all been leading to this, right here, in this very arena. Shall we chat a little bit about what to expect in tonight's finale, and reintroduce our remaining contestants?'

'I'm up for talking about anything other than Astrid, please,' Cinta called out, a fake smile plastered over her face.

Cass signed at her, swearing, and I smirked.

'Ha-ha, let's begin with the ever-fiery Cinta and her military-reject teammate, Reeta!' Cresta forced a fake laugh and a spotlight landed on Cinta. Her frown melted into a smile in a split second, directly looking down the lens of camera one, all perfect teeth and flawless skin. Bloody hell, Cinta was scarily good at this. As soon as the spotlight faded, she turned and threw me a laser stare.

'And we can't forget the deadly big brother Mills, with his loveable grandad of a teammate, Herrod!' Cresta continued. The spotlight switched to light up Mills and Herrod. Mills flexed his muscles and grimaced at the camera. Herrod looked more than a little worried.

'Next up we have the team that has won the most rounds in this game show, Cass and her gentle giant, Jupiter!' Cresta called, and the spotlight switched again. Cass had her arms crossed and rolled her eyes at the camera. Jupiter half smiled and waved.

'Then we have silver fox Noon, and his nerdy sidekick, Esmond!' The light switched to Noon. He nodded briefly to the camera and I heard Esmond muttering under his breath that he was not nerdy, he was just factual.

'And last but not least, our wild-card couple – the lovely Astrid and Luke!' The spotlight switched to us. I brought my hands up to protect my eyes as Luke managed a wave and a smile. There was a reason I'd struggled to trust him for so long, but after our condensed time together away from the cameras, I could finally recognise the different smile he had here. This one didn't quite reach his eyes.

'Fantastic.' The spotlight faded to the regular stage lighting and Cresta stepped in front of the camera again. 'Now we're all up to speed, let's move on to the finale. Let me explain the rules,' she said, grinning.

I had to hand it to Cresta. She certainly didn't let anything faze her, and nothing was going to stand in the way of her finally kicking off this finale. My stomach clenched in anticipation of what they were going to throw at us this time.

'Cinta and Reeta, you received the most votes during the cunning challenge and collected your golden boxes last night, and therefore were the only team to get a good night's sleep and full bellies. As our viewers saw, Cass, Jupiter, Mills, Herrod, Noon and Esmond all spent the night in our Chamber of Terror, listening to the screams of Pyres that we pumped in via loudspeaker.'

Cresta announced this as if they had spent the evening giving each other manicures. The bags under their eyes said otherwise. And Cinta and Reeta won the cunning challenge – that figured. In contrast to the others, they looked like they had been to the spa.

'But now, everyone starts this final challenge on an even playing field; pardon the pun,' Cresta continued. 'This is where we test the most important, if perhaps the most basic, attribute of anyone on this island: the ability to survive.'

I shifted from one foot to the other, wiping my sweaty palms on my trousers. The last few hours had been like a dream, a weird reprieve from the horror we had been living in. But now I needed to switch back into endurance mode. I needed to let the monster out.

'This is quite possibly the simplest round to explain,' Cresta continued. 'We are standing in what remains of the Colosseum sports arena. As you all know, this part of the island was the first to fall to the Pyres and is therefore the deadliest. We want to see what our contestants can really do. No gimmicks, no head starts and no public vote. You, my viewers, got them this far. Now it's time for the fight of their lives: the last team standing will win an islander one ticket off the island, plus one hundred thousand credits for their mainlander.'

'Or in my case, a one-way trip to become a lab rat,' Luke said under his breath.

'We won't let that happen,' I whispered back, but it was getting harder and harder to believe it. What was our game plan anyway? How were we supposed to finish this, to bring Bloodwatch down once and for all? I'd bluffed my way to this point, but we were quickly reaching the end. We had to come up with something, and fast.

'Over the last few nights, while our contestants were busy with their challenges, we used our technology to collect as many Pyres in the area as possible. They are currently locked in a holding pen at the away end of this very field.'

Cresta gestured to a tunnel at the far end of the playing field. The 'Y' in 'AWAY' had fallen at some point and no one was left to put it back up. If they had been collecting the Pyres for that long, it explained why they weren't as afraid standing in the forest yesterday during the cunning challenge. And if they could control the Pyres so easily, why wouldn't they use that technology for good, to clear the island and help us rebuild? Bloodwatch kept proving that they were pure evil, time and time again.

'There are no rules in this round. Every exit from the stadium is sealed, so our contestants will be trapped here until only one pair remains,' Cresta said.

'One pair remaining? As in we keep going until everyone else is dead, right?' Cinta asked, like she was checking a menu order in a restaurant.

My heart sank. Luke couldn't die, but neither could Noon. Cass. Jupiter. Heck, even Esmond I'd grown fond of. The thought of losing any of them now, when we were so close to being out of this hellscape of a game show, was impossible. If I wasn't so numb from everything that came before, I'd have thrown up. The last team standing. That meant that all the others were dead.

'There can only be one winning team, babe,' Cresta said with a wink.

'Once there is one team remaining, the safe room at the centre of the field will open. The winning team has to make it there and wait for our clean-up crew to release them.'

I looked at the familiar steel box set into the centre of the field, made from the same material as the one in the castle, with a flashing red light next to the sealed door. I could safely assume by *clean-up crew* Cresta meant kill squad – they'd need some ammo to cut down the crowd I could only assume they were about to let rip in here.

Cresta clapped her hands together to grab back our attention. 'All right. Let the finale of *Escape from Blood Island* begin!'

A black shirt called out and the cameramen lowered their lenses. Like we had seen a dozen times before, the crew quickly packed up their stuff and moved out. Just as the last car entered the tunnel, it came to a stop, and for a mad second I genuinely thought they felt sorry for us and were about to invite us back to safety. No such luck. A black shirt got out, slammed the gate closed behind the car, got back into the vehicle and drove off.

The whole time this was happening, all five teams stood in silence, watching as our best hope of survival disappeared and left us to die.

Cinta was the first to break the ice, unsurprisingly. She marched over to me and swiped at my head like she was about to slap me. Luckily I was faster, and managed to jump out of the way so she barely brushed my shoulder.

'Cinta, come on, man, what the hell?' Noon said, stepping out in front of her.

Cinta scoffed. 'Seriously, Noon? You think I'm the one who's out of line here?' She waved her arms around wildly. 'For god's sake, she isn't even supposed to be here. She and her boyfriend are just one more obstacle between me and walking out of here alive.'

'Not to solidify my reputation as a pedant of pedantry, Miss Cinta, but it isn't Astrid's or indeed Luke's fault you're here,' Esmond said. I raised an eyebrow at him. It was the first time I'd heard him speak up in front of the crowd, ever.

'Feeling brave behind Noon's scary arse, are we, nerd?' Cinta spat. In response, Esmond did indeed shrink a little behind Noon's shoulder. 'I hate to remind you of this, but you chose to be here. I didn't. You think what they offered us made this a choice? No way. They said they would cut off my crates, OK? If I hadn't accepted, and Bloodwatch had left me there, I would have starved to death. So excuse me for being a little bit pissed off that I'm now one step further away from walking out of here.'

Cinta glared at me, her chest heaving, and for the first time, in a tiny way, I understood where she was coming from. She was right. The choice I was presented with back when Bloodwatch recruited me wasn't a choice. The public chose us, and as I learned the hard way what the public wanted, Bloodwatch delivered. Bloodwatch had threatened to destroy the Burgh if I didn't take part. Behind all the make-up and bravado, Cinta was as scared and vulnerable as the rest of us.

'Enough playing with each other,' Mills said. He sauntered over to us, Herrod trailing behind him. 'We're standing here yelling and screeching when in just a few minutes the biggest brood any of you ever did see is about to tear out of that tunnel. Keep your bleedin' heads screwed on.'

'Mills is right,' Luke said. 'Why haven't they released them yet?'

'Probably waiting until they're far enough away for it not to be a problem,' I said slowly, looking around the field. In the far distance, barely visible over the top of the bleachers, I could see the ever-present red light of the broadcast tower. 'This is the first time they've done this, and I'm willing to bet they collected a lot of Pyres for their big finale. They want to make sure the Pyres stay here and that they're safely back at their base before they let them out. This place hasn't had any upkeep for eight years or more; who knows how secure it is?'

'The Executioner has a point,' Noon said. 'We've got a few minutes until they roll back to their little compound. We should look for weak points, any spots where we could escape.'

'Escape?' Reeta asked, hands on her hips. 'I want to win, not escape.'

Noon grinned. 'Well, good luck with that, girl. All I heard was "last team standing" and "there are no rules". Whether they thought we might try and break out is a whole other conversation, but I don't see a red line this time. If you wanna stand here and try and reason with hundreds of Pyres, be my guest. I'll be waiting outside the stadium for my crown when you go down first.'

Reeta's face paled.

'Again with the yapping.' Mills pinched the end of his nose. 'Cinta, Reeta, come with us if you want to live. I need someone to help keep this old millstone around my neck alive, and I'd rather it was the four of us duking it out at the end than one of these Chatty bleedin' Cathys. I'm sure the Pyres will appreciate you reasoning with them while they drain every ounce of blood from your bodies.' Mills addressed the last part to me, Noon and Cass. Then he winked at Cass. 'Except for you, sweetheart. At least you won't hear them coming.'

I launched myself at Mills, and Jupiter was the only one fast enough to catch my arm and the only one strong enough to hold me back. 'Leave it, sis. He ain't worth it.'

'See you in hell,' Cinta said, walking over to Mills. The three of them jogged off together, talking in whispers and dragging Herrod alongside, treating him as roughly as an old dog that couldn't keep up.

'I hope they die first. I hope they die first and they leave Mills until last so that he has to watch,' Cass signed, her movements and facial expressions so fast and angry I almost missed what she said.

'What did she say?' Jupiter asked.

'She said we should move before those gates open,' I said, signing at the same time so Cass could follow along.

Cinta, Mills and Reeta had raced off across the field to the far side and were now climbing the bleachers to the top. Herrod was struggling, though.

Not that I cared much about Mills, but Herrod was a decent enough guy to at least feel bad whenever Mills opened his mouth. I hoped that when he went, he went quickly.

'Listen. I think we should head downwards,' I said, gathering the other five members of our team around me. 'Cinta and Mills went upwards. It might give them an advantage initially, but it leaves them nowhere to go. If there's a route into the tunnels beyond the stadium, to the shops and concession stands, there might be a way out they didn't think of.'

'All right. I'm with the Executioner,' Noon said. Luke nodded at me and Cass; Jupiter and Esmond all agreed too. Just before we moved, Esmond caught my arm.

'Not to be a Debbie Downer,' he said, 'but if we all escape, and we're the only three teams left, then what happens?'

All six of us looked at each other. I took in a deep breath. 'Then we find another way out of this,' I said, with as much confidence as I could muster.

But none of us had a chance to think further, because a booming voice filled the air.

'Let the gaaaaaame begin!'

CHAPTER TWENTY-SEVEN

The old gates creaked as they opened. For a few seconds, nothing happened, and a fleeting thought crossed my mind. Maybe there were no Pyres. Maybe it was all a joke, and we would all win, and Cresta would be back any minute in her sparkly crop top and we would pop champagne and eat cake. Maybe Hild and Griff would be there and I could introduce them to Luke. Maybe we would all leave the island and find a cure for Pyreism, and Bloodwatch would become a charity to help rehabilitate us all into civilisation. Maybe we would rebuild. Maybe I could find Dad and Wynn and cure them and we could all be together.

The first screech echoed down the tunnel and my bubble burst. Who was I kidding. I didn't need cake and champagne right now. I needed the monster inside me, so I used all the mental energy I had left to blow the lid off its box. I was ready to pounce. Ready for anything.

There was no room for fear when you filled every part of your body with something else. The will to live. The first Pyre came sprinting out of the tunnel, running on all fours.

We didn't wait around to see the rest. 'Move, move, move!' I yelled, and all six of us ran across the field and past the safe-room box to the nearest stands.

I reacted the fastest so made it there first. I stopped before descending the staircase to the concourse and turned round to make sure everyone was following me. Luke was right behind me and I practically pushed him down the stairs, making sure he made it in. Shortly behind him was Noon, who followed Luke down without a backward glance, then Cass and Jupiter.

I scanned the field and saw Esmond was running behind. Standing by the staircase gave me precious seconds to assess how bad the situation was. Opening the gate at the away end of the field was like letting a dam burst and watching as Pyres flooded the stadium. Before tonight, the most Pyres I had seen at once had been back in North Point.

This was next level, though. We had been running for less than a minute to reach the stairs to the concourse, and in that time the Pyres hadn't stopped coming. There must have been thousands of them – the only reason they hadn't hit us yet being how huge the field was. We couldn't even see the safe-room box any more. Good luck to whoever tried to get to that.

I remembered watching a game on TV with Dad and there was a pitch invasion when the home team won. This was what the Pyres looked like, fans invading the pitch. But those fans were wearing team shirts and face paint, a riot of colour. Pyres were the absence of colour, what happened when you stripped a human being of everything they ever were. They were naked, hairless, pale bodies that made up a mindless mass. These weren't the same Pyres Noon claimed to have seen looking after the dog, or the same Pyres that Hild had seen collecting their dead. These were too far gone, only living for their next kill.

And they were heading for us.

On the opposite side of the stadium, Mills and Cinta's crew began to climb faster. Mills doubled back a couple of rows to grab Herrod by his shirt and drag him over the seats. Under the floodlights, their red and green shirts were just as visible as ours. The Pyre flood split in two as it ran, half racing up the stands and half heading our way.

'Come on!' I yelled at Esmond, not worrying about staying quiet any more. These Pyres were hungry. The floodlights and our smell alone were enough for them to notice us. I had a fleeting feeling that I should be more afraid. But it was gone as soon as it appeared. Being afraid was what would get us killed. Thinking like monsters was what would get us out of this.

I ran to Esmond and grabbed the back of his green shirt as the first of the Pyres reached the barrier to the field. It leaped the fence on all fours and ran directly at us.

Esmond made the mistake of turning to look and the colour drained from his face, his mouth forming a perfect 'o' of panic.

We ran, my legs straining with the effort of pushing both myself and Esmond towards the staircase. The sound of a dozen wet slapping footsteps, of bare flesh on concrete, kept me going. When we reached the mouth of the tunnel I pushed Esmond down first.

At the bottom were the metal bars of the turnstiles, leading to the concourse. They extended over the whole height and width of the tunnel, like the bars of a prison cell, and Jupiter, Cass, Noon and Luke were on the other side.

Esmond reached the bottom first and I forced him into the narrow turnstile. He struggled for a split second, but then he made it through and it was my turn.

As I rushed into the gap, the first Pyre caught up to me and lunged at my back. Noon thrust a broken umbrella through the gaps in the bars and into the Pyre's eye, catching it mid-air and killing it instantly. I pushed on, moving so quickly that I fell out on to the concrete floor. I rolled on to my back and brought my arm across my face to protect myself from the mass of Pyres inevitably about to rain on me.

Cass and Luke were ready, though. They ran forward holding what looked like an old flagpole, clearly heavy enough that it needed both of them to lift it. They forced the pole through the gaps in the stile bars horizontally. More Pyres had run in after me, and they were caught in the turnstile, so Cass and Luke speared a couple as they pushed.

The turnstile jammed, firmly fixed in place by the pole. The Pyres on the other side hit the bars, their arms stretching through the gaps, desperate to get to us. They screeched and pushed and strained, but it was no use. They couldn't get through. We were safe, for now at least.

'Gotta love a bit of old-fashioned crowd control,' Jupiter said, helping me to my feet.

'Thanks,' I said, dusting off my trousers. Now the adrenaline had worn off, I leaned my hands on my knees, catching my breath. Luke jogged over to me, putting a gentle hand on the small of my back.

'You OK?' he asked, forehead etched with concern.

'Yeah. I'm good. We made it,' I said, my voice ragged.

'The Executioner strikes again,' Noon said, resting his rusty umbrella on his shoulder. 'Looks like you bought us some time, but I'm assuming this isn't the only entrance back here. I remember getting lost in this place at games because they usually go round in a circle at stadiums, right? That's a lot of flagpoles to find to block up all those turnstiles.'

'Pretty sure you're right,' I said to Noon. 'As long as we stay fairly quiet, and Mills and Cinta keep some of the brood busy on their side, we should be OK while we come up with a plan.'

We lowered our voices and stood closer together to discuss next steps, with me interpreting for Cass. The Pyres were screeching loudly enough that it mostly covered our whispers. One good thing about Bloodwatch rounding up the most violent, and longest-turned, Pyres? They didn't have the brainpower to work out how to go around and find us.

Jupiter suggested we check out the food-concession stand behind us for any supplies. 'There might be some things we can use to defend ourselves, knives and stuff. Man, I wish you guys had those gnarly weapons from North Point right about now.'

'Same,' Cass signed, looking down.

'Hang on a minute,' Esmond said, holding up his hands. 'Before we start moving, can we hear what's going on with yourself, Mr Luke?' Esmond's eyes shone with curiosity.

'You don't have to tell them if you don't want to,' I said, putting a hand on Luke's arm.

Luke shook his head. 'It's OK. I've told the world I'm maybe, possibly, immune now. Might as well say how it happened.'

So Luke spent a few precious minutes filling in the others on what he'd told me. I at least persuaded everyone that we should walk and talk, so we loaded up on knives and carving forks from the hot-dog stand nearby while we listened to Luke's story. He told them about the bite, his symptoms, how he could run faster, like he was stronger now. He told them about how he worried he would lose control, but hadn't hurt anyone yet. He even showed Esmond his scar, careful the whole time not to make too much noise.

'I can't believe they let you come back on to some dumb reality show instead of sending you straight to a research facility. No offence,' Esmond said, shaking his head.

'None taken,' Luke said with a half-smile.

'I can't believe it either,' Noon said. 'Bloodwatch only make money while we're all under the control of the Pyres. Sure, I bet the mainland would love a cure for themselves, just in case the Pyres reach their shores. They still don't even know how it started. But even if they do find a cure, they won't give it to us. We're the moneymakers, right, Executioner?'

Noon grinned and punched me on the shoulder. I rolled my eyes, but I had no argument. He was voicing what we all already knew.

'Plus, there's the argument that Pyres are their own species now,' Esmond said.

We all turned to look at him.

'Hey, don't shoot the messenger,' he said, raising his hands in surrender. 'I never much cared for the Influencer stuff but I watched a lot of the nature documentaries Bloodwatch put out in conjunction with the Scientific Research League. They've been studying Pyres as an evolved animal for almost eight years, since after the fall. There are plenty of folks on the mainland who think they should be protected. Maybe even designated a real species and given a proper name.'

'Really?' I asked Luke and Jupiter.

Luke shrugged and Jupiter sighed. 'I mean, he's not wrong. I think it's wild, but there are some people who campaign to, like, save the Pyres and give them their own habitat to thrive in. Like a Pyre zoo or something.'

'A Pyre nature sanctuary,' Esmond corrected. 'A place where they wouldn't be hunted by humans and could be fed on 3D-printed blood.'

Noon burst out laughing. 'Well, now I've heard it all. A bloody Pyre sanctuary. Shame the mainland didn't offer us lowly humans sanctuary, eh, ladies?'

'All right. Enough chit-chatting. What's the plan, Astrid?' Cass signed.

All eyes swivelled to me and I gave them a blank look.

'Let's be real, Executioner. Pretty much everyone here would be dead without you and that big, brave noggin of yours. Where you go, we go. So, where we going?' Noon asked.

I looked at Luke and he smiled at me. For the second time that night, fear crept in again, sending my heart into overdrive, and not because of the Pyres. What was my plan? I had exposed Luke and got us into the finale, but for what? I stared over at the Pyres, still screeching and chomping their overgrown teeth at us through the bars. Beyond them, the night sky was clear, and a million stars dotted the landscape. The brightest star of all was the big red beacon of the Bloodwatch broadcast tower.

Without the viewers, Bloodwatch loses all power.

That was it. *That* was our plan.

'All right, gather round,' I said, motioning for the six of us to cluster together, shoulder to shoulder.

'Hmmm. Cosy,' Noon said.

I elbowed him in the ribs. 'Shut up,' I signed in the middle. 'We can't let the cameras see what we're up to, so we need to sign right here. It's the only way.'

Jupiter, Esmond and Luke would have to catch up later. They didn't move, though, so I had to trust that their faith in me was enough to keep them in position, because I didn't know what Bloodwatch might do if they got a whiff of what we were planning.

'Why is it important they don't see what we're up to?' Cass signed back.

'Because what I'm about to suggest won't win us the contest,' I said. 'It'll bring down Bloodwatch, once and for all. And they can't see it coming or we're all dead.'

CHAPTER TWENTY-EIGHT

'I'm so up for this,' Cass signed back, her facial expressions matching her fingers with enthusiasm.

'I haven't even told you the plan yet,' I signed back, smiling at her.

'If we can beat this shitshow, we have to do it,' Noon signed.

'It's pretty dangerous. And probably stupid,' I signed back.

'Because this entire game show is so safe and smart,' Noon signed, and rolled his eyes.

I smirked. 'All right. We need to look for a way out and I have a destination in mind. We're going straight for the broadcast tower. Pyres in tow.'

Noon nodded. 'We're going to take out the broadcast tower and shut down the whole bloody network. It'll take them years to get it back up, if it doesn't ruin them. That's pretty messed up, Executioner. I love it.'

'I think in the chaos we could try to escape using a raft or something too,' I signed. 'They won't be watching us. The mainland doesn't have the resources to patrol people washing up on shore like they did.'

'And after that?' Cass asked. 'We're basically celebrities, and Luke has a target on his back. Esmond and Jupiter will be accomplices. There won't be a place on the mainland we can go where we won't be recognised.'

'Then we find somewhere we *can* go,' I signed back. 'It won't just be us. Once the tower goes down, everyone on the island will see it. I'm willing to bet there are a few more islanders ready to get out of here and they might take that as the signal. It at least gives them a chance.'

'Astrid's right,' Luke signed crudely. He was at least following some of the conversation.

'Did you get any of that?' I signed, looking at Jupiter and Esmond.

'Cass teaches me. I understand a bit,' Jupiter signed, a little disjointedly but enough for us to understand.

We all looked at Esmond, who had gone beetroot red.

'I suppose this is a good time to tell you all that I did indeed take a number of classes in sign language before leaving the mainland after watching several hours of video of how often it is used here,' Esmond said, his hands fast and practised. 'I hoped by keeping my skill a secret it might aid myself and my teammate in overhearing battle plans and the like. But I guess now isn't the right time for pretending. In short, yes, I both understand and am metaphorically on board with the plan.'

'A simple yes will do next time, nerd,' Noon said, patting Esmond on the head.

We set off to find a way out of the stadium. There were a lot of entrances, but I was aware that the lights were on down here and cameras had been fitted, meaning that Bloodwatch thought we would sneak into the concourse some point – and that meant they would have sealed off any way out too.

We walked in a pack, only spreading out within shouting distance of each other, Jupiter staying with Cass so that they would both hear us if we found something.

'How do you think Cinta and Mills's teams are doing?' Luke whispered to me as we walked.

'Reeta is probably holding her own, but Herrod? I don't know how much Mills will be looking after him. Although they both have to live to win, so who knows. I'm sure it's only a matter of time before Cinta and Mills turn on each other. The way they're playing, there's only one winner, right?' I whispered back.

'That would certainly match their MOs.' Esmond made us jump as he crept between us.

'You always that stealthy, buddy?' Luke whispered, a hand on his chest.

'Apologies, friends. I have been told before that I am unusually light on my feet. Or, as Cinta once told me, creepily silent.'

'Well, don't listen to her. She's a total psychopath,' I said, putting a hand on Esmond's shoulder.

Esmond didn't look offended, though. 'Oh, she is absolutely a psychopath. She hits all the key markers in charm, manipulation and her general lack of guilt or empathy. I do however think that her general psychopathy probably stems from her trauma. Quite apart from living on this island for nearly a decade, she has been alone for the majority of that time, where many of the good islanders seem to have found their own families, so to speak. Even Mills had his brother. I would further hypothesise that Cinta's obsession with her looks has been fed by her reliance on so-called "Influencer" packages. Her fans, in effect, are all she has left, and she clings to them so tightly she's willing to kill for them.'

Both Luke and I blinked at Esmond.

'So are you saying we should forgive her?' I whispered. 'Because I don't think I can do that.'

Esmond actually chuckled. 'Oh god, no. She is, as I said, a psychopath. There are reasons she came to be that way, but there're also reasons that you went through hell and didn't. Monsters always come out.'

I thought about my own monster, the one that had been coming out more and more recently. But surely that was the difference between Cinta and me: I kept mine locked away while she relished releasing hers.

After a few more minutes of walking, we found what we were looking for. A STAFF ONLY sign. We opened the door and found an old loading bay for bringing in food and memorabilia, judging from the scraps we found in boxes nearby. What made it most useful, though, were the loading-bay doors. They were huge, a single one of them the size of a house – more than large enough to release the Pyres from the stadium back out into the night.

Esmond opened his mouth to say something and I shook my head, instead motioning for us to huddle again so that the cameras couldn't see us talking.

'We need to act fast,' I signed once we were stood shoulder to shoulder again. 'Bloodwatch won't like that they can't see what we're saying, and once they cotton on they might try and stop us. I don't even know if they can stop something this huge once it's in motion, but we can't give them the chance. So we need a plan, and we need to execute it ASAP.'

'I agree,' Esmond signed. 'And I think I have an idea.'

With Esmond's plan clearly explained, and making sure Luke stuck with me, and Jupiter stuck with Cass in case there was any confusion, we broke apart. We gave each other one last nod before running for our starting positions. This would be a team effort, and if everything went to plan we'd all make it out. This might be the last time I saw Cass or Noon. I'd even grown fond of Jupiter and Esmond in the end. We were a team.

Luke and I walked back through the staff doors leaving the others to their own jobs. The turnstile for this side of the stadium was opposite the staff entrance, so Luke and I crossed the corridor and pushed through. I moved the turnstile a fraction anticlockwise and winced as it let out a shallow whine. Carefully, I inched my way round, and then waited for Luke to do the same. I watched the entrance to the tunnel the whole time, waiting for a brood to come crashing down on us, but they didn't. And then Luke was through.

We crept up the stairs, ears straining for nearby footsteps – human or Pyre. We were on the side of the stadium Mills and Cinta had gone, so there were more than just Pyres out there trying to kill us. Every muscle in my body was tense with wanting to run back down the steps and through the turnstile to relative safety. But the others were counting on us, and we had to be fast. So I poked my head out of the tunnel entrance.

Pyres completely covered the field, so many of them that it was hard to tell where one of them ended and the next began. Unlike with the square, where they ended up crushed together, there was a bit more room for them to move here, despite there being easily upwards of a thousand of them. On the far side of the field, near the bottom of the bleachers, a clog of Pyres were pushed against the tunnel we had run down earlier. From this angle, it almost looked like a waterfall pouring out.

If waterfalls were made of corpses, that is.

Luke checked either side of the concrete entrance, over and above the tunnel we came out of. 'Can't see any Pyres up here. Where are Cinta and Mills?'

'Not sure,' I said, a small moth of anxiety fluttering in my chest. Just because we couldn't see them didn't mean they couldn't see us. This was their territory. If they were still alive it was because they had found a bloody good hiding place. 'Come on. Let's get this done before we have to say hello.'

We stepped out from the tunnel. It was risky, being this exposed, but as long as we were quiet until the time came, we should be OK. We had scoped out most of the concourse and Cinta and Mills definitely weren't there.

Where did they go?

I shook my head. Focus. I had to find something that would make a loud noise, and then be ready to run. On the steps in front of me one of the handrails was leaning at an angle. I pulled at it and it moved, but didn't come free like I hoped.

'Luke, help me get this. We can use it to bang against the concrete, get the Pyres' attention,' I whispered. We needed something loud to grab the attention of the brood, but that didn't mean I wanted to risk attracting them too early. When Luke didn't reply, I gave up on the pipe and turned round. 'Luke?'

Then everything stopped. Luke was by the tunnel entrance, and Mills was standing behind him, his arm across Luke's throat.

Mills grinned at me over Luke's shoulder. 'Well, well, well. I guess now we get to find out who's really the Executioner, hmm?'

'Mills, you don't have to do this,' I said, trying to buy time. My eyes darted to the old commentator's box behind him. It was high up, right at the top of the stands. There was a door to one side, and the glass was mirrored. Probably to stop the fans from looking in and distracting the commentators, but it would work today for confusing a brood of Pyres chasing after you. Smart.

I heard a high-pitched laugh that set my teeth on edge. Cinta stepped out from behind Mills, flanked by Reeta and Herrod. Reeta had one hand on her hip and a mean smile playing around her lips. Herrod looked like he would rather be anywhere else than here and shrugged apologetically.

'You don't really believe that we shouldn't kill you and your boyfriend, do you?' Cinta asked, laughing again as she spoke. 'This whole stupid finale has become a game of hide-and-seek. If the Pyres can't get the job done, we'll do it for them.'

Luke squirmed under Mills's arm, his face turning a deep shade of puce. He couldn't breathe. Mills was going to strangle him to death, and then they would all come for me. We couldn't take Bloodwatch down; what were we thinking? And with every second that passed, I was getting Cass, Noon and their partners into more trouble. Bloodwatch were always watching, and they always won. We were simply their puppets.

No. The monster inside me stirred. I couldn't give in to panic now. If I was going to die, I at least had to go down swinging.

What was it that Cinta said?

If the Pyres can't get the job done, we'll do it for them.

I opened my eyes and smiled at Cinta. 'I dunno. I think the Pyres still have a shot at killing us,' I said.

Cinta raised an eyebrow, confusion shadowing her face.

I turned to face the field and drew in a deep breath. There was more than one way to make a noise; I just had to hope I was loud enough.

I opened my mouth and screamed at the top of my lungs. I put everything I had into it: all the panic and anger and grief and fear and even hope that I had stuffed away inside me and let rip. I screamed until there was nothing left.

It was only a few seconds but, looking at the playing field, I could see that it had worked. The Pyres nearest to us spun and rose to attention like a group of meerkats. They started to run, climbing over each other to get to us, and the sudden movement alerted more of them. Within moments there was a stampede, hundreds of them turning to run at us, wave after wave of faces rushing in our direction as more and more sought out the source of my screaming.

'Oh shit, she's nuts!' Mills screamed.

He backed up, and in his panic loosened his grip on

Luke. Luke ducked under his meaty arm, dashed towards me and hauled me towards the tunnel and back under the stands where we came from.

I let him lead me, my legs moving faster than my brain could keep up with. Mills and Cinta ran up towards the commentary box, Reeta and Herrod close behind them. And then Herrod tripped and fell, and sprawled across the steps above us. Cinta tapped Mills on the shoulder, pointing to Herrod, and Mills swore before doubling back for him. And then we were inside the tunnel, them above us, and I couldn't see any more.

Had Herrod escaped? Some of the faster Pyres might go straight for him instead of chasing us down the tunnel. We wanted a Pyre brood down here, but nothing we couldn't handle. The turnstile would help us direct the flow and push enough down into the concourse for the plan to work. That said, we could do without a fist fight.

I didn't dare look back, tripping over my own feet as we raced for the turnstile. Luke got there first and pushed me through. Everything was moving too fast for me to protest, and he was right behind me anyway, pushing through the bars and falling through the stile so close to me that our bodies were pressed together in the rotating door for a split second before we were spat out into the empty corridor beyond.

'Oh god. They got the old man and now they're coming for me, wait, shit, please!'

Luke and I spun round at the sound of Mills's voice. Herrod was gone. It was a long shot that he got away, but the realisation still stabbed at my heart. And then there was Mills himself. It was unbelievable, but there he was, running towards the turnstile, a Pyre biting into his neck. For a second I imagined the Pyre as a child and Mills as a dad, giving his son a piggyback ride down to the concourse to buy a hot dog to share. But the screams coming from Mills were enough to shatter that fantasy.

Mills slammed into the gate and tried to push through, but the Pyre on his back got caught in the bars above. The Pyre pulled its head back as it hit the bars, tearing a chunk from Mills's neck as it went. Mills reached through the bars, his eyes wide with fear, blood pouring down his shirt. Even I could smell it, the sticky, metallic scent of Mills's life draining out of him.

And apparently, we weren't the only ones. Mills's wound had sent the Pyres that came chasing after him into a frenzy, forcing them up to the stile, crushing Mills against the bars. I watched, frozen.

And for a second, it seemed like the Pyres were stuck. Then the rusty metal of the stile began to creak. The bars spun round, moving fast under the weight of the bodies that began to pour into the corridor.

CHAPTER TWENTY-NINE

I raced towards the STAFF ONLY door, Luke right behind me. The noise of the Pyres piling through the stile was deafening, their shrieks echoing down the massive corridor. It was like they were everywhere, and I didn't need to turn round to know they were right behind us, enough of them to crush us underfoot before they even had a chance to suck us dry.

We bashed through the staff door with a bang and kept running. I could see up ahead that Noon and Esmond had found a way to force the entrance mechanism open, just as Esmond said he would, and the nearest of the massive loading bay doors had lifted, leaving a gaping hole in the wall. I strained my eyes as I scanned the car park beyond, hoping that Cass and Jupiter had managed to do their bit.

'Shit, look out!' Luke called. I risked a look over my shoulder and watched as so many Pyres burst into the loading bay that the staff door flew off its hinges. The force with which they were pushing through was enough that some of them were sent sprawling across the concrete floor, disoriented for a few seconds.

Then one of them looked up and locked their cold, dead eyes on me.

'Go, go, go!' I screamed. Luke and I ran to the open door and dropped down to swing our legs over the edge that led to the car park. It was a bit of a jump but I threw myself down and hurt my heel as I jarred my foot on the tarmac. I was soon sprinting again, no time for pain, the adrenaline working its magic as a painkiller.

I kept running, Luke beside me, scanning left and right for any sign of Noon, Esmond, Cass or Jupiter.

'Did they leave without us?' Luke panted beside me. Behind us, the Pyres had found their way to the exit, jumping down on to the hard ground to pursue their prey. Us.

'They wouldn't do that,' I said. Cass and Noon were islanders. They had our backs.

We were fast approaching the chain-link fence around the stadium and car park. There were gates open somewhere, that must have been how Bloodwatch got in, but they could be on the other side of the stadium for all we knew. Luke and I weren't jogging, we were sprinting, trying to keep a few precious steps ahead of the Pyres. My legs were already aching with the sharp pain of lactic acid building up in my joints. We'd never make it.

We reached the fence and slammed against it, futile, useless. Luke's eyes widened as he looked at me. Maybe he would survive this, maybe he could communicate with these Pyres and persuade them not to rip him limb from limb.

I wouldn't be so lucky.

I turned and looked at the mass of teeth and limbs and death running towards me. Luke reached out and grabbed my hand. I held my breath.

And then there was a car, a four-by-four truck cutting across the scene in front of me, knocking the Pyres out of the way, their bodies flying through the air like rag dolls.

The passenger door flew open and Jupiter peeped his head out. 'Get in if you wanna live!' he yelled, and we jumped in.

The truck was a six-seater, so we threw ourselves across Jupiter's lap and into the seats in the boot of the car. Jupiter slammed the door shut as the first of the Pyres made their way round, slamming themselves into the car window.

'Drive!' Noon yelled.

Esmond threw the gear stick into place and put his foot down. There were Pyres on all sides of the car banging on the windows, but as we picked up speed they almost all fell away. There was one hanging on to the right-side handle of the car, smashing its head over and over into the window, smearing it with blood.

'Esmond, bank left into the fence,' I said.

Esmond glanced in the rear-view mirror, saw what I was talking about and turned left. The Pyre hit the fence and came flying off, bouncing on the tarmac behind the car as we drove away.

'That was way too close,' Cass signed.

'I agree, but we need to lead the brood to the tower. If we don't get enough of them, they'll scatter and we've lost our chance of bringing Bloodwatch down,' I said.

It was weird, being somewhere with no cameras, being able to speak freely. But there were hundreds of abandoned cars in the car park; they couldn't bug every single one. They weren't expecting us to break out, after all.

'How much petrol do we have?' I asked Esmond.

He checked the dashboard. 'Half a tank. More than enough to get to Bloodwatch HQ, even with the potency dropping over time,' he replied, nodding to the tower that stood alone against the night sky through the windscreen. 'I suspect the petrol itself has been sitting there for the last eight years.'

'Watch it. We can't waste a drop,' Noon said, and I nodded. 'We have to circle round, get the Pyre brood rounded up like the good little sheep herd they are and get them heading for the broadcast tower. Oh, and maybe pray that we don't run out of gas. Where's that Godric guy when you need him, eh?'

'Probably still out in the square. Or in that sick building that they made us answer quiz questions in,' Jupiter said, his face downcast.

'Jupiter is right. They are the true monsters here. Bloodwatch have to go,' Cass signed, lip-reading what Jupiter had said.

'Agreed,' I said. 'So, Esmond, you need to drive back round and slow down just enough so the Pyres follow you, but don't catch up to us. Think you can handle that?'

'My ballet teacher at school always said I had very strong toes – if you need me light on the gas and heavy on the clutch, I'm your man,' he replied.

'OK, then,' I said, exchanging a look with Noon. 'Did anyone see an exit? I don't fancy our chances ramming down the fence if we have a brood close behind.'

'There,' Luke said, pointing out of the filthy window on his side of the car. It was hard to see through the grime but I spotted it, a gap in the chain-link fence that was even helpfully labelled EXIT.

'OK, let's do this. Esmond, you circle round until you've collected up as many Pyres as you can. Then lead them slowly enough towards the gate, and drive straight for the tower. And everyone else, be prepared to run. Even if this hunk of junk gets us all the way to the door of Bloodwatch HQ, you remember how high those walls are. They have snipers and everything up there. We don't want to be around when the Pyres arrive and the fun begins.'

'No, we do not,' Luke muttered, staring out of the dirty window.

I reached across and squeezed his hand. 'We've got this.'

Esmond circled round until we could see the brood once more, all still milling around by the loading-bay area.

As soon as they spotted the car, the ones closest ran straight for us, which alerted those behind, until they were all running, pale wave after wave of bodies coming our way.

My heart pounded at the sight of them despite the safety of the car. The truck hadn't been moved in years. It could conk out at any moment, the only thing separating us from the thousands of Pyres outside being a thin layer of metal and some very breakable glass. The window on Jupiter's side had even cracked already.

We could not fail. Not now, not after coming this far. This was going to work. It had to.

The first of the Pyres rammed into the front of the car,

its arms outstretched over the bonnet like it was giving the truck a bizarre hug.

'Esmond, turn round,' I said, my voice strained with panic. 'We need them close, but not that close.'

Esmond nodded and pulled the gear stick back into reverse, spinning the car with a squeal of the tyres and launching us back in the opposite direction. The noise was enough to attract more of the brood, and through the back window I could see we had quite the crowd following us. Esmond slowed letting some of the Pyres catch us up a little before moving again. Eventually he got into a smooth rhythm, maintaining just the right speed to keep the brood interested.

After a few minutes of playing cat and mouse, we reached the exit. The road ahead stretched into the forest, with the tower easily visible beyond, the red light blinking above the trees in the night.

Our way was lit only by the headlights. The gentle groans of the Pyres behind told us they were still following.

'You think there will be a big fight?' Cass mused, tapping me on the shoulder before signing. 'Bloodwatch. They'll know we're coming by now and they'll be shitting themselves.'

'Probably,' I reasoned, and Cass's eyes widened. 'But we won't be there. Let the Pyres get distracted by their loud noises and bright lights. We'll slip into the woods and head for the beach. Well, you will.'

'Where will you go?' Cass signed, and Luke raised an eyebrow.

It was the moment I had been dreading, because there was something incredibly tempting about sneaking to the beach and sailing off into the sunrise. But I couldn't leave Hild and Griff or even Judith behind. If I could reach the Burgh, maybe some people could get the word out, warn other settlements, send them to the beaches if that's what they wanted. I couldn't just leave.

'I have to go back to the Burgh,' I signed and spoke at the same time so Esmond could keep his eyes on the road. My heart was heavy, but I pushed the words out anyway. 'I have friends there. They need to know what's going on, give them a chance to leave too.'

'And I go where Astrid goes,' Luke signed.

His signing was getting better too, and my heavy heart lightened at his words. I leaned forward, the sudden urge to kiss him overwhelming.

'Hey, we will see the sun rise,' Esmond said, looking in the rear-view mirror. 'Did I say it right? That's the island's version of good luck, correct? I've watched enough of Bloodwatch to pick that up.'

'Yeah, spot on,' I said, smiling. 'We will see the sun rise.'

As if the universe was listening and had got sick of our crowing, the car stuttered and I lurched forward.

'The petrol on the island isn't as potent after sitting for years in corroding fuel tanks, but might it start to shut the car down?' Esmond asked. He was gripping the wheel so tightly his knuckles were white.

'Oh shit,' Noon said in reply. 'Get ready to run.'

I craned my neck to look out of the front window. It was too soon. The tower was still a good couple of hundred metres away. In a forest this dense, the Pyres would probably scatter and never find Bloodwatch at all.

'All right, new plan,' I said, picking a piece of broken glass off the floor of the car and pressing the sharpest part into my palm. A pinprick of blood appeared.

'What are you doing?' Luke asked, his face pale, pinching his nose.

'Sorry,' I signed at him, and then turned to tell everyone what I was thinking. 'I'm going to lead the Pyres towards Bloodwatch on foot. Last minute, I'll smear some blood on the gate and run into the woods and climb the highest tree I can, hoping that none of them spot me, and wait there until they invade the base.'

'That's suicide,' Luke said, his voice hoarse with the effort of looking at my face, not my bloodied hand. 'I can't let you do that.'

'I'm not asking permission,' I said, my voice gentle. 'We can't fail now. Our only hope of Bloodwatch not hunting us down is making sure there isn't any Bloodwatch left to chase us.'

'Now, that I agree with,' Luke said. He took a deep, heavy breath. 'That's why I have a better idea. I can talk to the Pyres, tell them where to go. They won't attack me if I let them in.'

'Let them in?' Cass asked.

'The Pyres, they don't talk . . . like we do,' Luke said, his eyes wide. 'It's hard to explain, but it's sort of like a voice in your mind. And if I open my mind to them, they can understand me, and I can understand them. It's just a bit . . . draining. When I do it, I don't let in their voice.

I feel everything – their thirst, their obsession with blood, their sadness, their loss. It can be overwhelming, so I can't do it much, but it will work.'

'We can't let you try that, if it's that bad,' I said.

'I wasn't asking permission,' Luke said with a half-smile, parroting my words back at me. 'Trust me, Astrid. I can do this. I won't lose myself.'

'No, you won't,' I said, gripping his shoulders. 'Because I'm coming with you. This is what you did before, right? When that Pyre was going to attack me in North Point and then suddenly stopped? You can do it again. We stay together and I pull you out of it if you fall too far into the darkness. Deal?' My voice was even, but my pulse wasn't. The only thing more terrifying now than facing down a brood of thirsty Pyres was losing Luke.

'Wait,' Esmond said. The car lurched again and I assumed that was what he was panicking about, but it wasn't. He was fiddling with the dial on the car radio. 'I didn't realise this thing was on because no one is broadcasting, but I think I can hear something . . . there.'

He let go of the dial and a static-riddled voice came out.

'ASTRID. WE HAVE YOUR SISTER AND YOUR FATHER. GIVE YOURSELF AND LUKE UP. THIS WILL BE YOUR ONLY WARNING.'

And then the car finally sputtered to a stop and died.

CHAPTER THIRTY

Run.

That was the only word that came to mind. The word that had overshadowed our entire time on the island, on this game show, our whole lives. Always on the run from something. And tonight it was from the biggest Pyre brood any of us had ever seen.

Luke clicked the passenger door open and pulled me out behind him. Cass, Jupiter, Noon and Esmond all jumped up from their seats, scrambling from the car. And all the time, the words on the radio echoed in my head.

We have your sister and your father. Give yourself and Luke up.

I wasn't self-absorbed enough to think it was me they wanted. They needed Luke, and they knew they could use me to get to him.

I straightened up once we were out of the car. We had maybe a thirty-second head start on the Pyres behind us, but Esmond had been following my instructions perfectly. The car was never too far ahead of the brood, and that meant less time to get away now.

Bloodwatch wanted me to give myself up? Fine. I'd walk in through the front gates. I'd just have a few friends with me too.

I took a deep breath and fought every instinct to stop as I pushed the jagged edge of the glass into my palm. The pain made me gasp, but it had the desired effect. Blood dripped down my fingers like melted ice cream down a cone on a summer's day. Noon and Esmond disappeared into the trees on one side of the road, and Cass and Jupiter sank into the bushes on the other. Luke stood by my side, bracing himself against the smell of my blood. I hoped with every fibre of my being that the others would get away, that they would be safe.

Several pale faces turned in my direction, their noses twitching in the night air.

'Come at me!' I screamed, waving my hand over my head. Warm splatters hit my forehead. The car headlights were still on, the path ahead illuminated. The road was as straight as an arrow, and in the distance I could make out the high arch of a reinforced gate.

'OK, that's close enough,' Luke said, yanking my uninjured hand and dragging me away from the car just as the first Pyre reached it.

I ran, a new strength in my legs forcing them forward, a straight foot race to our goal. The sound of the car alarm setting off and the smashing of glass told me that the Pyres had reached the car and the blood on my injured hand was turning sticky.

I took my eyes off the road and looked up, saw the gate up ahead, the soft glow of the lights beyond the tall walls. There was also a silhouette of a person either side of the gate, up high, with the long noses of guns in their hands.

'Open the gate!' someone beyond the wall shouted, and the guards lowered their weapons.

Luke had hold of me, pulling me into his side. They couldn't risk aiming for me when they might hit him, and I knew they didn't want me to surrender myself so they could throw me a party. I'd done too much damage now to keep alive. Luke, on the other hand, was too important to kill, and that's exactly what I had been banking on.

Before us, the gate creaked open with electronic precision. Behind us, the Pyres screamed with guttural desperation.

We reached the gates and I wiped my bloody hand on the surface before slipping into the gap, barely wide enough to let us through. The doors immediately shut behind us, and seconds later rattled and banged with the fury of a few hundred Pyres slamming into the other side.

We were surrounded by a semicircle of at least twenty armed guards, all pointing their guns at us. And in the middle of the guards, pink braids making her unmissable, was Nova. Luke ripped a strip off the bottom of his T-shirt and handed it to me, and I wrapped it round my bloody hand as Nova spoke.

'This isn't what we agreed, Astrid,' Nova said, spreading her hands wide. 'I'd go as far as to say you tricked us.'

I laughed, the sound hollow as I tied up my bandage, but still audible over the bangs of the Pyres behind us. 'We tricked you? What about what you've done to us?'

'Now, now, Astrid. We explained the rules of the game quite clearly when you agreed—'

'No, I'm not talking about the show,' I interrupted. 'I'm talking about the island. The entire Bloodwatch Network. You come here and you have special charges to draw Pyres, you can round up thousands of them at will, you bring weapons that could end them for good. And do you even try to help us to take the island back? No, of course not. You leave us to rot because money is more important than people.'

'That's not on me,' Nova said. 'I was still in university when Bloodwatch was formed. I don't make the rules, I just follow them.'

'So it wasn't you that had the bright idea to capture the Pyre bodies of my dad and little sister to bargain for Luke's life? That was you following orders?' I spat.

The soldiers moved in slightly and Luke took another step towards me.

Nova shrugged. 'I had to bring Luke in. The scientists are inbound and they were breathing down the network's necks. It's nothing personal.'

'Nothing personal about enslaving an entire island of people for your entertainment and profit margins?' Luke asked.

'Are Wynn and Dad even here, or did you lie about that too?' I asked, anger rising in my chest.

'This isn't some mothers' meeting; we are in a serious situation,' Nova snapped. I'd never seen her lose it before, but she wasn't her usual painted self. Her black T-shirt had a dust mark across the front and she wasn't wearing a scrap of make-up. 'Enough conversation. Luke, come forward or we'll shoot Astrid. Simple as that.'

'No,' Luke said, stepping in front of me.

'Listen, idiot. We have snipers behind you too. They could take out Astrid right now,' Nova said, rolling her eyes and pointing up to the wall high above the gate we came through. I glanced up and spotted the guards we could see from the forest. Instead of guarding us from the Pyres, they had their guns trained on us.

And then I saw a shadow move at the top of the wall.

'Seems like we're pretty dangerous if you're pointing this many guns at us,' I said, stalling, letting the shadow get a little bit bigger.

'Astrid, don't. I don't think they're pissing about,' Luke muttered in my ear.

I looked away from the wall and leaned into his shoulder. 'Get ready to run again,' I whispered.

'What?'

But there wasn't time to answer, because the goon at the top of the wall screamed, dropping his gun over the railing. It went off as it hit the ground, shooting a black shirt square in the chest.

'What the hell are you doing up there?' Nova shouted up, her eyes wild.

'Oh shit. They've climbed the fence. Oh shit!' another guard shouted out from above. He was running to the metal staircase that would bring him back down to us when another Pyre launched themselves over the wall, running at him on all fours and taking him down by his legs.

'They're in the bloody trees!' A black shirt's radio went off at their waist, broadcasting the tinny last words of another guard. 'Oh god, they're getting in. There's too many. They're coming in!' came the voice, then static.

All hell broke loose.

The first guard to be attacked fell from the wall, screaming as he flew through the air, only stopping when his neck hit the ground first. The Pyre on his back didn't flinch, protected from the fall by the guard's body, too busy drinking from his neck to even notice us.

Luke and I legged it. We ran straight at the semicircle of guards and pushed past them, their disorientation an invitation for us to get out of there. Then the shooting started, the guards firing rapidly. I looked back over my shoulder and watched as dozens of pale bodies came tumbling over the wall, landing where we had stood. Some of them died on impact with the ground, their bodies folded in impossible ways, but others landed on top of them and ran for the nearest blood bags.

The bullets slowed some of them down, red flowers blooming over their bare chests, but the guards weren't as practised as the islanders were with their shots. They aimed indiscriminately, missing the heart and head. The Pyres leaped into the air and landed on the faces of those stupid enough not to have run already. In the melee, I saw a flash of pink braids, a panicked face in a sea of pale skin, and then nothing.

'Come on!' Luke yelled. There was an alarm ringing out, a siren that signalled one thing: we're screwed. The paths between the makeshift buildings were filled with black shirts running this way and that, totally ignoring us. We pushed on, running for the one place we had in our sights the whole time: the broadcast tower at the centre of the compound.

'We need to think of a way to destroy it,' Luke panted.

'There has to be something here,' I said, struggling to keep up with him in the sea of panicked people. 'They have all sorts of stuff. When they recruited me, they set a whole package on fire with the flip of a switch.'

Luke tripped as he pushed through the crowd and fell, and I stopped to help him. When I looked up again, I could see the other three walls of the compound standing tall above the buildings, as high as the trees of the forest. All of them were lit with floodlights, and all of them were studded with tiny shadows, falling like dark raindrops as they topped the fence and fell to the ground.

'They're everywhere,' Luke said as I lifted him off the ground. 'We have to move fast if we want to get out of here alive.'

I swallowed hard. It hadn't occurred to me that I might not make it. I thought I might not get back to the Burgh, or that it might be too difficult for Hild and me to get to a raft to evacuate. I thought bringing down the tower would be hard. But to not make it? The thought made my veins turn to ice.

'Hey, Astrid?' Luke asked. His voice sounded far away. 'Astrid, stay with me. We can do this. Stay with me.'

I blinked in his general direction, the ice in my veins freezing my muscles in place.

Luke grabbed my face between his hands and brought his eyes close to mine. 'I need you. Are you with me?'

I blinked. Luke needed me. Cass and Noon and Jupiter and Esmond and Hild and the Burgh and the whole island, they needed this. The thought of each person brought me back to reality.

'I'm with you,' I whispered, looking at the tower. 'Come on.'

We ran through the crowds until we reached the base of the tower, the smooth concrete walls at the bottom stretching way over our heads.

'We can't climb it,' Luke said, frustration putting an edge on his voice. 'And even if we could, we need something big to make sure it breaks. We need to make sure it's impossible to fix.'

'Right,' I said, scanning the scene in front of us.

I don't know what I was expecting but there wasn't exactly a supply cupboard nearby labelled BLOODWATCH PYROTECHNICS. I tried to grab someone running past us, to ask them where the Bloodwatch weapons might be, but they squirmed out of my grasp, screaming, running away to . . .

Where *was* everyone running to? It looked like chaos, but that wasn't true. Now we were in the middle, it was easier to see that everyone was running to the same place.

The helicopter pad.

We had landed there on the first day, not too far from the tower. It was the only way out, both off the island and away from the Pyres that had them surrounded. I looked up and spotted the first helicopter taking off, rising from the other side of a nearby building. It lifted into the sky and sped away into the night.

'I have an idea,' I said, grabbing Luke's arm. 'Come on.'

Luke followed me without question as we now ran with the crowd instead of against it. In front of us, ten more helicopters sat waiting on the makeshift tarmac, their blades already whirring. A guard was directing everyone to the nearest helicopter and they were loading people up ten at a time before taking off.

'What's the plan?' Luke shouted over the sound of the helicopter blades.

'We need to crash a helicopter into the tower!' I yelled back.

Luke's mouth dropped open. 'Excuse me?'

'They're big enough, right? And these things have a ton of fuel in them. The propellors will do a lot of damage too!' I shouted back.

'And how are we going to do that?'

'I don't know, we figure something out!' I yelled, the panic taking over again.

Then someone screamed, and another, and another, travelling up the crowd like a ripple of terror.

Luke and I strained to see above the crowd. At the back of the helicopter queue, the first Pyres had reached the poor sods that were too late to the evacuation point. More Pyres flooded in through the gap between the buildings, all of them sprinting towards us.

Luke and I pushed to the side of the crowd while everyone else surged forward. A few people stumbled on to the tarmac, disoriented, and fell into the whirring propellor blades, spraying the crowd with blood. This had the undesired effect of making everyone panic even more and sending the Pyres into a frenzy. Luke reached out to grab my hand and we forced our way through, aiming for the side of the building ahead.

We stumbled out from the crowd. It was starting to get difficult to tell who was human and who was Pyre. My breath caught in my throat as person after person went down, Pyres looming over them, sucking them dry.

And then, in the crowd, I saw someone I hadn't seen in five years. Two people, in fact, holding hands, her wearing a torn plaid dress, him in a long shirt and filthy trousers, both with their hair hanging lank and in clumps over their shoulders, staring straight at me.

Dad and Wynn.

CHAPTER THIRTY-ONE

Dad and Wynn weaved their way through the crowd, ignoring the screaming of both humans and Pyres alike. They didn't even stop when blood splattered their faces from a nearby feeding frenzy.

'She hasn't aged a day,' I said, my voice catching as I spoke. I stared at Wynn, at her thick eyelashes and blue eyes that didn't match my hazel ones, the familiar red hair. It was thinner than I remembered, hanging lank around her abnormally pale face, but it was her. Teeth protruded from her bottom lip that didn't used to be there, but she was still Wynn. Wynn from four years ago. She was even wearing the same clothes from that night, her blue plaid dress with the daisies on the lapels, although they were so blood-soaked around her chin that they looked more like poppies.

'That's your dad and sister,' Luke said slowly, connecting the dots.

The crowd was so noisy and claustrophobic before, but it was like everything around me stopped. I could only see Dad and Wynn, and they could only see me.

'Do you want me to try and talk to them?' Luke asked.

'You can do that?' I asked, my eyes still on them.

'I can try. I don't think you want them here when we

destroy the tower; they could get hurt. And they're still . . . human-ish, after all these years. They could be some of the smarter Pyres we've seen. You could try and find them after this is all over, see what you might mean to them.'

I couldn't be separated from them again. Whether they were here because Nova found them, or whether they were swept up into the brood at the stadium, it didn't matter. I'd thought I would never see them again, or if I did, they would be unrecognisable. And yet here they were, in some ways the same as the day I left them, in others completely different.

For the first time since I could remember, the monster inside wasn't angry. It was there all right, but it was like it was reacting to Wynn and Dad too, reaching out to them. And that's when I realised it was never angry at all. It was sad. The monster inside, the toxic thing I had drawn strength from all these years – it was grief.

I blinked and my vision swam with tears. This was not the time to lose it, surrounded by Pyres and death and destruction. If I wanted to have any hope that I could one day be reunited with Dad and Wynn, Luke had to get them to leave, even if it broke my heart.

'Tell them to go,' I breathed, tears running down my face. 'Tell them to get out of here before they come any closer, and I'll find them later. I don't know if they can . . . control themselves. I don't want to hurt them.' The fresh blood dripping from Wynn's chin would haunt me forever. They weren't attacking us, but they weren't themselves either.

Luke nodded solemnly, studying my face. He turned and looked at Dad and Wynn, muttering something under his breath, maintaining eye contact. Dad and Wynn stopped walking and cocked their heads.

It was more pale bodies than black shirts now. We'd be able to move while they were distracted drinking their prey, but we wouldn't have long. Meanwhile, several of the helicopters were taking off, some with no passengers, eager to get away from the Pyres, abandoning those still scrabbling for help. For the first time it struck me how many people worked at Bloodwatch. Not all of these black shirts were as culpable as Nova. For some of them, it was just a job gone wrong. They didn't deserve this.

I wiped the tears from my face. I brought the brood here to end this, but I'd murdered innocent people along the way. And even if they thought they knew what they were signing up for, they couldn't have known the whole truth. And now they were all dead. Because of me.

It was like I was seeing it all for the first time, the carnage, the blood, the bodies. When I saw my first dead body as a kid, I cried for three days. Now it was merely part of the daily grind. I didn't want that any more. I wanted more for me, for them, for the islanders. For everyone.

Determination steeled my muscles. We had to bring Bloodwatch down, and we had to try and do it as quickly and as safely as possible. If I gave up now, all these people died for nothing. We weren't the only ones who had suffered.

I looked again at Dad and smiled at him. He was still focused on Luke, but his head moved slightly, his eye catching mine, his blood-splattered face softening.

'I love you,' I mouthed, blinking back the sting of more tears.

He stared at me, said nothing. Then he looked back at Luke, took Wynn by the hand and turned to walk away.

'I think they got the message,' Luke said, watching as they walked away through the crowd, trampling dead bodies as they went.

'Thank you,' I whispered, watching until Dad and Wynn disappeared behind a far building.

'You ready?' Luke asked, gripping my shoulders, his face etched with concern.

I nodded.

Luke led the way as we carefully stepped through the carnage left by the Pyre brood. The smell was the worst part, a mixture of metallic blood and open flesh. They ignored us as we picked our way through, too busy with their meals or genuinely listening to Luke's silent pleas to leave us alone, I wasn't sure, but we slowly moved forward towards the fence that separated the helicopters from everything else. I accidentally caught one Pyre on the shoulder with my foot, and it looked up at me and hissed, teeth dripping with blood. I froze, but one glare from Luke and it looked away.

'Why do they listen to you?' I asked him as we stepped over a dead black shirt with a permanent vacant stare and gaunt cheeks. 'I know they can understand you, but why do they take your orders?'

Luke shrugged. 'I think it only works with the stupid ones, like these.'

'What about Dad and Wynn, then?' I said, my voice cracking on my sister's name.

'I told them how much you loved them, and that was enough.'

That cleaved my heart in two, like a well-placed shot with a crossbow from Hild's guard watch.

We reached the helicopters and shielded our eyes as two more took off. There were a few Pyres here eyeing up the fence, but they held back, cautious. Were they . . . afraid of the choppers? It looked like it, and they were right to be, with what happened when the first few crowd members got sliced open by the blades.

Something grabbed at my shirt and I whirled round, arms up, ready to fight. Luke spun with me, searching for the danger, arm snaking around my waist.

I looked into the eyes of a blood-covered face, dark skin exposed between blood splatters. And the face was accompanied by another, a bigger guy with a familiar smile.

'Cass,' I said, bringing her in for a hug, relief piercing my bones.

'That was a trip, but we saw you guys run this way. We were able to fight our way through,' Jupiter said.

'I cannot tell you how glad I am to see you. How did you get in?' I asked

Cass signed. 'The main gate buckled under the weight of the sheer number of Pyres pushing through.'

I turned to Cass. 'Noon and Esmond?'

She shrugged and shook her head.

'We'll find them,' I signed. 'Luke can keep the Pyres off us. We need to get to the helicopters. I think they're big enough to take the tower out.'

Cass looked over my shoulder at the helicopter pad,

piecing together my plan. Then she grinned. 'This might help,' she said, bringing up a gun she had hanging off her shoulder.

'Where did you get that?' I asked, eyes wide.

'There were a few near the gate. We helped ourselves,' Jupiter said, raising his own.

I nodded. 'OK. We do this, but we try to take out the least number of people possible. These guys? They're just scared. We need that tower down, but we need to try and do it in the right way.'

Cass and Jupiter nodded and we moved as a unit towards the helipad.

The chain-link fence had been closed off and a couple of guards pointed their guns through the gaps, keeping any braver Pyres at bay. They hadn't noticed us yet, and I realised both Luke and I were covered with blood. For all they could see, we were Pyres ourselves, and that meant we blended in. I stared through the fence, looking for something that would help us with our plan, some clue as to what to do next.

And that's when I saw them. Nova, Cresta and Cinta, all heading to a helicopter on standby. Cinta even had her own long-nosed gun.

'You have got to be bloody kidding me,' I said.

'I guess because we left the arena and Mills died, Cinta is technically the winner,' Luke said. 'Un-bloody-believable.'

'Actually, man, very bloody believable,' Jupiter said sadly.

Cinta won by default, even without a partner. It only just occurred to me that I had no idea what happened to Reeta. But I could guess.

We watched as the three of them ran across the helipad. A black shirt from the other side of the pad climbed the fence and ran towards them, waving his arms above his head and shouting something.

Cinta stopped, lifted the barrel of the gun and pulled the trigger.

The black shirt crumpled to the ground, unmoving.

'She didn't even flinch,' I said, anger setting my teeth on edge.

'She has bigger problems. Check out Nova,' Jupiter said, nodding back at the others.

Nova held a bloody rag to her neck, and from the wild look in her eyes she knew she was done for. She was the authority Cresta and Cinta needed to get on that helicopter. They were all infected as far as quarantine was concerned. Everyone in that chopper would be killed as soon as they hit the mainland anyway, if Nova didn't turn first and finish the job herself.

The three of them climbed into the helicopter and slammed the door shut. The blades whirred faster until the chopper was hovering above the tarmac.

It was now or never. 'I'll do it if you don't want to,' I signed to Cass, my mind set. 'But you're the better shot. I saw what you did for Decke.'

Cass touched my shoulder. 'We're in this together. I'll do it.'

The helicopter rose higher, faster, and it banked over the next building to head towards the coast, a stone's throw away from the tower.

Cass raised her gun and closed one eye, lining up her sights. Then she gently squeezed the trigger.

The spray of bullets caught in the blades above the helicopter and sent it sprawling sideways, towards the base of the broadcast tower.

A fireball erupted from the side of the structure, parts of the helicopter spinning away from the blast zone. Even the Pyres looked up, curious, distracted by the chaos of fire and light. There was a loud creaking moan, and then the metal bars of the tower buckled, sending the entire building backwards. Finally, as the tower fell, the red light switched off.

Bloodwatch was offline.

There was a loud boom as the tower hit the ground on the other side of the compound. The last of the helicopters had already started taking off when they saw what was happening, and even the guards by the fence had finally abandoned their posts. As for Cinta, Cresta and Nova, I wasn't sticking around to find out if they'd survived.

'Holy shit. We did it,' Jupiter said, clapping Cass on the back in awe of her marksmanship. 'Now what?'

'Now we get out of here,' I said, nodding at Luke.

With Luke's help, it was surprisingly easy to escape. There was a gaping hole in the perimeter of the compound. Every now and then the odd Pyre would stop, sniff the air and look at us hungrily, their teeth dripping with blood. But one glance from Luke and they would back off.

The four of us helped each other over the rubble avoiding the dancing live wires that still sparked pathetically near the base of the ruined tower. And then we were out, free, running through the woods.

Right before we broke out from the treeline of the forest, I spotted something fast moving on my left and nudged Luke, alerting him in case it was a Pyre.

'What's up, Executioner,' Noon said, stepping out from the bushes. 'Quite a mess you left back there. I assume it was you anyway. Usually is.'

'I had some help,' I said, my heart swelling with relief at the sight of him.

Esmond arrived a few seconds later, his face ruddy with exhaustion. 'I understand this is a life-or-death type situation we find ourselves in,' he panted, 'but can we please slow down a little now? I believe most of the brood is participating in the all-you-can-eat buffet back at Bloodwatch HQ.'

He didn't mean to do it, but Esmond's words made my heart stutter with guilt. 'All those people,' I whispered, looking at the plume of smoke rising above the trees.

'But you will have saved so many others,' Cass signed. 'We just need to warn everyone. We may not have done the right thing, but we did the best thing under the circumstances.'

'Maybe,' I said, pulling my gaze away from the flames. 'Where are you going now?'

'I need to warn my settlement,' Cass signed. 'Then we can get word out to whoever we can to escape before the mainland get here.'

'Speaking of which, I feel like Esmond and I are done on the mainland,' Jupiter said. 'We can't be here when the army gets in, and you know they'll be coming.'

'Indeed,' Esmond said, nodding sadly. 'But it will be good to pair up with a friend such as yourself.'

'Yeah, I've got people to warn too,' Noon said, scratching his chin. 'So this is probably goodbye, kid.'

'I'll go where you go,' Luke said, slipping his fingers between mine.

I looked at the faces around me, these people who had become my family, just like Hild and Griff and everyone at the Burgh. And overhead came the blinking red and white lights of aircraft heading in from beyond the coast, probably sent to collect Luke for experimentation, or to get revenge on us all, or both.

'We aren't free until we all are,' I said, looking at them one by one. 'It's not just the Burgh. We have to warn everyone to escape while they can. Bloodwatch may be down, but this isn't over, not by a long shot. There's no way the mainland and the network are going to let us shut down their biggest investment. We need to be ready.'

And with that, we all gave each other one final look before splitting off in different directions, scattering under the roar of the Pyres, Luke's hand still warm in mine. He kissed me on the forehead. The monster inside me felt calmer now I knew Dad and Wynn were out there somewhere. And if Luke was the key to a cure, we could be together again. Maybe we could save Hild, and the Burgh, the whole island even. But for now, we had work to do.

ACKNOWLEDGEMENTS

I started writing *To the Death* in January 2024. It was part of a writing challenge I set myself every January, to write a first draft in a month. I needed something fast paced to keep my attention on the page, and before I knew it ninety-four thousand words had tumbled out of my brain. I am a meticulous plotter, so I didn't start the challenge without a plan. As my lovely agent Lucy Irvine said when she first started reading, 'You've always wanted to write a zombie story', and here I am.

I hope you loved reading this book as much as I did writing it. This is a story of escapism and high-octane action, but it's also about grief, and love, and not judging yourself too harshly. And I hope that you, dear reader, get some closure from poor Astrid – and maybe even from some of her friends she meets along the way.

This is the fourth set of acknowledgements I've written, and most read like a contacts list, a long record of people that I need to thank for helping me get the book over the finish line. To the team at Hachette, especially Katie Levy for believing in this book, and Laura and Anna for the late stage edits: thank you. To Lucy for never giving up on my hare-brained ideas: you are the best agent

I could ask for. To my writing groups and my family for early feedback and support: I couldn't keep doing this without you. To the writers that we lost along the way: I think of you whenever I sit down at my desk. To Paul Blow, my incredible cover artist: thanks for bringing the book to life.

And of course to you, my lovely readers, who keep coming back and supporting me book after book. *To the Death* wouldn't exist without you.

LOOK OUT FOR
BOOK 2

COMING 2027

Photo © Melissa Welliver

Melissa Welliver is a speculative fiction author who loves to write about how The End Of The World is never really the end of the world. She was born and raised in Stockport and now lives in the High Peak with her bassetoodle, Zelda. As a dual citizen of both America and the UK, Melissa enjoys writing fiction that bridges the gap across the pond. Melissa runs a podcast on her love of tropes alongside podcaster Jamie Greenwood and YA author Naomi Gibson called *The Chosen Ones and Other Tropes*.

She has previously published two standalone dystopian rom-coms and one darker dystopian book. Melissa's books have been longlisted for the Berkshire Book Award and won the Write Blend Bookshop award for YA fiction in 2022. Melissa's writing has also listed in the Mslexia Prize, the Bath Novel Award, the Northern Writers Awards and the Wells Book for Children prize.

'Welcome back, dystopia. Welliver delivers a razor-sharp assault on life, death, and media itself. *To the Death* doesn't just raise the stakes, it lights them on fire.'
– Bill Wood

'Melissa Welliver is redefining dystopia for a whole new generation. *To the Death* is a riotous, bloodthirsty triumph and her best work yet.'
– Cynthia Murphy

'*To the Death* is everything fans of *The Hunger Games* could want – but with much sharper teeth! Prepare for a fast-paced, heart-pounding horror adventure with monsters – both human and not-so-human – lurking around every corner. Buckle up, and let the games begin!'
– Kat Ellis

'Fast, fun, and bloodthirsty, *To the Death* brings the dystopian genre back to life with sharp teeth and cutting commentary on reality TV's hunger for spectacle. Melissa Welliver is on fire, and I can't wait to see what she writes next.'
– Kathryn Foxfield

'Perfect for fans of *The Hunger Games* and *The Last of Us*, this is a chilling, gory thriller with plenty of bite! Dystopias are back and Melissa Welliver is at the helm.'
– Amy McCaw

'*To the Death* is a wild ride from start to finish – you won't want to put it down. Welliver is in her element and is bringing dystopia back with an epic story of zombie vampires . . . Loved it.'
– Naomi Gibson